MW01133928

The Twilight of the Day

Ian A. O'Connor

Pegasus Publishing & Entertainment Group

The Twilight of the Day
Publisher: Pegasus Publishing & Entertainment Group;
2 edition (May 14, 2015)
2001© Ian A. O'Connor. All rights reserved.
Second Printing, May, 2015© Ian A. O'Connor. All rights reserved.

No part of this book may be reproduced or transmitted in any form or by any means, mechanical or electronic, including photocopying or recording, or by any information storage or retrieval system, without permission in writing from the author. Brief passages may be quoted by reviewers to be printed in a newspaper, magazine or online review site.

Cover art: www.SelfPubBookCovers.Com/BeeJavier

This is a work of fiction.

Visit Ian at: www.ianaoconnor.com
Contact Ian at: ianaoconnor@ianaoconnor.com

Manufactured in the United States of America

To my wife Candice Myers O'Connor
My compass

Fiction Titles by Ian A. O'Connor

The Twilight of the Day

The Seventh Seal

Nonfiction Titles by Ian A. O'Connor
With Howard C. "Scrappy" Johnson

SCRAPPY: Memoir of a U. S. Fighter Pilot in Korea and Vietnam

CHAPTER 1

"Max Epperman is dead."

The terrible finality of those words slammed into James Vincent Trader with a force that stole his breath away. Overcome with despair, he sank to the floor of his darkened cell, a pitiful, emaciated mannequin draped in a rude, ill-fitting, pajama-like prison uniform of purple and gray stripes. His head fell forward until it found a haven between wasted arms wrapped around skeletal knees, and thus hidden from the world he began an unconscious rocking back and forth as kaleidoscopic images of the free-at-last Max Epperman filled every convolution of his brain.

Time stood still.

"Jim, can you hear me?"

The question came a full five minutes later, not in the form of the spoken word, but rather as a muted, coded tapping on the century-old concrete wall separating him from a man he had never met.

Reluctantly, he willed himself to rise from the sanctuary of the hiding places deep within his soul and began a painful crawl toward the divide. As he reached out to get his bearings in the darkness, the ancient metal door at the north end of the hallway was violently flung open. It crashed into solid concrete, sending an ear-splitting thunderclap rolling down the long, dank corridor. In its wake came the dreaded sounds of running feet.

Trader's heart pounded in terror. "One, two…no…there's three of them," he counted aloud. *"Oh, God!"* It was an involuntarily wail, a terrified lament born of utter hopelessness.

The executioners were now coming for him.

* * *

Mukmahr Salaam Jallud was wringing wet. His clothing and body odor was totally offensive. Seated by the window on the left side of the aircraft, he managed an anxious glance across the aisle at his fellow passengers, taking little comfort in the knowledge that he was no more of a goat than the rest of them. He turned back to the window, desperate to catch a glimpse of the earth below. Nothing. The plane continued to thrash its way blindly through the monsoon storm.

Twice the Russian pilot had aborted his landing, and moments ago had announced in a strained voice that if he had to abandon this approach, then he would divert to an alternate airfield fifty miles to the north where the weather was reported to be marginally better.

"*No, you land here or crash trying,*" Jallud threatened angrily under his breath, "or I'll force you down at gunpoint if I have to," he added, meaning every word.

Twice he had postponed this trip. Then, six days ago, he had received an ultimatum from halfway around the world. If he did not present himself in this capital city by sundown today, October 15, then any hope of a deal was off, and there would be no reprise.

Jallud knew it was no idle bluff. The news from Paris had confirmed that. No, unless he could cement an agreement today, then all the hard work of the past several months would have been for naught—to say nothing of the millions of dollars already spent.

Without warning, the huge Ilyushin turboprop floundered, made a sickening rolling turn into its left wing, stalled, then plunged straight down toward the ground. Passengers screamed as the plane fell, all four engines howling. Pandemonium reigned. Then, at the last possible instant, a miracle. With wings suddenly level, the plane's main landing gear crashed onto a concrete runway and the airliner rapidly lost speed on the grooved, rain-drenched surface. They were on the ground in Hanoi, North Vietnam.

Jallud drew in a deep breath, held it for an eternity, then slowly exhaled. His had been a long journey, one that had originated in Tripoli, Libya, some forty grueling hours earlier.

He rose unsteadily from his seat and elbowed his way toward the exit. Rain cascaded over him as he made his way down the rickety, metal stairway. He was drenched by the time he reached the foot of the stairs and the two waiting army officers huddled under one umbrella while holding forth a second for his use. Jallud recognized the taller man. Colonel Ky.

"Welcome, Monsieur Jallud," Ky shouted out in French. "I'm sorry our weather could not have been more accommodating, but at least it's keeping the Americans from our skies.　Nature's helping hand is something we've come to appreciate."

Jallud glanced at his watch as he scrambled under cover. His face betrayed a sense of worry. "We must hurry, Colonel."

The trio dashed towards an ancient Citroen, and the moment they were inside the driver took off toward the city.

Colonel Ky could see that Jallud was agitated. "Relax," he said in a voice meant to soothe, "we'll make it before General Trang's deadline, I promise."

"We'd better."

But Ky's words had their intended effect. Jallud allowed a fleeting hint of a smile to cross his wet face. *He's right, I must relax.* Jallud held his up his watch and peered at the luminescent dial. 5:01 P.M. Daylight was fast fading. Sundown would come at 5:30 P.M. This was definitely cutting things close.

He had first met General Trang and Colonel Ky here in Hanoi back in June. Now, on the Ides of October, what had been but a germ of an idea four months ago was about to become a reality.　His breathing stopped as he contemplated for the hundredth time the enormity of what he was on the verge of accomplishing.　Even Colonel Muammar Gaddafi, the Supreme Leader of Libya, had openly marveled at what he was attempting. But Gaddafi had given his full blessing, telling the Revolutionary Council that Jallud's plan, once put into action, would rocket Libya into the forefront of the world's powers.　Jallud remembered the speech verbatim. *Rocket* was the word Gaddafi had used. That said it all. And it was nothing short of prophecy.

He was brought out of his reverie by Ky's announcement that the rain had stopped and the sky was clearing.

What a shabby city, Jallud thought, taking in the sights. The drab, monochromatic walls of most buildings were plastered with fiery party slogans and myriad pictures of Ho Chi Minh. The founder of the revolution, dead though he was these past three years, gazed down benevolently upon his subjects from a thousand pair of paper eyes.

He found himself again fascinated by the innumerable one-man air raid shelters that lined the curbs of every street, where at the first sound of a siren, people would scamper into those holes like so many rabbits, pull the covers over themselves, and patiently await the all clear. It was a way of life, and had been since the days of the Japanese occupation thirty years earlier.

It took fifteen interminable minutes to reach the ministry; minutes spent dodging untold numbers of people silently pedaling their bicycles as they went about their daily lives with a determined purpose.

The Minister for State Security, General Da Van Trang, met his Arab visitor in the lobby. He made a slight bow, offered a solicitous handshake, and inquired as to his health.

Trang was both an oddity and a rarity in North Vietnam, and he reveled in his uniqueness. His French mother had passed on to her six-foot-two inch son an elegance and refinement that made him stand apart from his much shorter countrymen. That a half-caste could have risen so high in the government was unfathomable to most. However, Trang was good at his job. But more importantly, he had been a confidant of Chairman Ho. No one in the country hated either the French or Americans more than he. Indeed, his animus bordered on mania, and when his name had circulated in the politburo in 1968 as a possible representative to the fledgling peace talks underway in Paris, Chairman Ho had nixed that notion. His rationale: eventually Trang would explode into uncontrollable violence.

After a simple meal of hot tea and sticky-rice cakes, Trang steered the conversation to the business that had brought them together again. He held aloft a slim manila folder. "Your proposal's been well received by the politburo, Monsieur Jallud," he began in a deep, mellifluous voice. "The men named on the list you presented to us last August in Paris are now housed in a single group, and in accordance with your wishes, none are in direct contact with any of the others. However, it's my sad duty to inform you that one has died, though we did all we could to prevent it."

Jallud's onyx eyes hardened. "Who?"

Trang opened the folder and extracted the list. He spent an inordinate amount of time in scrutinizing a sheet that held only ten names. Jallud could see he was stalling. The list held the names of men known to Trang by heart. "Maxwell Epperman, the Jew!" he finally spat out.

Jallud slammed his fist down on the desk, and rose from his chair. "May Allah damn you all to hell!" he shouted. "You were warned to make sure nothing happened to any of these men! Oh, how you assured me they'd be treated as family." He was apoplectic. "Apparently Vietnamese treat family like so much dog shit!" He paused to catch a breath. "And how many of the others are dying? Do you think you're dealing with a desert moron?"

"It was a tragic accident," Trang mumbled, fearful that maybe this volatile Arab would call the whole deal off. He knew what would happen if this plan should fail. He would be shot along with his wife and three children. Such were the rules of this winner-take-all high stakes game.

"General, that so-called tragic accident has just cost your government three million dollars."

"No!" The alarm in Trang's voice was genuine. "The agreed price of thirty-five million dollars stands firm, regardless of the fate of the Jew." Beads of sweat dotted his upper lip.

Colonel Ky squirmed in his chair, eyes darting from one to the other.

Jallud studied Trang with open contempt. For a man ten thousand miles from home and in a land surrounded by strangers, he showed no fear, no hesitation to speak his mind. "Just who in the hell do you think you're dealing with?" he asked the seated Trang, staring as if studying a maggot. "You don't demand a thing! *I demand!*" He pointed a finger toward his own chest for emphasis. "I'm the man with the money, and my money talks, as the Americans like to say, especially in this pigpen of a country. So you either accept or reject my offer, and I demand an answer right now, because if you think you're going to waltz me around like you have those two clowns Kissinger and Haig in Paris, then you're crazy. Just say, no, General, and the deal is off. I mean it!"

Trang took in a deep, steadying breath, held it for a long moment then slowly exhaled. He repeated the process. Finally: "I agree." Swallowing the last vestige of pride, he continued. "On behalf of my government, I accept your generous offer, Monsieur Jallud. I also promise you the rest of the American prisoners are in excellent health, and will continue to receive exemplary care."

Ky saw that Trang's conciliatory tone and defeated demeanor seemed to mollify the Arab.

Jallud returned to his seat. "Let's put this behind us," he suggested with a conciliatory wave of a hand. "We have much still to accomplish, and very little time." A smile creased his face. "My agents in Paris tell me you and the Americans are about to sign a peace treaty. Could this be true?"

Trang nodded. "It is true. We're confident an accord will be reached by this weekend, so our business must be concluded today." He allowed himself a hint of a smile. "Never before have prisoners-of-war held by one country actually been sold to another. Tell me, what makes these particular men so special?" The voice again flowed like honey.

Jallud understood that Trang knew the answer, but decided to humor him nonetheless. "My government spent many months studying a list of both missing and known captured American airmen, and thanks to the likes of *The New York Times* which has unwittingly aided our cause, we have been able to uncover the identities of a select few men with skills so...well...let's just say skills we are not in a position to acquire on the open market. All of the pilots on your list have degrees in nuclear physics, and, to put in the simplest of terms, my government needs their services. You in turn have need of our money, so we both prosper from a simple business transaction. More than that, I'm not at liberty to say."

"Of course." Trang shot a glance at Colonel Ky, then leaned toward Jallud, both hands gripping the arms of his chair. "I must remind you that our agreement calls for these men to disappear forever once you're finished with them. The Politburo is emphatic on this point. Even though we have beaten the

Americans and their South Vietnamese puppets, we do realize that we have never been subjected to the full effects of their potential wrath." He slowly shook his head for emphasis. "Because if it ever became known that we had sold some of their military officers to a third country, then the Americans would destroy us, swiftly, and without mercy. We remember what they did to Japan in nineteen forty-five."

Jallud instinctively leaned in closer. "I've made plans to cover every contingency. These ten Americans will do my bidding, and when I've finished with them they will die. It's that simple. My country has as much at stake in this as yours, so we're as one. The world will never know what became of these men. I, Jallud, guarantee it."

"That's what I needed to hear." Trang visibly relaxed. "Let's review the particulars." He shuffled through a thick pile of papers on his desk, finally pulling a sheet from the middle. "My representatives in Switzerland have been told to await the transfer of funds, and I do appreciate your thoughtfulness in using a money source that cannot be traced back to any government. Such professionalism is commendable." Trang flashed a greedy grin. "As soon as my people wire back that the dollars have been deposited into our account, I'll hand over the Americans."

"Excellent."

Trang allowed a frown to cross his face. "How you intend to get these men out of Vietnam? We both know the Russians and the Chinese will never permit you to overfly their airspace."

"Quite right." Jallud extracted a tightly folded chart from an inside pocket and spread it on top of the cluttered desk. "I've thought of everything, General. There's only one way for these men to leave, and that's by submarine. So, at the appointed hour, my boat will enter into Haiphong Harbor; take on its cargo and leave, all under cover of darkness. Then it'll run submerged until it's beyond the patrol zone of the American Seventh Fleet. In fact, my submarine is in these waters as we speak, awaiting my instructions as to when to enter the harbor. I can have it here within a few hours."

"And you, monsieur?"

"I'll leave with the Americans," Jallud replied. "How long will it take to move the prisoners to Haiphong once you hear from Switzerland?"

"A couple of hours at most."

"Then I'll make the arrangements to transfer the money, and alert my submarine to standby to enter Haiphong. Here are the short-wave frequencies we will be using," he said, pointing to the bottom of the chart. "Make sure your forces take the necessary precautions to see that my boat is not blown out of the water by mistake. Naturally, it's flying no flag; indeed it has no identifying markings whatsoever. That way no one could ever trace it back to Libya if anything ever happened to it. A small but necessary contravention of maritime law."

Both men parted company with the outward appearance of restored friendship, yet each knew he was no friend of the other.

Jallud was pleased but worried. The loss of Max Epperman could prove to be a major setback, because that particular naval officer had been a recognized authority on nuclear particle acceleration, and his work at Stanford University while on special leave from the U. S. Navy had been considered exemplary. It was a heavy blow, he begrudgingly conceded, but not a mortal one. The remaining nine pilots would just have to take up the slack.

Thirty hours later, Jallud's well-organized world blew apart.

rirf

navr

CHAPTER 2

Trader sat frozen on the stone floor for a full five minutes after the trio had pounded past his cell. They had traveled the length of the corridor only to exit noisily through the opposite door. Why? He had no answer. As his heartbeat slowly returned to normal, he allowed himself a whispered prayer of thanks. He crawled once more towards the wall and willed his thoughts back to Max Epperman.

If ever a man had seemed at first blush to be out of place in the military, that man was Max Epperman. However, Max had loved the Navy to a fault. Trader had met him several years earlier when they were both assigned to the Pentagon working with Westinghouse as liaison officers on the nuclear submarine program. Max was in his late twenties at the time. He was a newly minted PhD, and a mere lieutenant J.G., yet his knowledge of nuclear physics was that of a scientist ten years his senior. Trader had been roundly impressed with the young officer.

Three years later Trader received orders sending him to a staff assignment working for the Commander-in-Chief, Pacific, at Pearl Harbor, while Max went to a once in a lifetime plum assignment. He became a visiting fellow to Stanford University. Because of their sensitive technical backgrounds, such officers were always kept well out of 'harms way,' which at this point in history translated to mean the war zone in Southeast Asia. However, like all career officers, each was keenly aware that if he were ever to achieve flag rank, having a Vietnam tour on his records was *de rigueur*.

And, so, after several rounds of polite nagging, the Navy finally relented, and allowed them both—and others in similar circumstances—into the combat zone long enough to punch their ticket, as the saying went. But for some unknown bureaucratic reason, the Air Force had never been as strict with its scientist-officers, and several pilots with nuclear backgrounds had already successfully completed combat tours in Vietnam and returned safely home.

A handful had not.

Max Epperman, who was neither a naval aviator nor a naval flight officer/systems operator, was captured by the North Vietnamese when the helicopter he was a passenger in developed engine trouble and crashed into the Tonkin Gulf. He and one other survivor were picked up by an enemy patrol craft and taken prisoner. That had been slightly over a year ago.

Because he was a small, frail looking individual, and also because he was a Jew, Max Epperman had been singled out by the Vietnamese for special, sadistic abuse. His beatings were always more frequent and more severe, yet the feisty officer dogged his captors at every turn, and revealed nothing of himself or his job. On the few occasions he was able to pass coded messages to other prisoners, he told them not to worry. He assured them he was holding his own

Now he was beyond the pain.

Trader blinked back the hot tears. Picking up the small scrap of stone he used to tap out the code, he began to talk.

"W..h..e..n?"

"Two hours ago," the man next door tapped back. He was an Air Force captain named Mark FitzGerald, a prisoner since early 1967. Even though the two were but a four-inch wall apart, in the week Trader had come to this prison—the latest in a series of prisons—he had yet to meet the other man.

"How?"

The reply took several minutes to transmit.

"Word came down the line that Max told Gerry Glasstner earlier this evening he thought he was dying. Said he couldn't breathe properly; said he was spitting up blood. Also, he hadn't been able to eat or drink anything for the past two days because he couldn't swallow. He asked that the following message be relayed to you. 'Tell Jim Trader they didn't get to me.' Then about forty minutes ago Gerry heard the guards enter Max's cell. By peeking through his slop-drop grate he saw them drag Max's body away."

"Thanks, Mark. Try to grab some sleep, there's still a couple of hours until dawn. Pass the word back up the line tomorrow that I got the message. God bless America!"

Trader winced as he rose from the stone floor and hobbled over to his bunk.

What kind of a God would allow men to endure such hell? The answer lay far to the back of his consciousness, and the knowing made the situation that much harder to bear.

* * *

For three years Commander James Vincent Trader had pestered the Bureau of Personnel (BUPERS) with a shower of volunteer statements, begging for a duty assignment to the Seventh Fleet. He had kept current with his flying, and was fully qualified for carrier operations.

Finally, BUPERS relented, and offered him the chance to join an attack squadron on the aircraft carrier, *USS Ranger.* He was going as the squadron's operations officer.

Being a rather long-in-the-tooth full commander, he was over-qualified for the job and he knew it. He was told by a three-star admiral that the assignment would last only ninety days, and that his flying duties would be very limited. He would only be permitted to fly into safe areas in South Vietnam, and never, never, into combat over the north. Those were the rules, take it or leave it, because the Navy had no intention — no matter how slight the risk — of losing a man with his secrets to the communists.

Trader jumped at the opportunity.

Forty-nine days into his tour he learned that he was on the promotion list to captain, with an effective date-of-rank of December 1, 1970. Coincidentally, this was also his just-published return date to Hawaii for reassignment. No way was the Navy going to be placed in the uncomfortable position of having Trader outrank not only his squadron commander, but the air group commander as well.

On the last night of November, a heavy strike was ordered into North Vietnam in the area known as Route Package Six, and in the confusion of the moment, Trader was mistakenly chosen to partake in the mission. Route Package Six was the most dangerous area in North Vietnam for American pilots. Losses to ground fire and surface-to-air missiles were mind numbing. Trader kept his mouth shut and went.

It was a total disaster. Of the forty-one fighters and bombers launched, seven were shot down, including Trader's Skyhawk. He had had only seconds to transmit a message saying he was hit and bailing out. There was no thought of trying to nurse his plane out over the Tonkin Gulf for a possible pick-up by either the Navy Task Force or Air Force rescue helicopters.

The North Vietnamese were all over him the moment he hit the ground. Dozens of angry fists pummeled his prostrate form, and though he tried desperately to curl up into a tight ball, the mob beat him relentlessly. They tore off his helmet, cutting his forehead as the plastic visor gouged exposed flesh. He was being hammered to death and he knew it. Just as he was about to slip into unconsciousness, a wheezing army truck pulled up. Soldiers rushed the crowd, cowing them into submission with rifle butts. He was dragged by his hair and thrown roughly into the back of the vehicle. A pimply youth slammed him face down onto the wooden slats, then sat heavily upon his back, violently knocking the breath out of him.

"You no move!" the teenager yelled down at him, then cocked his pistol and roughly screwed the barrel into Trader's right ear.

Trader froze in fright. His flight suit was suddenly wet, and he smelled his own urine. Soon the soldiers became aware of his embarrassing predicament. They began to laugh and prod him none too gently with their rifles, but fear outweighed embarrassment. He started to shake uncontrollably.

The ride lasted about an hour. During that time he could hear, and sometimes see, the battle being waged around him. Bright flashes of light tore across the night sky as bombs fell and anti-aircraft guns hurled their sabers up into the black in answer to the attacking planes.

He had no idea where he was when the truck finally coughed its way to a stop. The one thing he knew for sure was that he was deep inside enemy territory, very much a prisoner, and his chances of long-term survival were almost nonexistent.

Again, he was dragged painfully to his feet by his hair, and heard himself cry out. With his head held down to his knees he was turkey-trotted into a dilapidated wooden building and dumped into a foul smelling, earthen-floored room. Expert hands rummaged through the many zippered pockets on his flight suit, emptying each treasure trove one by one. Then his watch was stripped from his wrist and his dog tags yanked from around his neck. The rickety door was shut and he was left alone; cut, bruised, and very, very, frightened.

Welcome to North Vietnam, he had managed to whisper to himself.

* * *

For three weeks he traveled from one location to another, always at night, always blindfolded and shackled in ancient irons. By now he was so rancid that he was physically sickened by the stench of his own body, and underneath the rotting flight suit, he could feel sores beginning to erupt and ooze. Things had taken up residence in his matted hair, things that moved, things which continually migrated to every part of his body, and these things were living off him. The revulsion nearly drove him mad, and for the first time in decades he began to pray.

At the end of his journey he was stripped, sluiced down with a fire hose, then thrown naked into a rancid cell that was the twin of his first, save for a concrete floor. Sometime during the night a guard appeared, and, without a word, roughly sheared his head and beard with a decrepit pair of manual clippers, leaving him feeling and looking like a convict in some medieval dungeon. For the finale, he was doused with a strong-smelling disinfectant, and after a five minute interval was again sluiced clean. While still dripping, he was sprayed with clouds of DDT. He had then been given a threadbare blanket. Wrapping himself into a tight cocoon, he sat on the floor, scared and cold in a puddle of water, and waited for God only knew what.

* * *

It was obvious that the film had been shot by a professional. Trader sat on a stool and watched the carnage unfold on the small screen before him. There was no question as to authenticity; the building was indeed a hospital, and its destruction was absolute. The cameraman had skillfully zoomed-in on the human misery, and the anguish on the faces of those with maimed and torn bodies was real. The voice-over detailed in excellent English how the American criminal pilots had systematically destroyed this medical facility on the outskirts of Haiphong. The footage had been shot for impact and shock value. Trader was stunned.

"You will read a statement denouncing the barbarous conduct of your government, Captain Trader," said the man standing beside his stool. "What we just saw was not warfare. It was murder, and you will let the world know that you do not condone such conduct. Your statement will be read this afternoon in front of many cameras, and for once in your miserable life you can do something that will be both honorable and just."

"I can't do that," Trader said, staring down at his bare feet.

"We'll see." The man motioned to two guards who immediately pounced on Trader. They were joined by two more, and within moments the four had him trussed in a long rope with his arms pulled up high behind his back. One end of the rope was threaded through a pulley anchored into the ceiling and Trader was roughly hoisted off his feet. As his arms were wrenched backward and upward to a point level with his head, the full weight of his body was now being excruciatingly supported by his shoulders. The pain was indescribable, and he screamed uncontrollably as he moved back and forth like some giant, broken pendulum. Then the foursome began beating him with bamboo staves. At some point he lost consciousness.

An eternity passed. Now semi-conscious, he was freed and dragged back to his cell. For a full day he lay where they had dropped him, every muscle and joint protesting the slightest movement.

And he had known this was but a prelude to a terrible journey into hell.

*   *   *

Over the course of the next few months his tormentors devised even more sadistic torture for him to endure, and though he now found himself praying for death, his prayers were never answered. During this time he saw only one other American prisoner, a black man and, if possible, was in far worse shape than he. The man was being dragged face up by his feet from the interrogation room, his head thudding loudly on the concrete floor. Their eyes locked for what seemed like an age, and then they were out of each other's view.

Trader never saw the man again, never knew what became of him. However, the sight of that stoic figure remained indelibly etched in his mind, and it gave him the strength to endure.

Three more times during those months he had been moved to other prisons and the beatings never ceased. He told himself he'd been singled out for special abuse because of his rank, but he really wasn't sure. He estimated that his weight had dropped from 178 pounds to about 130, and was aware that his salt and pepper hair was rapidly turning white. His vision was deteriorating, and he noticed that whenever he tried to focus on objects more than a few feet away, his eyes would begin an involuntary dance in their sockets, two demented demons loosed from inside some horrible inferno. He became truly alarmed, sure he was going blind.

James Vincent Trader knew the full meaning of despair.

Then, in either September or October of 1972, after almost two years of solitude, he finally spoke with another American. He had been trucked to a new prison, journeying at odd hours of the day and night for a week, and placed in a cell which for the first time in his captivity had a window. True, the glass was opaque, four feet above his reach and covered with years of encrusted grime, but still, it was cause for celebration. At least he now had the pretense of sunlight, a small luxury which overwhelmed him. He took inventory of his new home. He had a cot, a thin, straw-filled mattress, and one blanket. There was a metal bowl a spoon, a bar of lye soap and a washcloth. He saw himself rich, and gave thanks to the Creator for his bounty.

Late that night he communicated with a fellow countryman. The muted sound had puzzled him at first, a constant tapping on the wall, low to the floor, somewhere near the foot of his bunk. He couldn't make sense out of it. Was it an animal? No, too regular, he quickly reasoned. Morse code? No.

Then it hit him! Of course! *The man next door was trying to communicate in the prisoners' code!*

He had been briefed by intelligence officers as to the existence of this code and how the pilots communicated with each other. This information had been passed on by the handful of prisoners who had been released over the years by the North Vietnamese, and every U. S. pilot knew that the alphabet was arranged into a box five rows across, five rows down. Twenty-five letters filling the box, the letter K deleted, as the letter C could be used in its stead.

Yes! He was definitely trying to communicate!

Over the course of the next few nights Trader discovered he was in a place called An Bhat, about sixty miles north of Hanoi, and that there were nine other prisoners. His proficiency with the code rapidly improved, and by the end of the week he was transmitting and receiving messages with speed and accuracy. His first priority was to memorize the names and serial numbers of seventy other prisoners, while others in turn added his vital statistics to their memorized lists. He was finally part of a group, and his heart sang with joy. For the first time in almost two years he felt glad to be alive.

"I'm going to survive this nightmare," he whispered to the dark one night after the talking had ceased, the men signing off as always with the initials G.B.A., 'God Bless America.' "I'm going to survive," he repeated, "even if it kills me!" He chuckled at his own feeble attempt at humor, and then fell into a fitful sleep.

*   *   *

Six hours after Trader had been confirmed shot-down that December morning, the Secretary of Defense signed a priority directive for all branches of the military. Effective immediately, no officer with a master's degree or a higher in nuclear physics would be allowed to serve within two hundred miles of the coast of Vietnam. No exceptions would be entertained.

The fervent hope whispered within a very tight circle of senior leaders at the Pentagon was that Captain James Vincent Trader had perished.

CHAPTER 3

The peephole opened to dimly reveal a pair of expressionless eyes. Satisfied the prisoner posed no threat, the guard unlocked the heavy steel door, stepped aside, and stood at attention as Colonel Ky entered the cramped eight-foot by ten foot cell. The prisoner was none other than Mukmahr Jallud, and he was being held in a dungeon in the sub-basement of the Offices for State Security, in Hanoi, North Vietnam.

Jallud rose from the stone floor and faced Ky. He was dressed in week-old under shorts, a too-small cotton shirt, and wore leg irons. He was clueless as to why his fortunes had plummeted so far, so fast.

"Colonel Ky, my friend..." he began in French.

"Silence! Get dressed. You're going to see General Trang." Ky motioned impatiently for to the guard to enter and remove the restraints.

This was Jallud's seventh day in the dungeon, seven terror-filled days, and six dread-filled nights. Only seven days ago — it seemed more like seven years — he had been awash in the glory of his own greatness. Now this! In the name of Allah, what had happened?

As the guard worked on opening his restraints, Jallud thought back to how he had retired for the night a week ago smug in the knowledge that within hours he would have accomplished the impossible. He alone would bring American scientists to Libya, and with their arrival, his country would emerge as the Light of Lights among nations!

The arrangements had all been made. His emissaries in Switzerland had assured him the thirty-two million dollars would be deposited into the secret North Vietnamese account in Zurich. Satisfied that everything was on schedule, and secure in the knowledge that nothing could go wrong, he had contacted the submarine commander. A time was agreed to for the transfer of the prisoners, and he had retired for the night at eight o'clock, having instructed the hotel staff to awaken him at two o'clock the following morning. This would give him ample time to motor the short distance to the harbor at Haiphong, and join the submarine for the long journey back to its home half-way around the world.

He had been awakened from a sound sleep by the screams and blows of an irate Colonel Ky, kicking and punching him like a man possessed. Jallud had rolled away from his tormentor, wrapping himself in a self-made straightjacket fashioned from his tangled bed sheets and had fallen heavily to the floor. Two guards dragged him off into the night wearing only his shorts.

Now, here he was, shackled, still dressed in his filthy underpants, a prisoner in what had to be the meanest, most noxious cell in this foul excuse for a country. However, the worst indignity was that no one had informed him as to the nature of his crimes!

To occupy the endless hours, his mind had run rampant. He had painstakingly analyzed every conceivable scenario to explain away his predicament. But one very disconcerting thought kept percolating to the surface, crowding aside all other possibilities. Suppose the North Vietnamese had never intended to hand over the American prisoners? What if it had all been a charade, a stringing him along until the money was safely in their hands? If this was indeed the case, then Jallud realized his future did not look promising. But wouldn't they have already killed him, he quickly counter-reasoned, and then figure out later how to deal with the Supreme Ruler? There was no court to which Gaddafi could turn to press his claim, so maybe he was right, maybe the North Vietnamese had decided to steal the money and the consequences be damned! Maybe these cunning little devils had similar negotiations underway with several other sources, standing to make a hundred million dollars or more from a slew of unsuspecting parties. They were certainly sneaky enough to do just that. It was a chilling thought, and he was beginning to see Trang in an altogether different light. Begrudgingly, he had come to accept a sad conclusion. His future looked as bleak as his surroundings.

As the guard freed his legs, an army captain appeared and beckoned Ky to follow him into the corridor. The two conferred in whispers for several minutes, and when Ky re-entered the cell it was as if someone else had taken his place. Ky wore an exaggerated toothy smile.

"Mr. Jallud, I must leave for a few minutes, but I'll return momentarily, I promise. Then I'll take you where you can shower and dress in clean clothes." He paused long enough to rattle off instructions to the guard, then left. The guard followed fast on the heels of his superior, surprising Jallud, as he made no attempt to lock the heavy metal door. Jallud sat on his bunk, folded his arms across his chest, wrapped his one blanket around his shoulders, and waited.

Ky returned as promised, carrying two large, obviously new bath towels, as well as soap, shaving utensils, a comb and hairbrush, all cradled in his arms like one bearing gifts to a pasha. "Come, come, Mr. Jallud! We must get you out of this place at once!" he chided, all smiles and gaiety. "This won't do at all. Come."

Jallud followed Ky up two flights of dimly lit stairs to the ground level and his first glimpse of sunlight in a week. Down to the end of the tiled hall they trekked, Ky now in the lead followed by Jallud, who in turn was trailed by the guard manhandling Jallud's suitcase.

Events were moving too fast. Jallud was thoroughly confused. What had transpired in some great hall of power to have made his fortunes take so dramatic a turn? It was all too much.

Ky opened the last door on the left with a theatrical flourish and stepped aside for Jallud to enter. True to his word, Ky had delivered him to a bathroom. Not just any bathroom. This one was huge. He was greeted by acres of white tile and chrome, all blinding in its sheer cleanliness.

"This is General Trang's personal facility. He insists on nothing but the best for our honored guest!" Ky reverently laid his armload of provisions onto a white leather chair, and beckoned impatiently to the guard to place the large valise close by. "Everything you need is here, Excellency. I'll wait for you outside. Take as long as you need. And when you're ready, we'll go upstairs and see Minister Trang."

Jallud nodded, afraid his voice would fail him. Something serious must have taken place to precipitate this sudden turn of events, and he silently vowed to regain the upper hand. But, first, he would transform himself back into a human being.

He locked the door and spent the next forty-five minutes in paradise.

*   *   *

If Ky was exasperated with Jallud for the length of time he'd taken, he displayed no sign of displeasure when the Arab finally stepped into the hall. "We'll go directly up to Minister Trang's office," he said, leading the way to the main stairway. People were everywhere, scurrying up-and-down, to and fro, bees engaged in the important work of maintaining the hive.

"The minister is out on business, but he'll be back shortly. However, he instructed me to serve lunch while you wait." Ky beamed at the newly rehabilitated guest.

A half hour later Trang entered, accompanied by a middle-aged man dressed in starched hospital whites.

"Ah, Mr. Jallud, how nice to see you again." The kind words were indeed there, but the voice and eyes bespoke a different story. Jallud could see that Trang was not the least bit pleased to see him.

Jallud did not rise as Trang approached, a deliberate act of unspoken contempt. The two glared at each other.

Jallud finally broke the impasse. "What in the hell is going on here, Trang? Just what..."

Trang silenced him with a finger to his lips. "All in good time. Do you require medical attention? I hope you weren't mistreated during your period of protective custody..."

"I don't need a goddamned doctor, I need answers!" Jallud yelled. "I repeat. What in the hell's going on here? And I haven't been in protective custody. I've been locked in a goddamned prison cell like one of your American pilots!"

Trang dismissed the doctor, and hurried over to his desk. "Sit down, Mr. Jallud." It was a command. "You and I have much to discuss. Since our last meeting you've managed to create problems of such magnitude for my government that I honestly don't know if the situation's salvable. Because of your utter incompetence, you have single-handedly disrupted our negotiations with the Americans in Paris. So much so, that our delegation had to leave France empty-handed. We were prepared to sign an accord with Kissinger and his little Saigon puppet, but that's no longer imminent. And all because you couldn't carry out a simple business agreement." Again, he held up his hand, signaling that he wouldn't be interrupted. "Simply put, no money was transferred to our account in Switzerland, and no submarine came to pick up the Americans."

This can't be, was Jallud's singular thought.

"While we were debating whether or not to just shoot you," Trang continued, "we finally figured out what happened." He paused to pick up a sheet of paper.

"Two days ago a Russian freighter found evidence that a submarine had sunk in the Tonkin Gulf. The Russians think there must have been an explosion on board. We learned this from intercepted radio messages between the freighter and the Russian naval command at Vladivostok. We also learned that analysis of the debris proved the boat was neither American nor Russian, so the Soviets have concluded that it must have been Chinese. But we know better, don't we?"

Jallud could only stare, mouth agape.

Trang continued. "Late last night we received an urgent message from our emissary in Switzerland informing us that he had tracked down your money. It had found its way into a wrong account! You couldn't even do that right," he mocked. "So, as of today, *Mr. Ambassador,* there's no submarine, no money, and no peace treaty." His eyes were full of open contempt.

Jallud could only think of the money. *Thirty-two million American dollars placed in the wrong account?* If this was indeed the case—and he had no reason to doubt what he had just been told—then he may as well shoot himself, and save Gaddafi the trouble. "And where's the money, now?" Jallud asked in what he hoped sounded like an even tone.

Trang waved an impatient hand. "It seems your lackeys deposited the entire sum into an account controlled by Monsieur

'Papa Doc' Duvalier, the president of Haiti. And there it sat until a few hours ago. Fortunately for you, the Haitian president was unaware of his windfall, and it's my understanding the money is now back with your people." Trang shook his head in disgust. "You've left my government in a shambles, and the politburo is now looking for blood. But it's *my* blood they want, Mr. Jallud!" Well, you can be sure if I'm about to lose my head, then I'll damn well have yours taken first!"

Jallud walked over to the window and stared down at the street, playing for time. From his second story vantage point he could see that the city was a beehive of activity. The streets were crammed with pedestrians, bicycles, and pushcarts of every description. He spotted a lone civilian car, but there seemed to be no shortage of trucks inching their way through the confusion. Even though the windows were slightly ajar, little noise drifted up. He shifted his gaze to scan the rest of the city, and because there were few tall buildings in Hanoi his view was unobstructed. What he saw was truly depressing. Although the Americans had not bombed this capital, it was certainly a wretched-looking metropolis. How in the name of Allah had the Americans come to wage war on such a pitiful excuse for a country? What possible threat could this filthy little pile of dirt be to America, or anyone else for that matter? His face hardened as he thought of the man behind him, and in that moment knew he would get everything he wanted.

"General Trang," he began, his back still turned, "I have no time for exaggerated tales of heads rolling; yours, mine, or anyone else's. I came to Hanoi for one purpose, and I intend to complete my mission. The only change of plan that has taken place is the time element. Nothing more. You people been at war for so many decades that a couple of extra months won't make a difference. The Americans will sign the accords in Paris, and then leave this corner of the world forever. My original plan is still sound so we will stick to it." He turned to face the general. Nothing was going to stand in his way, certainly nothing as inconsequential as this mere speck of an excuse for a country hidden halfway around the world.

"Go back and tell your politburo the deal is still on. The American prisoners will be shipped back to my country by a submarine, and you shall have your money. I, Jallud guarantee it! Now, arrange for me to be taken to my legation, because I need to confer with my government." He glanced at his watch and quickly calculated. It would be about four o'clock in the morning in Tripoli, which meant he would have to awaken the Supreme Leader. Well, it couldn't be helped. Gaddafi would understand — he hoped. "Tell your masters that I will double the price to seventy million. That should more than make up for any inconvenience your government might have suffered by having to delay signing a peace treaty. But hear me well, General. Forget all you might have heard that Arabs get insulted if you don't haggle. There'll be no negotiation. Seventy-million, take it or leave it, as the Americans say."

Trang had no intentions of haggling. "How soon can you have your new submarine here?"

Jallud knew nothing about submarines. He had no idea how fast they could travel and no clue as to how long it would take to prepare the second craft. He blurted out the first thing that popped into his head. "January. Three months from now. Yes, January fifteenth, to be precise. Tell your politburo that I shall come back for the Americans on January fifteenth. Tell them that as an expression of my good faith I shall deposit an additional twenty million dollars into your account in Switzerland before I leave for Tripoli. Should I not return by that date, then the deal is off and you're free to keep all the money as payment for any inconvenience your government might have suffered."

"Agreed." Trang busied himself stuffing documents into his case, but Jallud could tell by the way the man moved that he was excited. "I'll arrange for transportation to your legation. Colonel Ky will accompany you. We'll meet back here as soon as you have all the particulars worked out with your government. It doesn't matter if it's three in the morning, we meet back here."

Jallud nodded his approval. "One last thing. I want the Americans moved from whatever pigpens you have them caged in at the moment to more suitable quarters. I also want them to have thorough medical and dental exams," he continued, "and starting immediately, I want them put on a proper diet. These men have a long journey ahead, and they *will* be fit when the time comes to travel. They're to be allowed plenty of exercise, sunlight, reading materials, and anything else within reason," he added. "And should they desire to write letters home, then see to it. Of course, those letters will never be posted, but they'll never know that." He smiled, but only for an instant. "Remember, I tasted your gracious hospitality for barely a week. These men have been your guests for years. I want to protect my investment, so before I leave for Tripoli, I'll want to inspect their new facilities. Do we understand one another?"

"We do. I'll give the necessary orders before I meet with the politburo." Anger crept over Trang's face, erasing the pleasure felt only moments ago. The thought of the Americans living in relative comfort for the next couple of months was almost more than he could bear. "Please wait here for Colonel Ky. He'll be with you shortly."

General Trang scurried off on a mission to save his neck.

CHAPTER 4

How strange these past couple of months, Trader mused, returning to his room one evening after supper. It was early January 1973. Instead of fetid cells, he and the others now lived in a converted convent next to a grammar school. The nine prisoners spent their days together, their Vietnamese guards all but ignoring them. He was both pleased and puzzled by their sudden good fortune. Every facet of life had improved, even to the point all were actually gaining weight.

The turning point had come dramatically and unexpectedly one night in October. It had been well after midnight when Captain Dong, their jailer, had come into the cellblock and announced over his ever-present bullhorn that the prisoners were to get up and assemble in silence outside their cells. They would have two minutes to comply.

They did as instructed and, like nervous schoolboys, furtively glanced about under the dim hallway bulbs. They were seeing one another for the first time.

"You will follow me in single file, starting with you, Captain Trader. There will be no talking. You're being trucked to a safer home."

The ride lasted an hour. At the end of the journey the Americans were ushered into a two story, faded red brick building.

"This is your new home. You'll be two to a room," Dong said, the word cell mysteriously disappearing from his vocabulary. "We will meet at six o'clock in the morning at which time I'll explain certain things." Dong nodded to his sergeant and the man sprang to life. He quickly paired them off until he came to Trader.

"Captain Trader, you will have this room to yourself. Rank has its privileges, if I have the American saying right," Captain Dong said from behind a stupid grin. He held the door open and Trader entered without a word. The door shut behind him, but for the first time in memory he didn't hear a bolt slam home.

*   *   *

Dong assembled his charges at six o'clock and marched them into a large room on the second floor. A table was set with nine places. He wordlessly shut the door, leaving the group alone for the first time. All stood like statues, none daring to make the first move toward the table. They stared at bowls of steaming rice, a platter of black bread and two pots of hot tea, luxuries they had only dreamt of. It was a veritable feast. Several seconds passed before Trader broke the silence. "Gentlemen, my name is Jim Trader, and I guess I'm the senior officer present. I've no idea what Charlie is up to," he said, using the slang name to mean any Vietnamese soldier, "but I'm going to command you all to eat. I don't see any of us being singled out for special treatment, so my instincts tell me to have at it. This spread may not be repeated, so enjoy the getting while the getting is good." He moved towards the nearest chair and sat. The others needed no second invitation.

They ate in silence. With mouths filled to overflowing they grinned stupidly at each other, all winking and waggling their eyebrows.

When Trader was finished, he pushed back his chair and stood. Eight pairs of eyes locked onto the tall, gaunt, white-haired captain.

"You know who I am, gentlemen, so while we have the opportunity, let's introduce ourselves, and put faces with names. I don't know when Dong will return, or what the future holds, so let's skip the formalities. Trader nodded to the man on his right to start.

The officer rose and gave a small nod to include them all. "Doug Gilchrest, class of sixty-eight," he said, a reference to the year he had been shot down. As an afterthought he added, "Commander, U.S. Navy."

So it went. And once finished, each man remained standing.

"Mark FitzGerald, Captain, Air Force. I joined this happy club in March, sixty-seven."

"Tim Sweringen, Lieutenant Colonel, Air Force, class of sixty-five."

"John Waltensperger, Navy Commander, class of seventy-one."

The last four were Air Force lieutenant colonel Walter Boyd; Navy lieutenant commander Gerry Glasstner, Navy Lieutenant Commander Niels Borden, and Marine Major Nick Wolfe.

Then it was back to Trader. Everyone was now standing, eyes glued to their leader. Trader spoke in a voice barely above a whisper.

"Max Epperman, Lieutenant Commander, U.S. Navy, class of seventy-one. Dead, but never to be forgotten."

"Hear! Hear!" the prisoners rejoined, remembering their comrade; seen by none except Trader, but known and admired by all.

* * *

Shortly after onset of darkness on the evening of January 15, 1973, Trader and the other eight were rousted from their rooms, blindfolded, handcuffed, and warned repeatedly to keep silent, as they were led out of the building and into a truck. They traveled for almost two hours. They had no idea what was happening, and Dong had offered no explanation.

We're somewhere close to the sea, Trader sensed, the smell of salt heavy in the air. Hustled into a metal shed, they were told to sit on the concrete floor. Again Dong reminded them to stay quiet.

Trader felt a sense of foreboding. They all knew the war was drawing to a close simply because they had heard the constant explosions of the all-out bombing missions of the past three weeks and had rightfully concluded there were no longer areas considered off-limits by the U.S. command in Saigon. For anything to happen to them now would be the cruelest irony of all. His mind conjured up a kaleidoscope of images, none comforting. He visualized them being executed as a group, in some mean-spirited retribution for the bombing campaign that had obviously inflicted heavy damage all across North Vietnam. To have endured so much, only to be killed on the eve of victory filled him with a sense of hopelessness. It just can't end like this, he reasoned, not really holding out much hope. So he did the only thing he could. He prayed.

He had no idea how long he'd been sitting, when he suddenly heard the protesting rumble of the doors being opened, and the sound of muffled footsteps. Then silence.

He held his breath in anticipation of the expected sound of gunfire.

CHAPTER 5

Captain Dieter Weir rose from his stool bolted to the floor at the small, fold-down Formica-topped table. "Time to go," he said to Jallud, then turned to his executive officer whose face had taken on a surreal cast in the red glow of the night-operations lights. "Mister Grundhauser, take the boat up slowly to ten meters and standby to raise the observation scope."

"Aye, Captain," then Grundhauser repeated the command for everyone in the control room to hear.

For the past twenty minutes Weir had studied his nautical charts of Haiphong Harbor; dubious copies made by the Soviets from already outdated French ones. All were at least ten years old and, because of this, Weir was skeptical of their accuracy. He knew that winds and tides changed the ocean floor over time, and although the North Vietnamese had made half-hearted attempts to keep the deep channels into this harbor clear, he didn't trust the information before him. He was keenly aware that his predecessor had failed in his attempt to enter this same harbor three months earlier. The result had been the loss of his boat and all hands. Today would not be a repeat performance.

"Ten meters; all stop, up scope." Grundhauser followed the rising periscope from a crouched position, extending the handles as the electrically activated tube rose with barely a sound. "Ready, Captain," he said, taking a step backward.

This submarine, originally named the *USS Seahorse*, was now owned by the sovereign state of Libya, who in turn had purchased it from Egypt, in 1971. Its new name was the *Sword of Allah*, and it represented fifty percent of Libya's remaining submarine force. One third of the underwater fleet had been lost off the coast of North Vietnam three months earlier with the mysterious explosion and sinking of the British-built boat, *Desert Wind*. She had gone down with all hands, an entirely Libyan crew. Captain Weir had been vehement in his opposition to sending a submarine such a distance under the command of a Libyan captain. He had insisted the man was not qualified but Gaddafi ignored his warnings. It was all about national pride. As a result, Libya had lost a fine boat and a crew of fifty-five.

This time, Captain Weir, an East German national, was in command. His officers were also East Germans, and Jallud had confidently stepped aboard for this trip to the other side of the earth. The officers had all served as submariners in the service of the Democratic Peoples Republic. Hired by Gaddafi as technical representatives to help train his fledgling underwater service, each had signed lucrative two-year contracts with incentive clauses outlining the possibility of extending the agreements. Other clauses spelled out provisions for hefty phase-point bonuses.

Life in Tripoli was life in paradise. This seacoast capital was a world away from the harsh winters of northern Germany and the harsher realities of a tightly regulated society. Erich Hoenecker, the president of East Germany, had approved the Libyan government's request for assistance, and saw in this the perfect opportunity to curry favor with the young, firebrand revolutionary, Lt. Colonel Gaddafi. None of the officers were currently on active military status, and Hoenecker's hope was that once he had a foot in the door, then other opportunities would present themselves. Libya had oil, and lots of it. Hoenecker coveted this endless sea of petroleum and hoped to buy all he needed at a price more favorable than that offered by the Soviets. Therefore, when the Libyans approached his government for technical assistance in training submarine crews, he quickly saw the possibilities and granted his unconditional approval.

Weir now positioned himself in front of the scope and pressed his face deep into the rubber mask. He scanned the sky, then the sea, making a full three hundred and sixty-degree sweep. He repeated the procedure, but more slowly. His eyes stayed glued to the scope. "We have a three-quarter sky," he announced to no one in particular, "along with a waning moon, and seas with light swells. Perfect weather." A moment later he asked, "Is the high gain antenna up, Mister Webber?"

"Aye, Captain," replied Lt. Heinrich Webber, the communications officer. "HF, VHF, UHF and short wave all operational. I'm engaging the HF antenna now."

"Time check."

"Eighteen-twenty-two, Zulu, Captain," Webber replied, a reference to the standard twenty-four hour navigation clock used by all ships at sea. "Oh-one-twenty-two local, sir," he added, confirming that Hanoi was seven hours ahead of London and Greenwich Mean Time.

Weir pulled away from the observation scope with a self-congratulatory smile on his face. "I'm within one minute of the time I promised the North Vietnamese I'd rendezvous. How's that for German efficiency, Mister Jallud, hmm?" He returned to the periscope, but continued to chatter. "I had to take my boat some eleven thousand nautical miles to be at this spot at this precise moment. Now let's hope our Vietnamese comrades can travel five nautical miles with equal precision."

Jallud humored the German. "I'm impressed, Captain. What more can I say?"

"*Contact!* Bearing, three-one-six degrees," the radar operator called out in a loud voice. "It's a small surface craft, Captain. Range, eight hundred meters."

"Thank you, good job," Weir praised the Libyan radar operator. "Mister Webber, let's see if this is our escort. Please give the recognition signal."

The electronic microburst from the *Sword of Allah* was answered within moments.

"Excellent!" Weir drew back from the periscope and collapsed the handles. "Standby to surface. Blow all ballast. All ahead slow. Steer three-one-zero. Ready on the hatch."

The submarine was now a hive of activity. It gently broke the surface and turned toward the North Vietnamese patrol craft, which was on an intercept course.

The moment the conning tower cleared the swells, Weir popped the hatch and scurried topside along with Grundhauser, Jallud, and two lookouts. The officers plugged earphones and microphones into jacks allowing them communicate with the crew below.

"Lars, as soon as we've secured our mooring lines I want bunkering operations to start at once," Weir said to Grundhauser.

As he spoke, he tracked the North Vietnamese craft through night-vision binoculars then turned to Jallud. "We must take on our passengers with a minimum of delay. I'd like to be well clear of the harbor and running deep before first light. It wouldn't be good to be spotted by American reconnaissance aircraft."

"Understood, Captain." Jallud was about to explode with excitement. Finally, after so many months and one disastrous false start, the goal was clearly in his sights. The American pilots would soon be his. All he had to do was make sure that the balance of funds was transferred in Zurich to the North Vietnamese account. No more screw-ups like last time. And once the word came back that it had been done, they'd be on their way. What a glorious day! This date would signal the beginning of a new Muslim millennium!

*   *   *

"American pilots, pay attention to what I say," Trader heard an unfamiliar voice call out. The English was right, but the voice somehow strange. Moreover, the accent was definitely not Vietnamese. "Everyone stand-up, please, so that we can remove your blindfolds and restraints."

The nine struggled awkwardly to their feet and stood at attention. One by one they were released from their handcuffs and blindfolds. They all rubbed chaffed wrists and squinted with curious eyes.

Trader counted two dozen North Vietnamese army troops stationed at various points around the perimeter of the dimly lit warehouse, but closer at hand stood a dozen Caucasian naval enlisted men. All wore blue helmets and conspicuous armbands on their right sleeves. They were emblazoned with only two letters. *U.N.* The men were unarmed. And in front of the sailors stood a solitary figure dressed in a plain tan uniform, devoid of insignia save for his shoulder boards, which bore four gold braids.

A naval captain, Trader thought, staring at the man. His musings were cut short.

"Gentlemen, for you the war is over. You are now in my protective custody. Please follow my instructions. We're leaving to board a waiting vessel that will take you home. We have very little time, so I'll ask you to form a line, and I'll escort you to the ship. Please, no talking. It's taken many months of negotiations to secure your release, so you must do nothing to jeopardize the process at this late hour." He motioned the men forward.

Trader couldn't believe his eyes and ears. *Free!* And under the protection of the United Nations! The men sprang into a line, and were led outside and onto a pier. Tethered before them was a submarine.

Flanked by the sailors from the United Nations, and observed by at least one hundred North Vietnamese Regular Army troops, Trader led his group aboard.

The unknown captain ushered them below, then forward. The space contained nine bunks already made-up with sparkling new linens and blue blankets adorned with the U.N. crest.

"Gentlemen, there are nine footlockers. They have your names on them and they contain everything you'll need during the voyage. There's a head to your starboard. Make yourselves comfortable. I suggest trying to sleep, but whatever you decide, I only ask you remain quiet. We'll be casting off momentarily." He smiled for the first time. "Welcome to freedom."

Trader stepped forward, brought himself to attention and saluted. The others followed his lead and rendered the same courtesy.

The captain seemed embarrassed. He returned the honors, and somehow his salute turned into a wave as he departed. "I must secure this hatch," he said apologetically, by way of explanation. The cylindrical door closed on well-oiled hinges, and the locking mechanism rotated smoothly into place.

On the other side of the hatch, Jallud grinned broadly, punched the air with a clenched fist, then hurried to the conning tower, the nerve center of the submarine. *Thank you, Doctor Bakktari,* he thought. *I was sure you were nothing but a crazy psychiatrist, but I now see I was wrong! My apologies!*

He headed in search of Captain Weir to say he was ready to get underway.

* * *

Unknown to Captain James Vincent Trader, USN, or any

of the other eight prisoners, on January 27, 1973, the governments of The United States of America and The Democratic Republic of Vietnam signed a peace accords in Paris, France. America's longest war was over.

One provision of the agreement specified that all American prisoners were to be freed from their jails in North Vietnam and sent home.

*   *   *

Several time zones to the west, and hundreds of miles deep in the Libyan Desert, Dr. Sikar Bakktari sat in his air-conditioned office sipping noisily from a hot demitasse of sweet Turkish coffee the color and consistency of glue. He was studying the contents of nine manila folders for the thousandth time. It was a task he never grew tired of.

Two days ago a cryptic radio signal birthed in the China Sea bounced off the stratosphere, returned to earth, and was intercepted in Tripoli, Libya, informing him of success. *The* Sword of Allah *is returning to its scabbard.* The message was simple and succinct, but it spoke volumes. Jallud had the Americans and was on his way home.

Bakktari was the one who had come up with the idea of having the submarine crew pose as United Nations forces. He had reasoned this was the one neutral symbol the Americans would recognize, rally behind, and trust implicitly. The ruse had worked. He actually giggled as he imagined the Americans trooping on board without protest, indeed, in all likelihood with unabashed eagerness. Oh, how he would have loved to have been there to witness it. But enough! He had worked to do. There would be time later to accept kudos from on high.

He turned his attention to the folders arrayed before him. They contained the histories of the nine American prisoners, and he knew each man's story backward and forward. As he prepared to dig in, his mind turned to Jallud. Jallud had been ordered by the Supreme Leader to take Bakktari into his confidence, and had commanded Jallud to follow any and all advice given by the doctor. Bakktari could tell from the moment he first met Jallud that he didn't care for that arrangement one bit. Nevertheless,

Jallud had been smart enough to realize he did not have a choice in the matter. He was taciturn, petulant and oftentimes downright rude when dealing with Bakktari, but he followed the doctor's suggestions.

Over the course of several meetings Bakktari had come to understand Jallud, and had made a clinical diagnosis. In layman's terms, the man was quite mad. No doubt about it. Jallud was a sociopathic, manic-depressive, fully capable of exploding at the slightest provocation. However, he had the ability and the capacity to restrain himself if circumstances proved beyond his control, or if he thought he was manipulating the other person for his own purposes. But if events did not unfold to his liking, or if he suspected he was becoming cornered or trapped, then the man was fully capable of extreme violence, possibly murder. He was a man the Americans would label a loose cannon. Not a medical term, Bakktari thought, but an apt one.

Bakktari took great pride in the fact that he understood Americans. He had trained in the United States for more than a decade. His undergraduate degree was from Cornell; his medical diploma from the University of Missouri, and his board certification was from the psychiatric residency program at St. Vincent's Hospital in New York City. Oh, he knew the American mind all right! He knew what made it tick.

He picked up the first folder and flipped it open, instantly engrossed in its contents. Stapled to the left side was a photograph of his patient. It was a picture of James Vincent Trader, taken approximately four years ago in Washington, D. C. The man staring back at him was slightly taller than average, clean-cut, the image of one born to command. Bakktari's eyes drifted to the right side of the folder and he quickly scanned the biographical sketch he had written in English.

JAMES VINCENT TRADER

Born July 5, 1928, St. Louis, Missouri. Graduate of the U.S. Naval Academy, 1950. Naval aviation graduate, 1951, followed by four years of duty as a carrier pilot. Two combat tours in Korea. Married to the former Patricia Parsons of White Plains, New York. Three children:

girl, boy, girl. M.S. degree in nuclear physics from Stanford University; Ph.D. in nuclear physics with original research in particle acceleration, UCLA, in 1962. Not much information as to his duties after graduation, other than to note that he was assigned to the Pentagon and traveled a lot.

Next came an assignment to Pacific Fleet Headquarters in Hawaii. Then in 1970, sent to sea as an air wing squadron operations officer. Shot down over North Vietnam that same year. Nothing heard of him since. The North Vietnamese did not acknowledge that he was even a prisoner, and his wife and children have no idea whether he is dead or alive. Neither for that matter does his government. However, the wife and children have 'kept the faith', according to newspaper articles sent from America. Said articles are a part of this file. (See attachments) The family has since moved to Denver, Colorado. Patricia Trader is currently working in a law firm and attending law school at night. Like her husband, Patricia Trader is a go-getter. No picture of wife or children available.

Bakktari gave an almost imperceptible shake of his head, closed the folder, gave it a good luck pat and picked up the next one.

TIMOTHY SWERINGEN

Timothy Sweringen, Lt. Colonel, Air Force. No picture available. Born February 12, 1933, Topeka, Kansas. Graduated Purdue, 1955, with a degree in mathematics. M.A. degree in physics from the same institution the following year with a heavy emphasis on nuclear partition theory. Joined the Air Force in 1956. Graduated from Officer Candidate School, and went on to learn how to fly at Williams Air Force Base in Arizona. Graduation was followed with several operational assignments. In 1961, selected to attend MIT, where he earned his doctorate in nuclear physics. In early 1964 he was assigned to Kirtland Air Force Base in New Mexico, which is the home of the Sandia Labs, a facility known to be deeply involved in the American nuclear program. Not much more is known until his assignment to Korat Royal Thai Air Force Base, in 1965, as a squadron commander, flying F-105s. On his first mission over North Vietnam he was hit by a surface-to-air-missile. His wingman reported seeing a good parachute deploy, but lost sight of him in a torrential downpour. No record exists as to Sweringen's fate after this point. The North Vietnamese refuse to confirm that he is a prisoner. Timothy Sweringen had been in Southeast Asia exactly one week. He is divorced with no known relatives.

A rather timid knock on the door interrupted Bakktari as he leaned to pick up the third folder. "I said I wasn't to be disturbed!" he shouted at the unseen interloper.

Through the closed door, a disembodied voice answered. "Yes, Doctor, but you also said you wanted to be alerted when the mail plane arrives. Well, it's about five minutes away."

"*Oh!*" Bakktari swept up the files, carried them to the safe and hastily locked them inside. These files were for his eyes only. There were several other folders containing information on Jallud and other members of the staff. He even had one on Gaddafi.

The American prisoners wouldn't be here for another five weeks. However, the mail plane was bringing him the latest issue of *Playboy*, secreted among mountains of Western medical journals. Oh, how he loved *Playboy*! The articles were always so provocative, so stimulating! He laughed at his own wit, rubbed his hands in anticipation of the pleasures to come, and headed for the flight line.

*   *   *

For forty-one days, The *Sword of Allah* sailed westward, heading back to its homeport in the Mediterranean. Four times the boat rendezvoused with Libyan tankers. The first coupling took place in the Java Sea just south of Indonesia; the next, a hundred kilometers off the coast of Ceylon; then ten days later, a third, shortly after rounding the Cape of Good Hope and abeam of Angola. The last took place within sight of Tangiers, Morocco. Each meeting was a repeat performance of the outward-bound journey. A fuel line was passed without incident and the two vessels would plod along at five knots, tethered by a rubber umbilical cord feeding precious fuel to the submarine like a mother to her growing embryo. Radio chatter was non-existent, and the tanker captains handled the tasks with aplomb. Weir was impressed. He gave thanks to the god who did not exist in his communist homeland for the weather, which was cooperating beyond his wildest expectations, even taking into account the fact it was summertime in most of the latitudes he was traversing.

Captain Dieter Weir sailed into the harbor at Tripoli late in the afternoon on the last day of February 1973. He was tired and not ashamed to admit it. The *Sword of Allah* had been at sea for eighty days, and had made a trip equal to a circumnavigation of the globe.

CHAPTER 6

Resplendent in a crisp white naval uniform replete with a United Nations armband, a visibly elated Jallud led the Americans off the *Sword of Allah*. Flanking the gangplank, the entire submarine crew stood stiffly at attention. When Trader and his men appeared, they saluted, and then broke out in a round of cheers and hand clapping. Captain Weir approached Trader and saluted. "We were honored by your presence, Captain Trader."

Trader brought himself to attention and returned the salute. "Thank you, Captain. Your hospitality has overwhelmed us, and I will convey that message to the United Nations."

Weir smiled and shook the American's proffered hand. "I hope the rest of your journey is both safe and swift, and to borrow a saying from the Irish, 'May the wind be always at your back.'"

Bakktari stood at the foot of the gangway, dressed in a U.S. Air Force flight suit. "Hi, I'm Shakir Bakktari," he called out. "I'm a medical doctor, and I'll be escorting you on the next leg of your journey." Looking from one to another he asked, "So, how's everybody? After so long at sea, my guess is it'll take a while to regain your land legs. The earth will rock-and-roll under your feet until your inner ears calm down. Anyway, it's really great to have you guys here."

"It's great to be here, wherever here is," said Mark FitzGerald, looking about like a curious child. "You're American, right, Doc?"

Bakktari shook his head. "Nah, but I may as well be. I've lived in the States so long that sometimes I even forget I wasn't born there. Nope, I'm a true-blue Libyan by way of Pakistan four generations back. But I do work for the U.N.," he lied smoothly, "so I get to spend most of my time in New York and Geneva."

"Well it's good to see you, Doctor," said Trader. "We appreciate everything your organization's done for us." Trader was tired, but visibly excited. "What's the plan?" he asked.

"More travel, I'm afraid, but not too long, I promise," Bakktari replied, apologetically. "This time we'll be going by air."

"To where?"

"Unfortunately, I'm not at liberty to say, Captain. We must follow to the letter the restrictions placed on us by the North Vietnamese. We do not want to jeopardize any possible future releases, so we must play the hand they've dealt us. However, I can tell you this. All your questions will be answered shortly, so let's get on over to the air base, shall we? It's about a forty-five minute drive, so if you guys are ready, what say we shove-off?"

Trader walked beside Bakktari to a line of three waiting cars, the rest of his happy band of warriors a couple of paces behind. Because of the late hour, traffic was light. The small caravan made good time leaving the docks. It headed west, following the coastal highway toward what used to be the sprawling U.S. facility known as Wheelus Air Force Base.

Bakktari sat next to Trader in the rear of the darkened lead sedan, thrilled at how smoothly events were unfolding. The Americans were not in the least bit suspicious! He silently congratulated himself again on the success of his well-thought-out plan. He had wanted these men relaxed, and had deemed it an inviting touch that he had met the travelers wearing an American flight suit. Pilots universally identify with other men in such dress, and based on his warm reception, Bakktari knew he had made the right decision.

The convoy passed through the gates of the air base, and once inside the perimeter followed a military jeep with a *Follow Me* sign printed in both Arabic and English. The Jeep led them to a remote corner of the field and drew up alongside a parked C-130 cargo aircraft with only its number three engine turning. A squinting Trader could just make out the large United Nations crest on the tail and the organizational letters stenciled underneath.

"Thank God that bird's not an 'A' model," Tim Sweringen piped up from the front seat. "I flew those dogs when they first came off the production line way back when. Not fun."

"Why so?" John Waltensperger wanted to know.

"They had three-bladed props," Sweringen explained, squinting as he studied the plane. "Those rascals would vibrate enough to shake all of your fillings loose. You see, the C-130, or

Hercules as it's called, is a straight-wing design, and a real forgiving airplane to fly, but that original 'A' model quickly turned into a bear if you let it get away from you. And noisy! *Phew!* You couldn't yell loud enough for the rest of the crew to hear. Anyway, Lockheed fixed it by simply going to a four-blade prop in the B model. Now the Herc is a sweetheart to fly."

"The sooner we leave here, gentlemen the sooner we get there," Bakktari politely interrupted, "so what say we climb aboard. Your baggage should be right behind us." He turned to look. "In fact, it's in the van pulling up now. How's that for perfect timing?"

Within minutes, they were airborne, nine worn-out souls sound asleep, winging their way into the dark unknown.

* * *

On and on the plane droned toward a spot five hundred and forty miles south of Tripoli. The next thing Trader knew the loadmaster was making his rounds, shaking each of the stretched-out, sleeping figures. "Ten minutes to touchdown, sir," he repeated as he passed through the cabin. It was still dark.

Trader pushed himself upright, fumbled with his seatbelt, yawned and stretched. He was still groggy from only two hours sleep.

The landing was uneventful. The aircraft commander expertly lowered the large transport onto the runway then kept it rolling at a high rate of speed, making no attempt to reverse the engines. For three minutes the plane taxied at a fast clip, turning right, left, and then left again, until finally coming to a stop. All four engines were cut.

Bakktari rose, but signaled for the Americans to remain seated.

"Listen up, gentlemen. It's been one helluva long journey and I know you're exhausted. There's a bus waiting to take you to your quarters. Now I want each of you to promise me you'll do nothing but rest." He looked around at the seated Americans. "You'll find refreshments in your rooms so eat and drink, but, really, I just want you guys to sleep. Doctor's orders."

Nine heads nodded as one. All were ready to collapse, too

tired to think, just grateful that the long journey was over. They trooped off the Hercules and into a factory-fresh, air-conditioned Mercedes-Benz bus.

Trader had not felt such relief in a millennium, but as he wearily climbed the steps, he felt a gnawing sense of foreboding. He shook his head as if to exorcise a demon. He was just too tired. I'll deal with it later, he thought, but only after a long, long sleep.

*   *   *

As soon as the small convoy was out of sight heading toward the airport, Jallud jumped in his waiting staff car and drove from the docks in the opposite direction. He was off to Tripoli to report to Gaddafi on the resounding success of his mission. He was beside himself with pride. He had literally plucked the Americans out of North Vietnam only days before the peace accord had been signed in Paris! The war was over, and the remaining prisoners were going home to America. But not this group. *Oh, no!* They would serve one final purpose, and then he would dispose of them like so much offal. He could hardly wait to get started on the next phase of his plan. He had no doubt there would be many trying days ahead, possibly weeks, possibly even months, but neither did he doubt for a single moment that he would deliver to the Supreme Leader the means for him to become the most powerful man on earth. *Allah be praised!*

*   *   *

Muammar el-Gaddafi was not to be found in Tripoli. When Jallud had telephoned the palace shortly after eight o'clock and identified himself, he had been told that the Supreme Ruler had left for his retreat in Misurata, a medium-sized town on the shore of the Gulf of Sidra, one of several retreats the colonel would disappear to on a moment's notice.

Peeved at the inconvenience of having to travel further, Jallud nonetheless motored the extra miles, arriving at an area on the outskirts of town where half a dozen colorful tents were pitched. However, there was nothing haphazard about their arrangement. Security was paramount, and it took Jallud several minutes to be recognized, processed, then finally escorted to the audience with his master.

Gaddafi was praying while pacing the interior of his tent when Jallud entered.

"*Asalaam Alaykum,*" Jallud bowed as he offered up the greeting. *Peace be upon you.* Now dressed in a rumpled safari suit, he felt a trickling of sweat coming from his hairline and also from under his arms. He stood like a supplicant awaiting the invitation to come forward, loath to admit that he was somewhat frightened of the colonel. Not to the point of paralysis; indeed, to an observer nothing of the kind was evident. But in his heart Jallud knew that Gaddafi was his master and, he knew too, that he would always do his master's bidding.

"*Wa 'Alaykum Asalaam.*" Gaddafi smiled for only an instant, his eyes boring into those of his visitor. *And peace be upon you also.* He stood dressed in desert garb, a simple nomad, but this was no simple nomad. Here was the man who at twenty-seven had led a revolt against King Idris in 1969 and had declared himself the head of state. No minister, general or member of the royal family had opposed him. He had the full support of the people and, more importantly, the support of the younger officers and enlisted ranks of the armed forces. Gaddafi had taken the reins of power as if it had been his birthright.

"Sit," he commanded as he made himself comfortable on the array of pillows. He looked expectantly at his visitor.

"The Americans should be at the facility any minute now," Jallud began, glancing at his watch. He paused, raised his eyebrows, then his face broke out into a wide grin. "Excellency, we have pulled it off without a hitch! Those pilots think they're going home to America. You should have seen them. They were like sheep during the entire journey, not a peep out of any of them. But of course, Dr. Bakktari had made sure that they were medicated at all times to keep them docile."

Gaddafi rolled a string of worry beads between the fingers of his right hand as he listened. He nodded at times, but his expression never changed.

"So far, so good," Gaddafi finally allowed, "but now comes the hard part. When do you plan to inform the Americans that they were brought here to perform a certain task for us?"

"I didn't have an opportunity to speak to Dr. Bakktari at the dock. There just wasn't a good moment. But you are right. This could well prove to be a difficult job. Bakktari told me weeks ago that he felt he should be seen as their friend and guardian, which means he must win their complete trust. Therefore, they must be given a few days of uninterrupted rest. Then they will receive thorough medical exams, because I want to make sure our investments don't die on us. And when the time is right, either Bakktari or I will tell them that we need a small favor before they return to their families. He feels that this will be a very delicate moment." A hint of contempt crept into Jallud's voice. "Quite frankly, Excellency, I think this is all so much psychological rubbish, but I'll try his approach first. If it doesn't work, then I guarantee you, my methods will get results."

Although he sounded bold, the reality was that Jallud was treading cautiously. Gaddafi had brought Dr. Bakktari into the operation, and even though he had no desire to work with Bakktari, he knew that the physician held sway with Gaddafi, and in all likelihood was reporting to him on a regular basis. He steered the conversation away from Bakktari. "Before I go into the desert to rejoin the Americans, I must first meet with those who will be working with our German friends to get the missiles we need."

Jallud was referring to the small, but highly dangerous group of West German terrorists called the *Baader Mienhoff Gang*. This fanatical group of urban terrorists had one simple agenda: see the Western democracies destroyed. To that end, their *modus operandi* included; assassinations, kidnappings, and highly visible bombings of public buildings. They had ties to a similar group in Italy known as the *Red Brigade*, and both organizations enjoyed the support of a very powerful and wealthy benefactor: Colonel Gaddafi of Libya. And as long as he channeled American dollars in their direction, they would gladly do his bidding.

Jallud continued. "Before I left for North Vietnam, my agents had been told that stealing three tactical missiles from NATO stores in Germany would not be a problem. Nevertheless, the Germans were quick to point out that these missiles are not stored with their nuclear warheads attached. Like we are some sort of fools!" he added, angered at the obvious belittlement of his Arab agents by the haughty Germans. "My people assured them it was just the missiles we wanted, and that we would to pay handsomely. The price we all agreed to was two million dollars. I can set this task in motion on your command, Excellency. The Germans promised delivery within ninety days of the time we send them the word."

Gaddafi rose and began to pace, lost in thought. After several long moments he nodded. "Make it happen, my friend. I want those missiles by the end of this year, and it must be three of them. The Americans have got to complete their task by June of next year because I want everything ready for me at that time to announce to the Western leaders just what it is I have planned for them. Make it happen, my friend," he repeated.

Jallud stood, aware that the meeting was over. He bowed. "I'll get started right away, Excellency. *Fi Amanallah." In Allah's protection.* He backed deferentially out of the tent.

As he walked over to his car his thoughts were on the timetable Gaddafi had just laid out. It was all according to plan, of course, but it would be cutting things close, nonetheless. There simply was no more room left for the unexpected. The three-month delay in getting the Americans out of Vietnam had used up all of his maneuvering time. Everything would have to be ready by the start of June 1974, and regardless of how hard he pushed his Arab scientists, and no matter how much help they got from the Americans, this would be a challenging deadline to meet. He shrugged his shoulders. No matter. Allah would not forsake him now.

CHAPTER 7

It was barely nine o'clock and the temperature was already well into the upper eighties. The Americans had been playing basketball, but because of the heat they decided to call it quits.

Walking back to their rooms in small knots of two and three, they were content. Still, this routine had been going on for eight days now, and all were anxious for change.

Bakktari followed them from his office window, marveling at how well-adjusted they were. All had been given comprehensive medical and dental checkups, and he had spoken at length with each in an offhand, non-threatening manner, searching for any sign of post-captivity trauma or psychosis. So far, he had found none.

He now had their files spread out on his desk plus a couple more on the floor within easy reach. He was working his way back and forth among them making notations in a shorthand of his own invention, but gibberish to prying eyes. Specifically, Jallud's. He had just listened to the BBC top-of-the-hour international newscast on his short-wave radio, and had learned that the last group of Americans was to be released from North Vietnam within a matter of days. The war had now been over for almost two months. Five hundred and ninety men had been accounted for; all others were either dead or missing in action. This was the word from Hanoi Radio. In the last few days, the American media had begun to speculate that the number was far short of what had been expected, and journalists were calling for an accounting of over two thousand such missing service members. This was going to become one very hot potato, Bakktari thought as he bent down to retrieve a folder from the floor.

He studied the subject's photograph taken a day or so ago at the hospital. It showed a man in his early thirties wearing a big smile. Settling deep into his leather chair, Bakktari scanned what he had written.

MARK FITZGERALD

Mark FitzGerald was born in Colorado Springs, Colorado, on December 31, 1940, the last of seven children, to a novelist/playwright father, and a retired actress mother. In 1958 he was accepted into the first Air Force Academy class to begin its four-year course at the newly constructed campus in Colorado Springs. Because he was an honor graduate, he was enrolled in the Graduate School at the University of Chicago, where he exited five years later with a Ph.D. in physics. Shortly after his twenty-sixth birthday, and just shy of the mandatory cutoff date for entrance to flight school, he was sent to Vance Air Force Base in Enid, Oklahoma, for pilot training. Upon graduation, (first in his class) he went on to advanced fighter school in F-100s, and in 1967 was sent to Vietnam. Flying out of Pleiku, he was hit by ground fire only a few thousand meters inside North Vietnam, and captured by a company of North Vietnamese Regular Army troops. No word of his fate has ever been made public by the government in Hanoi.

The phone rang. "Dr. Bakktari here." His ear was assaulted by mind-numbing static, but through the onslaught, he recognized the faint, tinny voice of Jallud.

"Bakktari, I'll be arriving late this afternoon. Fun and games are over for our guests. The time has come for them to earn their keep."

Not even so much as a simple greeting, Bakktari thought angrily. The man was such a cretin!

Well, two could play this game. *"Hello! Hello!* Is anyone there? Goddamn telephone! Nothing works in this miserable place!" He slammed the receiver down in its cradle and laughed loudly. "Hope that shattered your eardrum, you monkey turd!"

Clearing his mind of the anger he felt, he concentrated instead on the problem at hand. This was going to be a very delicate undertaking indeed. The Americans would soon learn that they were not going home after all, and had instead traded one prison for another. And when they learned what was expected of them, well, only *Allah* could predict their reaction.

Bakktari had come to like these Americans, and now felt a twinge of guilt. Unless he handled this coming transition from so-called free man back to prisoner carefully, then they would treat him as a traitor. He would have to play his role flawlessly. It would have to be a performance worthy of an Oscar, because if he failed to maintain their trust, then quite possibly the whole plan would disintegrate. If that happened, then their collective fates, including his own, would be at the mercy of a very unstable Jallud.

Bakktari exhaled nervously. He would not fail! He would show Jallud just why Colonel Gaddafi had picked him to be a guiding force in the project.

While staring out the window at the trackless waste of concrete-hard desert sand stretching to the horizon, a land seemingly as devoid of life as the surface of the moon, it was in that moment that Bakktari mentally began to prepare for the showdown soon to come.

*   *   *

If Captain Mark FitzGerald had asked Bakktari the same question today that he had asked at their initial meeting on the docks of Tripoli, namely, *where is here?* he would not have been comforted by the answer. "Here is the end of the world," Bakktari would reply, and that would not be far from the truth. However, the factual response would be: "Here, is Tejerri, an imperceptible dot on a map in the Sahara just one hundred miles north of the Tropic of Cancer."

Tejerri was one of the most inhospitable spots on earth. Far from any trade route, it was bordered to the east by the rugged Tibesti Mountain Range which meandered southward into an equally trackless and desolate region of the Republic of Chad.

In 1964, The Royal Petroleum Company of Libya in partnership with British Petroleum was granted rights by King Idris to explore the region for oil. Promising readings taken the year before by a small prospecting team suggested that the probability of striking oil was better than eighty percent. It took ten months to prepare for a protracted stay in the region.

By the time the search began in earnest, a 9000-foot landing strip had been cleared and graded, and a tent city erected by the Libyan Army. Because the project was important to the king, he had dispatched a company of soldiers to provide security against the scattered bands of nomads in the region; desert wanderers with a history of unpredictable behavior toward strangers. The captain in charge was a young officer by the name of Mukmahr Salaam Jallud.

Work started on the first borehole on the second day of March, and the roustabouts and roughnecks drilled around-the-clock for thirty-one days. The strata they encountered chewed up the best diamond-tipped drill bits that the Hughes Company, of Houston, Texas could produce. Then, on the thirty-second day, the drill broke through the bedrock at the thirty eight hundred-foot level. The bit was painstakingly extracted from over a half-mile beneath the desert floor. They had hit a pocket of water. The workers still had faith in the geologists who continued to assure them the probability of finding huge reserves of oil was excellent.

They spent the next seven months drilling nine wells within a thirty square mile area, and all they had to show for their toil was the discovery of a vast underground lake, definitely not the treasure they had spent millions to uncover. BP made the decision to abandon the project.

The wells were capped, the tents were struck, the planes were loaded, and three weeks later there was not the faintest sign of life on the desert floor. The only evidence of man's presence in the region was the 9000-foot airstrip; a horizontal monument to what might have been.

*   *   *

Four years later, a professor of physics at the University of Benghazi came up with a brilliant idea. He approached his cousin by marriage, the seventy-seven year old monarch who by this time was well into his dotage. The professor told the king of his scheme to turn the southern Sahara Desert into an oasis. His grand design called for a partnership with the United States and its 'Atoms for Peace' project to build a nuclear-powered facility to generate electricity. Once completed, they would fertilize the earth and nurture it with huge quantities of water pumped from the subterranean lake, creating a veritable Eden. He laid out plans for the construction of a rail link to Tejerri, and prophesied that within a period of ten years, there would be a hundred thousand people happily tilling the earth. The monarch gave his approval to prepare a proposal for consideration by the United Nations Grand Poobah in charge of such matters, as well as the proper authorities in the U.S.

The professor's plan quickly germinated and took on a life of its own. But before the well-connected academic could dazzle the United Nations' scientists with his brilliance, he was killed in a plane crash along with three other souls attempting to land in the middle of a blinding sandstorm at the deserted airfield near a spot on the map marked Tejerri.

The dream died with the dreamer.

Until Jallud remembered.

*   *   *

That year was 1970. Jallud had stood shoulder-to-shoulder with Gaddafi during the coup the previous September, and was rewarded by being brought into the inner circle of power. Old King Idris was trotted off to Egypt along with his family, sycophants and other hangers-on. The first order of business for the newly formed government, known as the Revolutionary Council, was the expropriation of all foreign holdings. Next, tens of thousands of non-citizens were hustled out of the country with efficient dispatch. The entire oil generating, refining, storage and distribution apparatus was now firmly in the hands of the state. It had all happened so fast that the international oil community soon found itself on the outside looking in, and wondering how such a thing could have happened.

Those were heady days for Jallud. Gaddafi gave him the title of Minister At Large. He was not a member of the cabinet despite the title, but the ministerial rank—although impressive in theory but ephemeral in fact—made him a force to be reckoned with. Three months later, Gaddafi promoted him to major, and concurrently awarded him the diplomatic rank of Ambassador at Large, conferring upon him full diplomatic status, and thus immunity from prosecution while in a foreign capital, should the need ever arise.

It was obvious to all that that Gaddafi had seen in Jallud a kindred soul.

*   *   *

Jallud had been born into a life of wealth and status, and so apologized to no one for his superior ways. The only child of a third generation banker and entrepreneur, his was a privileged existence. By his twelfth birthday he had visited all the capitals of Europe and thanks to the introduction of an English governess into the Jallud household on the boy's second birthday, he was fully conversant in French and English, as well as his native Arabic. His primary education was at St. Brendan's Episcopal School in Tripoli, a school founded by a retired headmaster from Harrow. The youngster excelled at his studies without effort, did well on the playing fields, but was not popular with the other boys. Jallud was a bully, and displayed a sadistic streak that went beyond typical boyhood pranks. The other children gave him wide berth, even those older boys who could, and sometimes would, beat him up on occasion. He did have a smattering of pals from his own privileged class, and along with other elites, learned the social graces.

His secondary education began when he was thirteen. He was accepted into Harrow, in England, the result of a strong recommendation from his headmaster and a gift to the school of one hundred thousand pounds from his parents.

This was post-war England, and the days of an empire where the sun never set were but a distant memory. However, the well-to-do who attended Harrow and Eaton were not affected by the deprivations being felt by most of the inhabitants of that Sceptered Isle.

Life could not have been grander. Summer vacations were spent in leisurely travel with his parents, and oftentimes with a friend brought along to keep him company. The Jalluds became familiar figures in New York and Washington, and even made it as far south one summer as Buenos Aires, the invited houseguests of President Juan Peron and his immensely popular young wife, Evita.

At eighteen he was accepted into the Royal Military Academy Sandhurst at Surrey, England. That he had even wanted such an appointment had surprised his parents, but they recognized it for the honor it was, and heartily approved his mature decision. Sandhurst was the school of ministers and kings. Indeed, their English acquaintance, Winston Churchill, had graduated out some fifty years earlier.

Jallud graduated, but not without incident. He managed to survive a scandal where a young local girl had been found brutally murdered after a rather raucous party involving several of his classmates. The authorities had placed Jallud as the last person to be seen with her, but the investigation soon came up against a solid brick wall. He was never charged with any crime, but the incident put him under such scrutiny that his final months at Sandhurst were nothing short of exemplary. He graduated near the top of his class and returned to Libya to accept an appointment as a subaltern in the army of the king.

Jallud would later insist that he had a vision that morning in January 1970, a vision as real as any recorded by the Prophet. In a blinding flash, he saw the future. Gaddafi might be his temporal master, but Allah, the one true God and Master of all creation had decreed that he, Jallud, would show the way for Islam to guide mankind to everlasting salvation. In the vision he was shown the means to subjugate the decadent Western democracies and their despised puppet, the unholy State of Israel.

A few days later, he met with Gaddafi, and over the course of several hours, laid out his plan as seen in the vision.

Gaddafi was enthralled. If Jallud could put all the disparate pieces together—and he was confident that he could—then he, Gaddafi, would become the preeminent power on earth. Of course it required some manipulation of events, and, yes, people would die, but for the most part they would be Jews and other infidels who couldn't gain entrance into paradise anyway.

Jallud spoke of a site deep in the desert, a place perfect for their purposes. There was water in abundance buried deep within the bowels of the earth, but more importantly, it was a spot far from prying eyes. Here they could perfect their plan and bring the dream to fruition. He mesmerized Gaddafi with how he intended to capture the 'fire of a thousand suns,' and the Supreme Leader immediately saw that although risky, it was indeed doable. He decreed that no expense would be spared to make the dream a reality.

Jallud had left the meeting feeling that Gaddafi had somehow usurped his vision.

CHAPTER 8

Trader concluded that he must have been daydreaming. Wallowing in the simple luxury of just lying on his bed, his mind had tiptoed off to wander freely. It had been years since he'd felt so at peace. Floating in a twilight state, he had drifted back through time and space.

The eldest of five, and big brother to four sisters, much had been expected of him while growing up on a farm in Missouri. His father had inherited the six hundred and forty acres from his father, who in turn had been handed the homestead from his father. There was never any doubt that when the time came, young Jim and his family would be the fourth generation to draw their sustenance from this corner of heaven on earth.

It was a hard existence, but life was secure for the Trader clan as America entered the 1930s. The Wall Street crash of 1929 had not yet cast its tentacles of destruction as far west as the town of Clayton, Missouri, but when it did in late 1933, it came with a vengeance.

Just before Christmas, Trader's world changed forever. He was in kindergarten, and the school of one hundred and fifty-seven students was evenly divided between sodbusters and townies. There existed a definite pecking order, and sodbusters were not ranked high on the social totem pole of juvenile life in Clayton. But they were a tougher bunch of kids than their brethren who lived in fine houses on paved streets — sons and daughters of doctors, lawyers, shopkeepers, insurance salesmen, bookkeepers — thus the child of the land more often than not won the few brawls that did erupt. This is not to imply they were constantly at each other's throats. They weren't.

Arriving at school that cold December morning, young Trader noticed the students gathered in a large group on the playground. Buzz Harris, an eighth grader, and big, held center stage. "My dad heard it on the radio," he was saying, "and I heard him tell it to my mom. He said that Mr. Wallace had blowed his brains out. Locked himself in the bank after he'd closed early yesterday because he'd ran out money, and that's when he did it. Dad said he used a shotgun, and that Old Man Wallace had to be scooped off the floor and walls. He said it meant that the bank had gone belly-up, and that a lot of people in town were going to be in for the surprise of their lives."

Trader looked around for the Wallace twins. Charles and Cynthia Wallace were also eighth graders, and although considered somewhat snobbish and sometimes snooty, they were generally well-liked. They were nowhere to be seen this cold morning.

Mrs. Harrington, the principal, appeared on the edge of the field. With feet planted firmly inside orthopedic lace-up shoes she blew an earsplitting blast on her ever-present whistle.

"Attention children! Everybody, pay attention! We will all meet for a special assembly in the gymnasium. Now I want you to line-up by class, and go quietly like proper ladies and gentlemen. Your teachers will lead, and no talking!"

Trader had no idea what this all meant, but he soon found out. Within a matter of weeks many of the children had dropped out of school simply because their parents had suddenly found themselves penniless. All were forced to move in with relatives in other cities and towns. By June, there were sixty-one students left.

Hard times befell the Traders and all of their neighbors. Farm prices plummeted, and remained depressed for years. Still, the family somehow managed.

By the end of his junior year, Trader had embraced a plan that would allow him to continue his education. Unless he could win a scholarship, college was out of the question. But such scholarships were few, and almost impossible to come by. He had a natural bent for mathematics, and he thought he might like to become an engineer of some sort. He knew for sure that a farmer's life wasn't for him, but said nothing of this to his parents. He bided his time.

In the spring of 1946, he announced his plans.

"I've been accepted to Annapolis," he announced matter-of-factly one evening at dinner.

His father paused, soupspoon halfway between bowl and mouth. He stared at his son, then said, "The hell you say!"

"Thomas! Your tongue! The children!"

Ignoring his wife, Thomas Trader repeated himself. "The hell you say!"

"I'm going, Dad. I've got to."

"You don't *got* to do any such thing! Your home is right here, boy. You have work to do here. Anyway, I won't sign whatever papers I have to sign as your guardian, so no more talk of joining the navy. You're staying put, and when the time comes, you'll have the farm."

Trader threw down his fork. "I don't want the farm! I hate the farm! And I'm sure as hell not going to spend the rest of my life shoveling shit in Missouri!"

His sisters were paralyzed with fear. Dad and Jim had argued before, but never like this. The youngest began to wail.

His mother was beside herself. *"Stop it this very instant! Both of you!"* She, too, burst into tears.

Trader left the table without another word and went to his room. He began to pack. He would go to Annapolis even if he had to forge his father's signature.

The next morning Thomas Trader capitulated. He looked a hundred-years-old as he faced his son. "If that's what you truly want, lad, then I won't stand in your way. If it doesn't work out, Jim, promise me you'll come home. Just come home, son, okay?"

"I will, dad, and thanks. I promise I'll do you proud."

Annapolis was everything he had hoped it would be, and more. Plebe year was a nightmare, but daily he reminded himself how men had endured the hazing for over a century and a half. He, too, survived.

Almost twenty percent of his Plebe classmates were not around to celebrate graduation four years later. Academic deficiencies took the highest toll. A three-year course referred to as *wires* by the Midshipmen but officially known as electrical engineering, wreaked havoc in the ranks. *Wires* was the nemesis of generations of Middies. *Wires* was a giant killer.

In the summer of his second year he decided he wanted to be a pilot. Along with the rest of his class, he spent two months at the flight-training base in Pensacola, Florida, and after his first heart-pounding landing on a pitching carrier deck in a huge propeller-driven Skyraider, Trader found himself hooked.

In May 1950, he graduated in the top five percent of his class, his assignment to flight school assured. Eighteen months later, he was fully qualified in jet fighters and carrier operations, again finishing among the top five percent.

He met a girl named Patricia Parsons at a social mixer early in his second year. What she saw in him he dared not ask for fear it might drive her to pose such a question to herself, and in the process find him woefully lacking. But their relationship blossomed, and twenty-four hours after graduation James Vincent Trader married Patricia Parsons in the chapel at the U.S. Naval Academy at Annapolis, Maryland. Life was indeed grand.

Three children came in seven years. Hard years. Years where many of those months were spent away from home, including two sea-deployments to Korea, and aerial combat. He returned safely from each tour and was now a seasoned professional. At the end of his sixth year, scores of his classmates left the service, lured by the siren's song of the booming aviation industry. They flocked to the airlines in droves. He, however, was still hooked on the Navy and decided to stay in. If his wife was disappointed with his decision, she never said.

He was accepted to graduate school at Stanford University, and the family moved to California for the year it took him to complete his master's degree in nuclear physics. A few years later it was back again to California, this time to UCLA, where he obtained a Ph.D., his original work being in the field of particle acceleration.

It was now the spring of 1962.

Trader was given greater responsibilities as he became more senior in rank; his background and knowledge in things nuclear was highly treasured by the Navy. But in his own mind he was first and foremost a pilot. Trader had the best of both worlds.

The conflict in far-off Vietnam had heated up over the years to the point it was now a full-blown war. By the advent of summer in the year 1970, he had placed three volunteer statements requesting to serve, to do his part. His requests had been denied, and Trader was fast-becoming a very frustrated commander. He saw classmates being promoted to captain, and with those four gold braids on their sleeves came commands he would have died for.

Finally, someone at the Bureau of Personnel relented, because he was given orders sending him off to a limited flying assignment in the war zone with the understanding he would not partake in any combat missions.

James Vincent Trader was elated.

*   *   *

The ringing of his alarm clock brought his wayward mind home. It was time to meet the others and go downstairs.

Trader rapped on the door next to his. "Come forth," he commanded in a mock-stern voice.

Gerry Glasstner opened the door and grinned. "Good evening, Captain. Looks like this could be it."

"Gerry, the name's still Jim," Trader reminded his friend.

Glasstner shook his head. "No, sir. We all need get used to being formal again. We're heading back to the real world, Captain, which means we better get used to the ways of the military again and the formality of rank." They marched in step to the next door in line, but before Trader could knock, Tim Sweringen opened it and almost bumped into them on his way out.

"Hi, guys. Y'all going somewhere?"

"*Home!*" they said in unison, then laughed like little kids. Other doors began to open and soon the hallway was filled with nine expectant Americans.

Trader held up a hand for silence. "Fellows, I need a minute of your time before we go down." He paused, and looked at each man in turn. The men looked back, some solemn, some smiling, but all happy. "Gentlemen, this day's been a long time in coming. A lot longer for some than for others, but let me just say that I'm proud beyond words to have been associated with every one of you. There is not a finer group of fighting men anywhere, with the possible exception of our brothers still in captivity." He paused for but a moment, then continued. "Why we were chosen by the enemy for such a special release, I have no idea. However, we must not feel guilty at our good fortune. Our release is something none of us had any control over, and it certainly didn't come about as a reward for collaborating with the enemy."

Trader allowed time for his words to sink in with the subdued band of warriors standing before him. "Gerry reminded me a moment ago that we're going home, and he insisted that he address me as captain. He said that the world we're returning to demands the adherence to such protocol and, of course, he is right. However, there has never been the slightest lapse in proper military bearing or lack of adherence to proper protocol on anyone's part here, and the only reason we survived was because of our strong sense of discipline and our common bond as brother officers in the finest military establishment the world has ever seen." His voice broke, forcing him to pause.

He cleared his throat. "My only hope is that I will always be Jim Trader and not just Captain Trader to every one of you, because I intend to go to my Maker proud to have been able to call each of you my friend. Speech over. God Bless America!"

Tim Sweringen, the man held captive the longest and the second in seniority, stepped forward, and extended his hand to Trader. They shook hands, then embraced. Finally, Sweringen held up his hand, winked to break the solemnity of the moment, and like Trader, cleared his throat of the emotional logjam rendering speech almost impossible.

"Jim, on behalf of all of us, I say thank you for your leadership and your inspiration. It's no bullshit when I tell you that your fortitude and character helped us all in every way and did so every day. We are proud to have served under your command. Now, I was going to say that although you're a great commander, it's obvious you're a shitty pilot or you wouldn't be here. But then I realized that if I said that, then by default I would have to admit the same thing about myself. Well...that will never happen simply because everyone knows *I'm the world's greatest stick!*"

They broke out in loud whistles, jeers, cheers and catcalls, then the happy group made its way to the meeting room on the first floor.

Captain Jallud, the Libyan naval officer who had accompanied them on the submarine from North Vietnam was waiting. He wore a subdued look as he nodded solemnly to each as they entered then motioned them into seats. He was accompanied by four large men, each positioned in a corner. There was nothing casual or sloppy about their persons or in their demeanor. To Trader they looked ominous, almost like guards.

Jallud waited until the pilots were seated then he walked over to the door and shut it. He was not in uniform, but rather was dressed in an impeccably tailored English-cut suit, a crisp white shirt, a silk regimental tie, and shoes shined to a mirror finish. He slowly retraced his steps to the front of the room and faced the nine seated, silent figures.

"Please allow me to reintroduce myself. My name is Mukmahr Jallud, and it is my duty to inform you that there's been a slight change of plans." He held up both hands. "No, no, I'm not suggesting you will not be going home, I'm only saying there will be a slight delay in the timetable, that's all."

"What does a slight delay, mean?" Niels Borden asked. "Better yet, why any delay at all? And one more thing. Are you really a naval captain or was the uniform we last saw you in some kind of hoax?"

"Where's Doctor Bakktari?" someone else called out.

Jallud ignored the questions. "Gentlemen, if you'll please keep quiet I'll explain." He waited until he had their attention again. The men in the corners remained motionless.

"Thank you. Now let me tell you what all this means. First, you are at a university research laboratory deep in the Sahara, and although the work done here is currently classified, the results of that work will be used one day to benefit all humanity. Because of the sensitive nature of what we are doing, few people even know of the existence of our complex. And we're rightfully proud of the fact that we spared no expense gathering the best minds in the world to come here." He smiled, but only for an instant.

"A little over two years ago this was barren desert," Jallud continued, but I'm sure you've noticed that's far from the case now. All the buildings, all the electrical generating capability, all the things necessary to support a sophisticated undertaking such as we have here, all these things were accomplished with much sacrifice. What you behold, gentlemen, is a nuclear research facility as good as any to be found in Europe, or even America."

Trader had heard enough. He stood up. "Hold it right there, Mr. Jallud, Captain Jallud, or whatever the hell your real name is. I don't like the turn this conversation is taking. Now, we might not be the smartest guys in town, but it sure sounds to me like you're telling us in a fancy, roundabout way that we're now your prisoners."

"For shame, Captain Trader! You gentlemen are honored guests of the Libyan government," Jallud cooed, repeating the words General Trang had used to explain away his wretched week in captivity in North Vietnam. "You are our guests," he repeated, slowly, one word at a time. "Have you not been treated like guests? Have we, your hosts, been lacking in either hospitality or good manners? If that is so, then I will correct the deficiency immediately. Is it the food? Is it..."

"Knock it off, Mister..."

Jallud whirled to face his nemesis. "No, you knock it off, Captain Trader! In fact, shut the hell up and sit down!" Jallud had done what he had vowed to Bakktari he wouldn't do! That damned American naval captain had made him lose his temper. "You have no idea what is it that we want of you, what small favor you can do to show us your gratitude for rescuing you from that snake-pit in the jungle that was your home these past few years. We only ask for a little bit of help before sending you on your way to rejoin your families. Well, you, Captain Trader, you do not speak for the others. These are all free men, and they can speak for themselves without any bullying from you. Especially when you don't even know what it is I would ask of you."

"*Wrong, Jallud!*" Walter Boyd was on his feet, facing the enemy. "You're wrong to the tenth frigging power! Captain Trader *does* speak for all of us, and don't you ever forget it. I don't know what your little plan is, but I don't want to hear another word."

"Sit down, Colonel Boyd," Jallud said as if rebuking a child, but underneath he was struggling to stifle his anger. Oh, how that little shit Bakktari would gloat when he heard how things had fallen apart. That son of a bitch Trader would pay dearly for this! He started to seethe. It was useless to continue.

"Go to your bloody rooms," he roared, *"and stay there.* Don't leave for any reason tonight, even if the damned building catches fire, because if you do you will be shot. I, Jallud, guarantee it." He paused long enough to glance at his watch. "You will have breakfast at the usual time then you will re-assemble here at seven. Dismissed." He motioned to his four companions. The last man out slammed the door.

Trader rose, shaking his head. "I'm sorry, guys, but I think it's fair to say we won't be going home any time soon. Even though that slimy thug hasn't said specifically what it is he wants from us, we can reasonably conclude it's nothing good. And we must all now assume that he knows about our backgrounds, so my guess is the son of a bitch thinks we can build him a nuclear bomb!"

Under any other circumstances that comment would have triggered gales of laughter.

*   *   *

"All I need is your expertise in perfecting an initiator," Jallud said at ten minutes past seven the following morning. "You men wouldn't give me the chance last night to tell you the reasons why we in Libya have to take this step. However, I must remember you've been away from world events for so long that you have no understanding of the true threat the entire Arab world now faces from a nuclear power in our very back yard. Of course, I'm referring to the Zionists and their illegal state of Israel.

"We Arabs *must* balance the equation," he continued. "Once the Jews know we will retaliate if they try to expropriate more of our lands—and that we would retaliate with nuclear weapons—they will be less inclined to try to steal these lands. We, of course, have no thought of unleashing such a force," he added, "but this is the only way to bring about a lasting peace. It's really no different than your well-known American policy of Mutual Assured Destruction, vis-à-vis yourselves and the Soviets. *MAD.* Such an apt acronym. But, gentlemen, that MAD policy actually works. Your own country is living proof of what I speak. Well, we, too, are looking for just such a guarantee for peace."

Jallud looked like a long-winded prosecutor who had finally rested his case before the jury. The speech had left him parched. He took a long drink from a glass on the lectern before him, then wiped his mouth with a pristine handkerchief. "Gentlemen, what I ask is not unreasonable," he continued. "You will be true instruments of peace. Oh, I could accomplish my goals without your help, but it would take a while longer. I want to bring the fighting and bickering in this part of the world to an end as quickly as possible, and that's why I beseech you to help me. Because with each passing day, more innocents die. You must help me help them."

It was a calm, deliberate, and most persuasive Jallud who was talking this morning. He could have been in a university lecture hall conducting a seminar in political science — except for the four statues again stationed in each corner. Jallud even glanced at his notes from time to time. The entire scene had an almost surreal quality about it.

Reality, though, fairly shouted to Trader that there was nothing otherworldly about what Jallud was proposing. Trader found himself thinking that his comment yesterday had been bang-on. *Jallud wanted them to help to build a nuke. It was madness on a grand scale.* How in the hell are we going to escape from this lunatic? His mind raced. What are the chances of just one of us getting out of here alive? Not too promising, he realized with a sinking feeling.

Trader said nothing as he sat listening to Jallud drone on, spouting the most convoluted logic while hoping it was being accepted as persuasive argument. He certainly has the gift of gab, Trader thought, but it was gibberish nonetheless. All the talk of peace on earth and goodwill to men was so much bullshit. This clown wants to become a nuclear power; a one-man nightmare stalking the international community with demands which would escalate to a point that the unthinkable would one day become reality. He would never be sated. How could he be? *Jallud was utterly and hopelessly mad!*

Finally, Trader rose. "Mr. Jallud, on behalf of all of us, I must decline your heartfelt invitation to join you in this noble undertaking." There was no hint of sarcasm, no condescending tone in his voice. Trader knew this was an unbalanced mind before him.

"Ah, Captain Trader, thank you, but I must insist that you not be too hasty in reaching your decision. You still do not yet have all the facts at your disposal, so I cannot in good conscience accept your answer as final. He smiled a most insincere smile. "Here is what I propose. Talk it over among yourselves. I'll give you two days to reach a consensus. I truly regret having to detain you for a short while longer. I know you are eager to return to your families, and you have all earned that right. However, you can be finished with your task here in a matter of months then be on your way. A few more months is nothing in the great cosmic scheme now is it, gentlemen?"

Mark FitzGerald stood. "May I suggest that Captain Trader is right, but possibly for the wrong reasons. You mentioned that we don't have all the facts, so, on that score I defer to your judgment. But there are certain realities that just cannot be avoided."

FitzGerald began to tick off points as he made them, using his fingers to keep score. "First, you must recognize that none of us have had any hands-on experience in the field of nuclear physics in years. It's a fast-moving discipline and unless one keeps up to date, knowledge quickly becomes passé. Sad to admit, but we now know less than most third-year university students. Second, you must have a fissionable material such as Uranium or Plutonium and, with all due respect, that would take you years to acquire, starting with milled Uranium oxide, more commonly called yellowcake. It's something you cannot just go out and buy. Plutonium is definitely not for sale on the open market, you know. It's the most controlled substance on earth and can't be purchased at any price. Even the Russians won't part with the stuff. Therefore, what we have is an academic exercise that cannot be brought to a physical conclusion. Which means we can't possibly be of any value to you. I'm sorry, but those are the facts."

"An excellent summary, Captain FitzGerald. My compliments! That's exactly what I'm looking for. A rational discussion of the scientific process at work. Thank you." Jallud beamed. "But, remember, *you* do not have all the facts at your disposal just yet, so unfortunately, your conclusions are invalid. But thank you for your input."

Jallud then made a show of stuffing his notes into a slim eel skin briefcase. As he snapped it closed and nodded to the four guards, his mask dropped. "We will meet again in two days, so use the time well, my friends." His voice could have cut diamonds. He left with his entourage in tow.

As he walked down the hall he issued orders to the man beside him. "Tell our people in Colorado they must be ready to act. I will want the task completed with a minimum of fuss, and I'll want the results in the diplomatic pouch and back here within twenty-four hours. Now go."

Jallud strode into the blazing sunlight and headed for his limousine. *I shall soon find out whether or not you're the big, brave pilot you think you are, Captain James Trader. I really hope you force my hand, because I cannot wait to see the look on your face when I present you with my little surprise.*

CHAPTER 9

Seated in the back seat of the Mercedes, Jallud's thoughts hearkened back to the spring of the previous year and the extraordinary vision that had led him to the American pilots.

* * *

May 1972
(Ten months earlier)

The call to prayer, *Salat,* was sounded on the loudspeaker system throughout the desert research facility, piped from the minaret of the mosque by the *muezzin.* It was high noon, and all activity stopped. This ritual, performed five times a day following a strict adherence to the Koran and the teachings of the Prophet, beckoned the faithful to gather for worship.

Jallud made his way to prayer alongside the rest of the population. Dr. Hadid the head of the research staff accompanied him. There were a few infidels in residence, and they were encouraged to pray to their own god if they so chose. Jallud was delighted to be going to prayer. He was a true believer, and readily admitted a need for guidance from the Creator.

Forty-five minutes later, both were back in the director's office.

It was May 12, 1972, and Dr. Mohammed Hadid had a big problem on his hands. He took no joy in having to discuss it with Jallud, a man who did not react well to bad tidings. And what he was about to say most definitely came under that heading.

"You were saying?" Jallud prompted.

"I was saying that we have a major obstacle in our path, Minister, and I need your wisdom in helping me find the answer. Speaking bluntly, we cannot detonate a nuclear device because we have no expertise in such matters. We have read all the available literature on the subject but it's woefully inadequate, I'm afraid. The detonator, or initiator, if you will, is at the very heart of any nuclear bomb, and the method of assembly of such a component is a very closely guarded secret." Hadid threw up his hands in a sign of despair. He glanced cautiously at Jallud, and then hurried on. "Minister, permit me to refresh your memory with a synopsis of the history of atomic power. That way you will have a clearer understanding of the problem we now face."

"Go ahead. Educate me. Tell me what I need to know," Jallud replied, settling back in his chair.

"Think of the nucleus of an atom as doing for the physical world that which *Deoxyribonucleic Acid* does for the biological world," Hadid began. "Both are building blocks. They represent the essence, the being, the beginning and the continuum. Within both lie the secrets of the universe."

"Yes, I'm aware of all that."

Hadid nodded. "It's only been in the twentieth century that man has been able to look inward and, in so doing, made matter part grudgingly with its secrets. Not all of its secrets, mind you, but a tantalizing glimpse. It was through the study of certain atoms that men began to speculate as to whether the power of these building blocks of nature could be harnessed to create what we now refer to as nuclear weapons."

Jallud had no stomach for a long lecture. "Move on. Tell me something I don't know."

Hadid picked up the pace. "Such weapons have the ability to yield three separate types of explosions. The first two are fission weapons. They are called atom bombs and include all fusion-boosted weapons, which are also called H-bombs. The third class, however, is a combination of the first two, and they are called thermonuclear weapons. These weapons derive their incredibly destructive power from a combined use of fission and fusion. It all began with European and American scientists working in theoretical physics laboratories in the late 1930s. These physicists reached the same remarkable conclusion at about the same time: only one form of Uranium, the isotope of mass 235 played a significant and dominant part in fission. You see, it was already generally known that neutrons released through the fission process had the capability of initiating further fission, which in turn proved that it was theoretically possible to start a chain-reaction using this material called U-235. It was also believed that Plutonium-239 could likewise serve as a fissionable material."

Hadid paused long enough to take a gulp of water. "The adage, 'necessity is the mother of invention,'" he continued, "was never more aptly applied than when used to describe the total American commitment to build an atomic bomb shortly after the United States was dragged into the Second World War. The year was 1942. Codenamed the Manhattan Project, all the resources of all the research labs were brought together under one roof and President Roosevelt appointed one man to take charge. He was a no-nonsense U.S. Army brigadier general named Leslie R. Groves, and his task was daunting.

"That a nuclear explosion could make the quantum leap from the theoretical to the practical was very much in doubt. However, Washington gave the green light for the building of huge facilities to start the process of gathering fissionable material. Three methods were employed and each showed equal promise. They were the electromagnetic-separation and gaseous-diffusion methods for producing U-235, and the reactor-method for producing Pu-239."

By now Jallud was rocking back and forth on his chair, truly engrossed in what Hadid was explaining.

"Under the direction of Enrico Fermi, a brilliant man, an Italian, just like your lovely wife," Hadid added hastily, hoping to curry favor, "the first nuclear reactor was built on the grounds of the University of Chicago. Using a pile-layer of graphite bricks, the scientists embedded a quantity of Uranium Metal near the core, and Uranium-oxide pellets on the outer fringes. On December 2, 1942, the pile 'went critical,' which meant that the reaction had become self-sustaining. Plutonium was being produced at a constant rate.

"Shortly thereafter, General Groves gave the order to start construction on two huge facilities to painstakingly produce the quantities of Plutonium needed for bomb production. One facility was located in Oak Ridge, Tennessee, and it was used to produce material employing both the electromagnetic-separation method, and the diffusion process. The second was built near the town of Hanford, in Washington State. It was ideal. Extremely remote, but more importantly, it was situated on the Columbia River whose huge volume of water was critical for maintaining the cooling process inside the reactor. By 1944 the reactor at Hanford was producing Plutonium.

"Meanwhile, the site chosen by General Groves for the theoretical scientists to assemble was a place buried deep within the American Southwest, in Los Alamos, New Mexico. The scientists' marching orders were fivefold. First: discover the method by which fissionable material could be made to explode; two: define the measurements of the new fissionable materials from which said bombs were to be made; three: design the bombs themselves; four: construct them. And fifth: test the finished product.

"Yes, yes, go on."

"They went to work with a vengeance," Hadid said. "Their combined efforts resulted in a bomb which was exploded at the Trinity Test Site at Alamogordo, New Mexico, on July 16, 1945, at 5:30 A.M. For better or for worse, the nuclear age was born."

Jallud nodded. He was aware of the history surrounding the first atomic explosion. He made an impatient gesture for Hadid to speed things up.

"Contrary to popular belief," Hadid continued, talking even faster, "fission reactions do not require spectacularly high temperatures or densities for an explosion to occur. What is necessary is the assemblage of what we call critical mass. This we must have in order for an uncontrolled chain-reaction to develop, and it can be accomplished in two ways. One, employ a chemical explosive to compress a sphere of sub-critical mass of fissionable material into a critical mass, or two, drive two sub-critical masses together in a barrel. The mass then becomes critical, and the chain-reaction is initiated by injecting neutrons into the fissionable material at precisely the moment that the fissionable material approaches its critical configuration. This is accomplished with a device called an initiator, and both methods cause a nuclear detonation to occur." Hadid paused to study Jallud's face. Are you still with me so far, Excellency?"

"I'm with you."

"Good, because this is the important part. If too many neutrons are present as the critical configuration is approached, or if the critical configuration is approached too slowly, then a premature chain-reaction will cause the material to disassemble, or pre-detonate, if you will, before a full explosive yield can be achieved. This problem is especially significant for Plutonium where a small fraction of nuclei spontaneously undergo fission resulting in the premature introduction of neutrons as the weapon is assembled. Through trial and error, the implosion technique was favored to counter this tendency of Plutonium bombs to pre-detonate."

And this very real probability of pre-detonation occurring was the problem now facing Hadid. Nobody on staff had any expertise in this area. True, they did not yet know what type of delivery system they were going to employ, and also true, they were nowhere near the assembly stage. However, this was something they would have to address eventually so better Jallud know all the ramifications now while there was still time to back out of the project.

Jallud rocked back on the rear legs of his chair. Hadid had no way of gauging just how much the man had really understood. Even if he grasped only a fraction of what he had just been told, he would still deduce that Hadid was saying the present scientists did not have the resources to go beyond a certain point; a point soon to be reached.

Jallud leaned forward, causing the legs of his chair to slam down with a bang. His quizzical look suggested that Hadid was unable to see the obvious. He laughed aloud. "You *buy* what you need, my friend. Do not worry about cost; that's my job. Your job is to get results!"

"Minister, I'm not making myself clear. This is one area of expertise that's not for sale. There are but a few people in the entire world who have the knowledge to create the initiator we require. It is probably the best-kept secret of the atomic age.

Because if and when this secret becomes public knowledge, then it'll only be a matter of time until every country has the bomb. Providing, of course, that they also have the means of gathering enough fissionable material. That in itself is nearly an insurmountable obstacle. Fortunately for us, and thanks to your brilliance, we don't have that problem." Hadid reasoned that a little flattery went a long way when giving someone like Jallud a strong dose of bad medicine.

"So where would we find such experts?"

"America."

"And everyone knows Americans can be bought, right? It's only a matter of price."

Hadid shook his head. "Not these Americans, I'm afraid. And even if you did make an offer and even if they accepted, such people are so closely monitored that if they quit their jobs and came to Libya, everyone would put two-and-two together in an instant and know that we were attempting to build a bomb." Hadid shook his head. "If the Americans did not put us out of business in short order, then you can rest assured the Zionists would!"

"How about the Russians? You have told me often enough that their scientists are top rate. Or maybe the East Germans?" Jallud challenged.

"The Germans are top rate theoretical physicists but they're not scientists with any practical experience. Their Soviet masters don't allow them to dabble in this particular field. They can work in theoretical labs to their hearts content, but *no practical experience with nuclear material is tolerated!* Moscow controls all uses of atomic energy with iron fists. The Soviet scientists who *do* have the know-how are virtual prisoners inside Russia."

"So, you're telling me that after all the trouble I've gone through to secure the weapons-grade Plutonium; and the untold millions of American dollars I've spent building this place; after all the money used to transport the scientists here; after all these things we are at an impasse? *For your sake you'd better be wrong!*" Jallud was now screaming at the top of his lungs; out of breath and beyond reason. Panting heavily, he gasped; "You'd better come up with an answer because your miserable life depends on it!"

*   *   *

Hadid did not come up with the answer, Jallud did. And it came in a dream. Not a dream but a vision, he would later insist, because two nights later he awoke from a sound sleep yelling for joy and thoroughly frightening his Italian wife, Sophia. He hopped out of bed and began dancing around the room, alternating between uncontrollable laughter and shouting out the Shahada: *"There is no God but Allah, and Muhammad is the messenger of Allah."*

"Yes, yes, yes! *That is my answer!* I've found my scientists, and they're all Americans! *Allah be praised."*

He telephoned Hadid even though it was two o'clock in the morning. A worried Hadid came on the line.

"Sleep well, Doctor, for you shall have your scientists. *Allah* has shown me the way. When the time is right I shall deliver them to you and they will all be Americans." He paused to catch his breath. "Hadid, you are one very lucky man," he said, then severed the connection.

*   *   *

MARCH 1973
(The present)

March 29, 1973, was the day of reckoning for Trader and the others. True to his word, Jallud returned to hear their final answer.

Trader stood and faced his nemesis. "No! That's our answer, Mr. Jallud. We will neither aid nor abet you, nor your government, in any fashion. We are still prisoners of war, and won't willingly give comfort to the enemy. You can torture us, kill us, or you can return us to North Vietnam where we'll take our chances with the rest of our friends. But we will not help you."

Eight pilots were polled and each re-affirmed the words of their commander.

Jallud stared at the group, saying nothing for a full minute.

It was if he refused to believe the verdict just rendered. Finally, he spoke. "You are all fools. Fools," he repeated, but without a trace of anger in his voice. "You say that you are willing to return to the squalid camps in North Vietnam? Don't make me laugh! The war is over! It's been over for two months! The other pilots, five hundred and ninety men in all have been released in two groups over the past eight weeks. Your captors informed the world that no Americans are left in their filthy little jungle kingdom. Think about that!"

The nine were stunned into a mind-numbing silence. Those standing sat, and those already seated, slumped lower into their chairs. All stared at Jallud, looks of disbelief reflected on every face.

"You disappoint me, gentlemen, you truly do. I admire your courage, but condemn your stupidity. I asked so little from you. But you now force me to take other measures to change your minds. I would have preferred your voluntary cooperation, but in the end it is the results which matter, and I will get the results I want. I Jallud, guarantee it!"

His face was grim. "You're all free to return to your activities. Don't worry, I won't have you beaten and tortured, thrown into dungeons, or taken out and shot. You can continue doing what you've been doing; playing your childish American basketball, and football, and baseball. But mark my words, when we do meet again, you will most assuredly do my bidding."

He led his four guards out of the room without a backward glance.

* * *

Ten minutes later, perched rudely on the corner of Bakktari's desk, phone pressed to his ear, Jallud gave instructions to an underling in Tripoli.

"Tell our people in America that it's time to take action in Denver. I want the package delivered as quickly as possible and I want the newspaper article which will surely follow taken to the embassy for wire transmission to the capital. Get going."

Bakktari heard it all. He let his breath out slowly. "I prayed it would not come to this."

"Well, it has! They had their chance to do things the civilized way but they're not reasonable men. Now we do it my way."

Bakktari did not like where this was going.

"Maybe I could speak to them…"

"Absolutely not," Jallud answered, cutting Bakktari off midsentence.

"Then at least let me know when you plan to meet with them again so that I can prepare for that possible demonstration we've discussed many times. I'm going to have to come across as their only friend, so we must make our show convincing. Just don't kill me in the process. Remember, I still enjoy the full faith and confidence of Colonel Gaddafi."

It was a threat, and Jallud knew it. He let loose a short, mirthless laugh. "Don't worry, my good doctor, I will not kill you. However, you remember this; we must convince the Americans that you are their only friend in court, so, regretfully, there must be some pain. Nevertheless, you'll survive. This is for the future of Libya, and Libya is all that matters."

Bakktari looked glum. "I suppose you're right, but I must admit, I am not looking forward to our next meeting with the Americans. Not the least little bit."

Jallud had heard enough whining for one day. *"Salaam,"* he said, jumping off the desk and heading for the door.

CHAPTER 10

The men walked back and forth in a tight group on the sprinklered expanse of grass which served as a playing field. It had been marked to accommodate the game of soccer, a game enjoyed daily by various members of the research teams, a game that the Americans had spent many delightful hours watching and cheering on the participants. But not today.

Trader was speaking when Nick Wolfe interrupted him in midsentence. *"Of course!* It's so obvious we should have spotted it immediately! How could we all have been so stupid?"

"What, Nick?" a puzzled Trader asked. "What have we missed?"

"Our building. Look at it. What do you see?"

"A two-story concrete structure that's painted shit-brown and parked in the middle of nowhere," Trader replied.

"No, sir! What you see is a shit-brown building that was constructed just for us! That son of a bitch was built to house ten men, but there are only nine of us now. There's one extra room! These bastards have had this planned for a long time." He pointed an accusing finger at the structure. "Notice how it sits apart from all the others? Remember when we first moved in and everything smelled brand new? Damn right it was! These bastards have known for months we were coming. Only they'd planned on Max Epperman being with us. Ten men; ten rooms. *Son of a bitch!"* he yelled in utter frustration.

"Son of a bitch is right," Trader said, his jaw hardening. He motioned for the group to gather closer. "Gentlemen, as of this moment we're back at war and the rules we lived under in North Vietnam apply once more." He paused for a moment to gather his thoughts, then continued. "We must assume all our conversations indoors are being monitored, or soon will be, so, as of right now, it's back to using the prisoner's code to pass any vital information between us." He allowed a couple of seconds for this to sink in, then added in a whisper, "It's now obvious that Jallud plans to use us then lose us. We do what he wants, namely help him build a bomb, then he gets rid of us. We're a problem, and as such we sure as hell will never be allowed to leave this place alive. All that talk of sending us home after we help him is just so much bullshit! So as of right now our thoughts and energies must be focused on one thing, and only one thing."

"Escape," Tim Sweringen whispered back.

"Correct. And if only one of us gets out to blow the whistle as to what's really going on here, then we'll have done our job."

"That's one tall order, skipper," John Waltensperger murmured, giving voice to what each was thinking. "About all we know for sure is that we're somewhere in the Sahara, hours away from civilization, even by air. There are only two ways in or out; plane and rail. No one could make it out of here on foot; he'd be dead in an hour. Hate to sound like a party-pooper, boss, but that's my read of the situation."

"You read it correctly, John," Trader said, starting forward again. The group hovered close. "Remember, we're successful if only one of us makes it and one of us has *got* to make it. End of story."

"No wonder we didn't see any guards," FitzGerald said. "Everybody here knows we are prisoners except us. And everyone knows there is no way out."

"What do you think Jallud meant when he said that next time we meet he'd make us change our minds?" Doug Gilchrest asked.

"Don't know," Trader said, shaking his head, "but I can tell you this. He is one dangerous *hombre*. Quite possible the guy's a psychotic, or worse, but heed me well. We cross him at our own peril. I have a feeling that he's going to make our little sadistic friends back in Hanoi look like amateurs."

"Guess we'll know soon enough," Niels Borden said, kicking a clump of sand at his feet. He paused to watch it explode into a small cloud of dust.

Trader also watched the little cloud of dust as it slowly disappeared in the windless air. He found himself identifying with it in some strange sense, making him understand how insignificant it was in the greater cosmic scheme of things. And in that moment he realized that in essence, he, too, was that little insignificant cloud of dust. It was not a comforting thought.

As Trader walked back to their building, he realized that no one in America had an inkling as to their whereabouts. By not being repatriated they would have been written-off as dead. Had to. Ergo, no one was even looking for them. They were alone and waiting for God only knew what.

They waited four days.

* * *

Jallud came accompanied by six heavily armed soldiers. A very unhappy Bakktari shuffled in behind them.

For some inexplicable reason Trader thoughts raced back to a time months ago in North Vietnam. The Christmas bombings had just started, and somebody had yelled in a voice filled with unadulterated joy from one of the cells: *"It's showtime at the Palladium, folks!"* A smile flitted across his face. Well, it was showtime once more.

"Captain Trader, front and center," Jallud commanded without preamble, sounding every bit the no-nonsense drill sergeant on the parade ground.

The abruptness of the order startled Trader. He stepped forward and Jallud handed him a package. It was neither large nor heavy, and as he held it Trader felt a strange coldness seeping from within.

Jallud made an elaborate show of unfolding a newspaper page then held it aloft. "All of you listen carefully to what I'm about to read. It's from the *Denver Post* dated three days ago."

* * *

WOMAN BRUTALIZED IN BROAD DAYLIGHT

Denver police are looking for two men who attacked a woman on a downtown street yesterday, severely beating her before escaping in a waiting car. The horror of the incident is magnified by the fact that the two cut off her ring finger, and took it with them. Stunned onlookers said the attack was over in less than thirty seconds. The men were gone before anyone could react to aid the woman, identified as Patricia Parsons Trader, 43, of Denver. Mrs. Trader, who was conscious as she was taken by ambulance to Letterman Army Hospital, is the wife of Captain James Trader, a navy pilot who has been listed as missing-in-action since 1970 when he was shot down over North Vietnam. Captain Trader was not among the pilots recently freed by Hanoi.

"This was an act of mayhem," said police detective Jules Martinez, who has been placed in charge of the investigation. "We will find the individuals responsible for this," he vowed. "These animals cannot hide from me."

Mrs. Trader was described as resting comfortably by a hospital spokeswoman, who also stated that the injuries suffered, while serious, were not life-threatening.

*   *   *

"Open the box, Captain Trader, and see what's in it. Just pull on the string."

Time stood still. No one spoke. No one moved. Then all hell broke loose.

Bakktari sprang forward and hit Jallud with a closed fist, striking the taller man soundly on the side of his chin, sending him crashing into a metal folding chair. *"You barbarian!"* he screamed, but before he could utter another word two of the guards were on him, clubbing him with their weapons. The other soldiers leveled their rifles at the Americans and began to advance as the group of enraged pilots flung their chairs aside, ready to tear into Jallud.

Trader slid to the floor, clutching the obscene package close to his chest. He knew to the core of his very being that it did indeed contain Pat's finger. He began rocking back and forth. Tears coursed down his cheeks and not a sound escaped his lips.

A badly shaken Jallud slowly staggered to his feet and

turned hate-filled eyes down to Bakktari lying unconscious on the floor. He walked over and kicked him in the side with such force that Bakktari was lifted off the tiled surface. He spat at the prone figure.

"Get this traitor out of my sight!" he bellowed at the guards while cradling his jaw with both hands. Two men jumped forward, grabbed Bakktari by his feet and dragged him off, the limp figure offering no resistance as it cleaned a path through the film of dust on the linoleum.

The remaining four guards held their rifles at the ready, daring the pilots to make the slightest move.

Tim Sweringen broke the silence. Looking Jallud squarely in the eye, he said, calmly, "Bakktari's right. You *are* a barbarian." He then crouched down beside his friend. "Jim, give it to me, please. It's okay, I'll take care of it." He slowly pried the unopened box from his weeping friend's hands. Trader didn't resist.

"Captain Trader, hear me well! Patricia Trader's finger is indeed inside that box and it represents what I can and will continue to do until you and your men agree to help me. I will mail your loved ones to you piece by piece until there are enough parts brought here to constitute a family reunion. Wives, children, mothers, fathers, it makes no difference to me. They will all come, piece by piece, by piece. That is my promise to you. I was reasonable, but you wouldn't listen. Well, now you know where matters stand." He paused long enough to gingerly probe his swelling jaw. He shook his head slightly, as if to clear his mind, then said, "I am going to get cleaned up and I will be back in fifteen minutes for your answer. For your families' sakes you had better be prepared to give the answer I want to hear." He lurched away, followed by his guards who kept their rifles at the ready as they backed out behind their master.

Trader rose to his feet helped by Gerry Glasstner and Niels Borden. His face was like death, and his red-rimmed eyes never left the box in Sweringen's arms. "I can't make the decision; I just can't," he whispered through his agony. "Whatever you guys decide I'll back you all the way."

Sweringen motioned for the men to huddle tightly.

"Jim, let me tell Jallud we'll go along with what he wants," Sweringen whispered, hoping the room wasn't yet bugged. "Boss, we need to play a stalling game in order to sabotage his project, and we need time to figure out a way for one of us to escape. We have to get the upper hand. The guy's already proved he's a frigging maniac, crazy enough to carry through on his threats, so let's pretend to give in. Of course he'll be suspicious of our answer, and of course he knows we'll try to torpedo him, but what choice does he really have? We get to buy time. What do you say?"

Trader looked around the circle.

The men began murmuring, each adding a comment or two in hoarse whispers, but a consensus had already been reached. Sweringen was right. They would tell Jallud that they agreed to his terms, but with each man knowing they would all do everything possible to ensure that any bomb they made would never work.

When Jallud returned, Trader had Tim Sweringen announce the decision. He still couldn't trust himself to speak.

"Good, then I don't need to say any more on the subject." Jallud tossed a vial to Sweringen. "Sedatives," he explained. "Make sure Captain Trader takes both pills before retiring. He has had a stressful day."

Through eyes still clouded with pain, Trader saw Sweringen hand-off the medication to Niels Borden, then turn to Jallud and announce in a voice as cold as death, "I want shovels, and I want them now for a Christian burial service. Have them brought to us outside."

Trader saw that the demand had taken Jallud by surprise. He started to open his mouth, but obviously thought it the wiser course to say nothing. He simply nodded and walked out.

Sweringen said to the group, "Give me a couple of minutes, then we'll meet in the middle of the playing field." He headed for the stairwell cradling the package tenderly in his arms.

He went to his room and closed the door. Taking in a deep bracing breath, he opened the box. His worst fears were confirmed. Lying on shards of dry ice was a bloodless, desiccated finger encircled by a plain gold wedding band. Hot tears welled. Steeling himself, he gently worked the ring off the severed digit and placed it in his pocket. Lovingly, he wrapped the finger in a clean facecloth, sealed the box, then set off to the playing field.

By the time he rejoined the others, Mark FitzGerald and Nick Wolfe were busy digging up the lush imported sod exactly in the middle of the field. Below the sod was soft sand, going down for several feet. The others stood in silence until the task was completed.

Trader nodded his approval, then, for the first time since leaving the building, he spoke in a voice that was still weak. "Let us pray."

For the next several minutes each took turns reciting prayers and memorized passages from the bible. Trader was unabashedly moved to tears, touched by their kindness.

He was the last to offer a prayer, choosing Patricia's favorite psalm. *"Yea, though I walk through the valley of the shadow of death..."* His voice was clear, and when finished, he gestured for Sweringen to give him the remains. He brought the box up to his lips and lovingly kissed it. Getting down on his knees, he placed it firmly in the ground. Rising, he brushed his hands together, and with an unspoken command, gave permission to fill the void. The task was completed within minutes. The sod was replaced, and the area brushed clean by nine sets of willing hands. It was impossible to tell that the ground had ever been disturbed.

"Group! At-*ten*-shun," Trader called out.

The pilots stood at attention, eyes forward, backs rigid.

"*Pre*-sent, arms." Nine hands rose as one in salute.

Ten seconds later Trader gave the follow-on command. "*Or*-der, arms."

With their arms again by their sides, he rendered the last command. "*Pa*-rade, rest."

Sweringen turned to Trader. "Jim, I selected this spot for two reasons. First, it's the only grassy area within a million miles, and any time we're out here we will all feel a special closeness to Patricia. We have promised her — and you — that this act will not go unpunished. And it won't. Because the word will pass like shit through a goose throughout this entire complex how we have turned their only grassy field into a hallowed Christian burial ground. I want all these superstitious, heathen bastards to know they'll be playing in a graveyard from now on, and trust me, they'll be uncomfortable every second they're out here. However, my guess is it won't be used all that much, starting today. Serve the pricks right." He then handed Patricia's wedding ring to Trader.

Trader smiled weakly as he slipped it onto his left pinkie finger. "Thanks, Tim, and thank you all. I know Pat wholeheartedly approves." After a moment's silence he added a final thought. With eyes riveted to the ground, he made a vow for all to hear. "Pat, as God is my witness, I will see that man dead for what he has done to you."

He turned and led the grieving prisoners back to their building.

*   *   *

Jallud had watched the entire proceeding. Standing by the window in the small infirmary and holding the venetian blinds apart with splayed fingers, he commented every few seconds to Bakktari who was lying on the bed behind him. He kept up a running commentary until the Americans disappeared inside their building. He released the slats and as the blind swayed back into place, he turned and faced Bakktari.

"I thought you rather enjoyed hitting me, Doctor. Maybe you displayed a little too much exuberance." He started to grin, but immediately winced at the effort. His face was already markedly discolored and noticeably swollen. He walked three steps to the small bedside table and picked up a washcloth from a bowl filled with ice water. He held it gingerly up to his jaw, and while it dripped onto the floor he looked down at the figure on the bed.

Bakktari had fared the worst. "You could've killed me," he groaned. "I can only thank Allah that I had enough sense to make sure I was somewhat padded. I know we had to make it look convincing, but that last kick was definitely not called for,

Jallud. You could've ruptured my liver. As it is, I know you've damaged my right kidney. I might have to be flown to a hospital in Tripoli."

"And so you shall, Doctor. Come now, look on the bright side. We both did our duty, painful though it was. I guarantee you those pilots now see you as their only friend." He dropped the cloth into the stainless steel dish. "I, on the other hand, am now their mortal enemy, and they will spend their nights dreaming of ways to kill me. And that's good, because I have delivered a purpose into their miserable lives. I've become a lightning rod for their anger." He snorted. "So be it! As long as they do what they were brought here for, I'll happily take on the role of villain. As for you, Doctor, I'm certain they now look on you as an ally and friend. So you see, we both got what we wanted. Anyway, we must prepare to move forward. Their holiday is over. Tomorrow they begin to earn their keep." He moved towards the door, paused, and added an afterthought. "Those fools in North Vietnam should have asked me years ago how to make an American do one's bidding. The little bastards could learn a thing or two from me, wouldn't you agree?" He actually managed to produce a full-throated laugh as he stepped confidently out of the room, leaving Bakktari to wrestle with some very troubling thoughts.

CHAPTER 11

Doctor Mohammed Hadid breezed into the conference room willing himself to appear relaxed and confident. He had not yet met the Americans and was nervous at the prospect. He felt inferior having to rely on prison labor to solve a problem. He had lost face, and it galled.

Two assistants accompanied him, and all three wore smiles frozen on their faces. They were dressed in matching starched, white, full-length cotton lab coats replete with nametags, (English and Arabic) and radiation badges— the universal uniforms of geniuses.

"Good morning, gentlemen. My name is Doctor Hadid and it is my honor to be the director of this remarkable facility. And it's also an honor to be working with all of you. I know there is much you can teach me." The words stuck in his craw.

Perfect English, Trader thought, as he listened to the welcome, even though it came in a somewhat singsong delivery.

Hadid's audience sat impassively. He noted that the Americans were wearing summer-weight military styled uniforms, pressed to perfection, but devoid of any insignia of rank. "First, I would like to take you on a tour of our facility here by film. That's so much easier than a long, time-consuming walk-through. I think you'll be very impressed." He turned to one of his assistants and directed him in Arabic to turn on the projector.

For the next fifteen minutes Trader and his group watched the forbidding desert become magically transformed into the state-of-the-art-engineering marvel they were now forced to call home. Construction had taken just a little more than two years, Hadid explained proudly. There was a running voice-over commentary in Arabic, and five minutes into the footage Colonel Gaddafi appeared at what was obviously a dedication ceremony. He addressed a crowd of five hundred attentive, adoring workers. Toward the end of his speech the Supreme Ruler began gesticulating with both arms, the flailing tempo speeding up to keep time with his rapid-fire delivery. Then: abrupt silence. But not for long. Seconds later the demigod was serenaded with thunderous applause.

Hadid's eyes never left the screen as he translated. "Colonel Gaddafi is telling the workers that they have all embarked on a project to help the poor of the earth by showing the world how to use nuclear power for the good of mankind."

Then the audience was taken on a tour of the sparkling building housing the nuclear reactor and many impressive labs, all equal to any found in the West. Trader identified an early 1960s single stage 2MelV linear Van de Graff accelerator in the second lab, but could not tell from the footage whether or not it was functional. And he saw a technical library stacked with the latest journals authored by the world's leading minds in physics.

The narrator droned on in Arabic.

Next was a tour of the nuclear reactor. Trader noted that it was on-line and supplying the electrical needs of the entire facility. Not a breeder type, Trader could tell, looking for clues.

The reactor was housed in a huge structure built deep into the earth, and when the cameraman first panned it from ground level and then moments later from the vantage point of an aerial shot, it was obvious the announcer was explaining how the building could not be identified for what it truly was.

The tour ended with an intimate look at the living quarters. Everything was bright and clean; bedrooms, common areas, and dining halls. Trader could almost smell the newness. Here each frame was filled with happy, contented faces; workers playing and eating; or eagerly performing their duties for the betterment of man. It was a masterful presentation.

"So, gentlemen, that was just a brief tour, but of course you will get to see firsthand much more in the days ahead. However, it does give you an idea of what we have here and what we do." Hadid was all smiles. "Which brings us to the reason you'll be with us before continuing your journey home. I sincerely hope that day comes quickly. Now, which one of you gentlemen is Captain Trader?"

"I am."

Hadid knew who was who, but was genuinely shocked at how much older Trader looked in the flesh than the man he had seen in a photo taken four years earlier in Washington. *Why, his hair's completely white!* He could easily be ten, even fifteen years older than his true age of forty-five. Here is a soul who has truly experienced the absolute worst life had to offer.

"Would you prefer to be addressed as Doctor Trader, or Captain Trader?"

"I'm a naval captain and a prisoner of war. As such, we will all be addressed by our military ranks."

Hadid had not expected this response. He thought he was being civilized, but this American had just let him know where he stood.

"And so you shall. Tell me, what do you think should be the first order of business?"

"None of us has worked as physicists for years, so what we'll need at the very least are a few weeks of intensive reading of the most recent materials available. We'll need to spend several hours a day just bringing each other up to speed. Then, and only then, will we be ready to move onto the next step, which is to design and fabricate an initiator. However, as time goes on, we'll let you know what we think we'll require. But frankly, we won't know ourselves for at least several weeks."

"I see."

Gerald Glasstner stood. "You know, it would sure be a big help if we knew what kind of weapon we'll be designing the initiator for. What I mean is, will it be to trigger an airdropped package, a torpedo, a missile, or will it be for a static, platform-mounted device? There's a big difference in designing for each, you know." Glasstner was talking mumbo jumbo.

The others nodded; nine wise minds in total agreement.

Hadid spoke rapid-fire to his assistants and soon all three were embroiled in a heated discussion. They argued in Arabic, and all the while the pilots sat, saying nothing.

Finally Hadid turned to the Americans. "I can't answer your question at the moment, but I will in due course."

"What fissionable material are you thinking of using in your device?"

"And you are, who, may I ask?"

"Commander Gilchrest."

Hadid stared long and hard at the man, seemingly at odds with himself. He made his decision. "Plutonium. We will be working with Plutonium."

"When do you think the Plutonium will be ready?" Trader asked. "Of course, I'm referring to weapons-grade Plutonium."

"Of course, Captain. We have it now."

In spite of himself, Trader had to chuckle. "Oh, I rather doubt that. Anything short of weapons-grade Plutonium would be so unstable it would be impossible to work with. And frankly, I wouldn't want to be within a hundred miles of the stuff."

Hadid broke out in a little laugh. Trader could tell immediately the laugh was genuine. "How true! No, rest assured we have the proper grade of refined Plutonium on hand. I am not confusing weapons-grade material with reactor-grade material. Furthermore, we can replenish as we need it."

Trader did not know what to believe so he just shrugged his shoulders.

Hadid glanced at the clock on the back wall. "Let's call it a day. We'll all come back tomorrow to start in earnest. I shall have an index of all the literature in our library available for you to study at that time. You only have to ask what books and journals you want to see and they'll be brought to you at once. I'll also make sure you have blackboards, pens, paper, and calculators. Anything you require, you shall have. Any questions?"

"How about a gun for each of us and an airplane to share?" Mark FitzGerald asked in a most sincere voice.

"I'm afraid that's something I cannot provide." Hadid looked from one to the other. "Any other questions?"

"How about coffee for tomorrow?"

"Excellent suggestion, Captain Trader. Yes. You shall have gallons of hot coffee every morning. Also, tea, sodas, and any kind of food you desire. It will be here. Just tell me what you want." Again he eyed the clock. "So, we will meet tomorrow at seven sharp. You will all get your radiation badges issued then."

What choice do we have? Trader thought as he led his men to their waiting bus and the two-mile drive back to their quarters.

Four ripe guards crowded onto the bus with them.

Climbing off, Niels Borden fell in beside Trader. "How about a once-around, Jim?"

Trader shook his head. "Going to ask for a rain check, Niels, okay? I'm flat beat."

"Captain, I need five minutes of your time. It's important."

Their four guards stood bunched under the eaves, out of the sun's blinding glare.

Trader looked at them and motioned to Borden with his head. The two separated from the group and strolled casually away from the building.

"What's on your mind, Niels?"

"We're in a heap of trouble, boss. I mean big trouble. This place isn't the bullshit peace palace that Hadid character wants us to believe. It was built for one purpose only: to make nukes by the dozen. The guy in the film, the one with all the frizzy hair and dressed like some cartoon movie character field marshal? He admitted as much in his little speech. And when Hadid began arguing with his assistants after Gerry asked about delivery systems, he was telling his pals that we don't need to know about the missiles just yet."

"How in the hell do you know all that?"

"I speak Arabic, sir."

Trader stopped walking, stunned by the announcement. "Say again?"

"I speak Arabic, sir. I learned it growing up. My mother's Lebanese, so my sister and I learned to speak, read, and write Arabic along with English. We also had a Lebanese nanny until we started school. She was a cousin or something; lived with us for years."

"Why didn't you say so before this?" asked an incredulous Trader.

Niels gave a shake of his head. "Everybody we've been in contact with speaks English. I didn't think about it until I was watching the film and hearing the guy off-camera droning away in the background. Then, a couple of minutes later as I'm listening to *El Supremo* carrying on, bam, all of a sudden it's thirty years ago and I'm thinking in Arabic."

"*Son of a bitch!*"

"Yes, sir. Son of a bitch!"

Trader turned to Borden, am ear-to-ear grin lighting up his face. He slapped Niels on the shoulder. The years seemed to fall away. "Hot damn! This proves there is a God! I can't believe it. Now we can know what the enemy's up to and they'll never suspect."

"That's my thinking too, skipper."

"Niels, I don't want you to say anything to the others just yet. Let me think about it for a while." They were approaching the front of the building, ignored by the guards. "They've all got to be told, of course, but I want this thing as closely guarded a secret as the prisoners' code, because if Jallud ever found out, he'd have you shot. We've got to make sure you're never compromised."

"Thanks. I'll leave that up to you. Meanwhile, I'll keep my ears extra clean from now on."

"Roger, that."

Niels held open the door and the two stepped into the blessed comfort of air-conditioned coolness.

As he mounted the stairs, Trader realized he'd been just dealt his first ace, one from the top of the deck and not from up the sleeve of a card cheat. He was elated.

* * *

Jallud strode through the airline terminal with the confidence of a king. He had flown from Tripoli to Geneva along with his country's delegation to the OPEC conference. This was the cartel's second meeting of the year and the decisions to be announced later this week would rock the industrial world to its very core. *About bloody time*, he thought. He allowed himself to be escorted to a waiting Rolls Royce, a Libyan pennant attached to its front bumper snapping impatiently in the freshening breeze.

Geneva was a city ready for its wealthy visitors. Security was highly visible and highly mobile, evidenced by the number of police officers in cars, on motorcycles, and on foot. Special military types added to the numbers, all carrying machine pistols slung over shoulders.

Jallud entered the back of the car alone. The door was closed by a lackey who imperiously waved to the driver to proceed. The rest of his delegation scrambled into lesser limousines.

"Will you be going directly to the Hotel Intercontinental, Excellency?" asked the electronically transmitted voice coming through a speaker just below the glass partition.

Jallud drummed his fingers absently on the rich mahogany serving tray before him as he looked around, taking in the beauty of the lake and the majestic backdrop of the Jura Range on one side, and the precipitous Mont Salève on the other. What a difference a day makes, he thought. Yesterday nothing but sand; today the postcard beauty of Switzerland.

"Yes," he finally said. "The hotel. I don't know if I'll need the car again today but wait for me in case I do. If I decide not to go out I'll send word through the concierge desk. The just make sure you're back at eight in the morning."

"Very good, Excellency."

Arriving at the hotel, Jallud was spotted by the concierge who needed only to snap his fingers once and a liveried bellman sprang forth.

"Welcome back, Monsieur Jallud. How very nice to see you again. Will you be staying with us for the entire conference, sir?"

"Unfortunately no, Gerard. My loss, but duty calls for me to be constantly in motion. Today, Switzerland; tomorrow, Italy. And the day after that, who knows?"

"Ambassador, you work too hard," Gerard clucked sympathetically. "Whatever I can do to make your stay more comfortable, just ask, and it will be so."

"As always, Gerard. Thank you."

*   *   *

Twenty minutes later an envelope appeared on the carpet by the heavy oak door of Jallud's twelfth floor suit.

Tearing it open, he read the short message.

Excellency: Restaurante d'Hermes, Aubonne, 20:30 hours.
Wily

Aubonne was twenty kilometers away on the western shore of Lake Geneva. Good choice, Jallud thought. Wily had insisted that the final negotiations take place between the two of them alone. Jallud had been miffed when told of these conditions only four days earlier, but swallowed his anger and sent word that he would come. The date was June 18, 1973.

Wily had been right, he now realized. This was a time when the country would be swarming with Arabs. Any meeting between the two of them alone would not draw any untoward interest.

Jallud set out for his rendezvous at a little before eight. He had dismissed his driver earlier, reasoning that taking a taxi to the rendezvous would be appropriately inconspicuous.

The ride along the shore of Lake Geneva was uneventful, and eight-thirty found an impatient Jallud seated and waiting.

At ten minutes to nine a man in his late forties, dressed like the banker he claimed to be, approached the banquette, nodded once, and plunked himself down across from Jallud. No apologies for being late; no inquiry as to the state of his health; no little spark of civility whatsoever. This was to be a business meeting and the newcomer was all business.

Jallud had met Wily von Haart twice in the past two years, both times in different cities. No one would have thought that the slight, balding, pasty-faced man was anything other than the capitalistic banker his business card presented him to be. Jallud knew differently.

Wily began without preamble. "The middle of October. That's when I can fill your contract. Three items. You just tell me when and where you want them delivered." Wily sat back and took a long pull on the Beck's he had brought with him to the table.

"You sure?"

"Of course I'm sure," Wily replied, hackles rising at the very suggestion that his word might somehow be suspect. His pale, undemonstrative gray eyes bored into Jallud's.

Two can play this game, you little piece of shit. "Remember your friends, Wily. Especially friends with deep pockets. I have always been generous to you and yours, and I want to continue. I was not questioning your truthfulness; I was merely expressing surprise that it could come to pass so quickly."

A mollified Wily got the hint. "My apologies, Herr Jallud. I certainly didn't intend to be rude." He leaned across the table. The stale breath of cigarettes and beer washed over Jallud causing him to involuntarily draw back.

Wily continued. "In the first week of October our selected target will be removing three batteries of *Longbow* missiles from Regensburg and taking them back to Stuttgart for what the Americans call field-level, depot maintenance. To do this, the missiles will be loaded onto tractor-trailers and moved on the autobahn. They're never convoyed, but rather are trucked three to a load in separate vehicles. Three missiles make-up one battery, you see, and they are moved as unobtrusively as possible. The Americans are very conscious of image, and God forbid the German people should in any way suspect that their country is sinking under the weight of all these American nuclear missiles. As if we Germans don't already know it!"

Jallud could care less about the politics involved. "Your informant can be trusted?"

"He's an American army officer, so, yeah; I'd say the information is solid. As to trusting the man I would ask: how much trust can you place in a traitor, hmm?"

Jallud nodded. *Touché.*

"All the components will be intact," Wily was saying, "except for the warheads, of course. And the fuel. But everything else will be there."

"Like guidance systems?"

"Just so."

"Excellent!" Jallud then frowned. "Where do you suggest we take delivery?"

"That's up to you, but my people tell me they want to be out of Germany and the NATO countries as quickly as possible.

We would like to move them through Czechoslovakia, into Hungary and on into Yugoslavia for delivery at the docks in Dubrovnik. Our contacts have assured us of safe passage. All it takes is a little grease," Wily said, rubbing his thumb and forefinger together.

Jallud sat back and digested the information. It certainly sounded good. "How long do you think before the authorities will be alerted that three of their missiles are missing?"

Wily shrugged. "Who knows? Maybe one hour, maybe two hours. Certainly no more than that. By then we'll be well inside the Eastern Bloc and you will have your missiles as promised. It will go off without a hitch. You'll see."

"Can they be loaded onto a submarine?"

"That, sir, is your problem to solve. I promise delivery. It's up to you to figure out a way to cart them home."

Jallud refused to be baited. "You're right, of course. Now, the amount agreed to was two million, U.S.?"

"Half now; half on delivery. We have some major expenses to contend with before October."

"I shall deposit the funds tomorrow before I leave Switzerland."

"It is always a pleasure doing business with a professional." Wily drained his beer, and looked around to catch the waiter's eye. "Shall we order?"

A very contented Jallud got out of his taxi at eleven fifteen and ambled into the glass and marble lobby of his hotel. He strolled to the elevator bank and a made a solitary ride up to his suite. However, his day wasn't over just yet. Oh, no! Hours ago arrangements had been made to have a certain French female join him for the time between midnight and dawn. He smiled in anticipation of the night, and as he crossed his threshold he deliberately let the door slam shut, waking every guest within earshot.

The king was back in residence.

CHAPTER 12

The Americans had never experienced such heat. It was June, and daily the temperature soared to 120 degrees and beyond. Right now, this was one of the most dangerous spots on earth. The dry desert air could virtually draw the moisture right out of a person's lungs, leaving a man dead, to mummify, in less than a day. This monotonous, perilous weather pattern could be expected to last for another three months.

Bakktari had returned from Tripoli early in the month and had made it a point to speak to the prisoners one-on-one. He apologized for Jallud's behavior, and confided in each that he thought Jallud to be insane. He went to great lengths to assure them all that he had had no idea what was in Jallud's twisted mind when they'd been brought here originally, and nine times he made whispered promises that he'd do all in his power to see them freed. "I am your friend."

During his meeting with Trader he made an offer that took Trader completely by surprise.

"You know," he began, "I saw a film in Rome last month which got me to thinking. It was called *The Dirty Dozen*. Lee Marvin led a great cast and the story was about a group of prisoners all condemned to death—not that you men are, of course," he added, immediately mindful of his faux-pas. "Anyway, these dozen guys were offered a chance at full pardons and freedom if they agreed to become commandos on a dangerous mission against the Germans. Well, towards the end of their training Lee Marvin brought women into the camp for a party...it made me think of you. I can arrange it..."

Trader was thunderstruck. "No thank you," he finally managed. "No whores, Doctor, and don't you *ever* broach the subject again."

Bakktari's hands danced uncontrollably at the ends of his wrists like two deranged butterflies. He turned crimson. "Captain, it shall never be spoken of again." He raced to change the subject. "Now, is there anything else I can do for you?"

"We need sunglasses. The men are starting to complain of

headaches."

"I should have thought of that. My apologies. You will all have sunglasses today." Bakktari walked Trader to the door, desperate to make amends. "Please, get your work done as quickly as possible, Captain. All I want is to see you men out of this place and back in America with your families. I pray for that every day."

"Good. Keep praying."

* * *

The pilot-scientists immersed themselves in their learning. They read everything available on the subject of weapons construction and initiators, and each took turns lecturing his fellows on individual areas of expertise. All added to the accumulating body of knowledge. Save one. John Waltensperger, the group's lone astrophysicist. It became their sacred mission to make sure he was seen to be fully integrated into their ranks so no suspicion would befall him from the Libyan staff.

Trader had informed the others of Niels Borden's ability to understand Arabic, and they were elated. Whenever the Libyan scientists began conversing among themselves, the Americans would fall silent, allowing Niels to eavesdrop. All secrets learned were shared in the dead of night using the prisoners' code.

The men worked and waited, hoping that an opportunity would present itself for at least one of their number to escape.

* * *

One day in early July, and after a particularly trying discussion of the physics package to be manufactured, an exasperated Trader sought out Hadid. "You know, I think it's about time we get a look-see at the metal you're planning to use to fabricate the housing for the initiator. We need to give it a thorough analysis to make sure it's structurally flawless."

Hadid scratched his chin to hide his annoyance. Did this American really take him for a fool? Of course he knew the metal needed to build the sphere had to be perfect. The best metallurgical team in the country had been working on the problem for months.

"I know, Captain. I shall have samples brought for your

analysis and your blessing."

"I also think we should go to work in the labs," Trader pressed. "That way the equipment we'll need will be close at hand. If you don't have specific items, then we can tell you what to order."

Dammit, the man was trying to take over. So typical of everything he had ever heard about know-it-all Americans.

Trader continued. "We'll have to spend a few months designing, building and testing prototypes. Only then will we know what type of HE, or high-explosives, to use to initiate the reaction."

"A few months you say?" Hadid did not like the sound of that. And he knew Jallud would like it even less. This American was obviously stalling. "Oh, Captain Trader, I'm sure we can speedup that timetable considerably. You'll see."

Trader realized that Hadid had to answer to a very mercurial Jallud. He opted out of any hint of confrontation.

"Well, let's hope that's the case, Doctor. Now, if you have nothing more for us at the moment, I suggest we get another couple of hours of work in before calling it a day."

*   *   *

Seated on the bus going back to their building at a little past six, Trader found himself staring out the window, watching a supply plane line-up on its final approach.

"Sure would be nice to hop on that bird and fly out of here, eh, boss?" Doug Gilchrest said from the window seat behind.

"Sure would, Doug." As he followed the planes' progress, Trader pondered what Gilchrest had just said and a wheel started to turn ever so slowly in the recesses of his mind. His eyes remained glued on the C-130 until its main gear settled on the concrete runway amidst puffs of white smoke thrown off from its tires. It rolled rapidly behind a string of buildings and out of sight. An idea had been born.

After dinner Trader asked Tim Sweringen to join him for a walk. The men were completely free to do so; theirs was a prison without walls. By ten o'clock, the temperature usually plummeted into the forties, sometimes even into the thirties, another strange fact of life in the inhospitable environment of the desert.

They walked in silence enjoying the cool, windless, bone-dry air of the night. They gazed in unison towards the heavens, awestruck by the infinite blackness; a sky seeded with untold millions of shimmering diamonds. It made each reconfirm his belief in a creator.

Trader broke the reverie. "Tim, you used to fly the Hercules, right?"

"Roger that."

"I remember when we were on our ride from the sub to the airport you said it was a pretty good bird once Lockheed Aircraft went to making it with four-bladed props."

"That's correct. I must have logged about six hundred hours in the Herc before I got my request for a fighter assignment approved. But, hey, the Herc was an all-right bird."

"Could one guy handle it by himself, or is it strictly a two, or even a three-man plane?"

"Well, in a true emergency one guy could get it off the deck and put it down somewhere else in one piece, but he'd sure have his hands full! It's really a two pilot show just to fly it well. A complete mission crew calls for two pilots, a navigator, an engineer, and at least one loadmaster. What do you have in mind?"

Trader pressed home his question. "If the opportunity presented itself, could you take the supply plane out of here all by yourself?"

That stopped Sweringen in his tracks. "Boss, it's been *years* since I've flown that old workhorse. Shit, even if I got it off the ground, which way would I point the nose? I haven't..."

"Forget all that for a minute. Could you do it?"

Sweringen didn't hesitate. "Yes, but I'd need to bone-up on the dash-one again," he said, referring to the plane's operating manual. "I'd need to memorize the emergency procedures until I had them down cold. But, hell yes, I could do it."

"Well, we have a dash-one!"

Sweringen's face lit up, and his voice betrayed his sudden excitement. "Are you shitting me? Where did you get your hands on that?"

"I didn't, you did. It's stored in your head. All you've got to do is ferret it out from between your ears and put the information down on paper."

"Ah, you had me going there for a moment, boss!"

"Tim, I'm serious. This could be our only ticket out of here. I want you to start putting a manual together from memory. The information's all there, pal. It's up to you to get it out."

"But that could take months."

Trader let loose a dismissive snorting sound. "We've sure got the time. Look, I know it's a tall order, but I want you to give it a go. What do you say?"

Sweringen walked in silence for several seconds, grasping for an understanding of the enormity of such a daunting undertaking. Finally he said, "Of course I'll give it a shot, Jim. But no promises or guarantees as to results."

"Can't ask for anything more than that."

"I'll have to commit everything to paper because if something should happen to me, at least you guys will have a manual to try your escape. Jallud could find it. Could be real risky."

"I know, but I've weighed the consequences and the pluses outweigh the negatives."

"Then I'll get started right away." Sweringen chuckled. "Wouldn't it be a bite if we pulled it off and we all rode out of here together?"

"That's a hell of a thought. Make that your inspiration, okay?"

"Yes, sir. One brand new C-130 dash-one coming right up."

They solemnly shook hands.
* * *

"I had no idea you were an expert in metallurgy, Captain Trader." Hadid was furious upon hearing Trader's pronouncement that the prototype sphere was of inferior quality and would not perform as required. The high-tensile metal composite had been painstakingly analyzed during each tedious step of the fabrication process by his engineers, and it had been machined to exacting specifications. Now this American was suggesting it was inferior. What gall! A delaying tactic, nothing more.

"We assemble and detonate on schedule." Hadid's tone signaled the issue was closed.

"Then be my guest," Trader replied. "But let me tell you this. The high explosive package will not be uniformly contained which means your sphere will explode prematurely instead of holding the force internally long enough to create the necessary heat and pressure to start a thermonuclear reaction. You will get pre-detonation, and if there was a Plutonium core at the center of the globe you would have all of that deadly shit plastered over the desert rendering life here off limits for the next thousand years!"

"Enough of your doom and gloom predictions, Captain Trader. We test Friday."

*   *   *

The nine o'clock test firing was delayed four times until finally everything was ready at one o'clock in the afternoon. Even though it was now late September, the temperature at the test site read 112 degrees. Water consumption was being recorded by the gallon, and not by the liter, per man. There were three dozen specialists gathered, including the Americans.

The Libyans were in a festive mood, congratulating each other with much back-slapping, hand-shaking, and even a kiss or two in the Moslem fashion of greeting.

The maze of electrical measuring test leads attached to the sphere was finally pronounced operational by Hadid. The critical juncture was at hand.

Everybody on the range was accounted for and then ordered inside a stifling concrete bunker set one thousand meters away from the metal platform and the suspended sphere.

Hadid started the countdown, calling off the numbers in the traditional reverse order from ten down to the magical command of "Fire" when he closed the circuit and triggered the device. The current flowed at the speed of light and ignited the high explosive package resting inside the sphere. At its core lay a metal globe, mimicking the weight and density of a Plutonium heart.

Trader's eyes were glued to the tower through high-powered German binoculars. He clearly saw the sphere disintegrate, which meant the package had exploded long before implosion could have initiated a chain reaction. There hadn't been sufficient heat and pressure generated to detonate a Plutonium bomb. The sensors confirmed that fact in a nanosecond. The test was an abysmal failure.

Trader was the first to speak. He lowered his glasses, pursed his lips, and blew out a long breath with a dry, whistling sound. "Let's go see what we've got." He pulled open the metal door and headed toward the nearest Jeep.

Hadid was visibly shaken as he studied the wreckage strewn at his feet and far beyond. The sphere had failed miserably. Analysis of the high speed film would show that it had first separated into hemispheres, and then the halves themselves had been blown to bits. But enough pressure and heat had been forced inward to tear the ersatz Plutonium core into an untold number of fragments and had scattered them helter-skelter over the desert floor. There would not have been a chain reaction.

Trader found himself thinking that if this had been the real thing, then the ensuing damage from radiation contamination would be catastrophic. With a half-life of 24,360 years for the isotope Pu-239, well, he didn't want to even think about it!

He glanced at the speechless Hadid and knew the man's immediate concern was Jallud. He had been instructed to telephone the good news. Hadid began to shake. It was very possible that with this failure he had just signed of his own death warrant.

An hour later they all assembled in the conference room. Hadid had spoken to Jallud who had responded with screams of rage. The conversation ended with Jallud informing the director that he would arrive at the facility within twenty-four hours. "Expect heads to roll," he had thundered.

"You must be very pleased, Captain Trader," Hadid said in a defeated monotone. "The test went as you predicted."

Trader shook his head. "I feel no sense of satisfaction knowing I was right." He paused long enough to pour a glass of water and down half its contents. "I think, though, we've all learned a valuable lesson today, so it is definitely not the failure you see."

"And the lesson is…?"

"That there are no shortcuts. Mistakes made in the field of nuclear physics aren't habit forming, Doctor. The lesson reinforced by today's test is there's no room for error."

"What do you propose we do?" Hadid was grasping at straws.

"We start from scratch. We analyze all the data, but I can hazard a guess that we already know the answer. The hot pressing of the powder metallurgy and the die used to create the coupled half-spheres was flawed; not even close to the necessary tolerances. Plus, the high explosive was contaminated. That stuff also needs to be manufactured to the most exacting standards and under clean-room conditions every step of the way. There can't be the slightest hint of an impurity in the final product."

"Maybe we should go to an initiator of a different design?" Hadid suggested, his voice taking on a pleading tone.

Trader studied the man. "Sure, we can do that, but the results will be the same. If your materials aren't up to the job then all the design changes won't mean diddly. For example, you still haven't told us what sort of delivery system we're designing for."

This statement set off a round of discussion among several of the Libyans. The silent Americans sat and watched.

Finally, Hadid said, "I can't tell you just yet. I'm sorry. I know it would make your task easier, but until I am authorized by Jallud, well…"

Trader shrugged his shoulders. It was time to wrap this thing up. "You have your work cut out for you, Doctor, so I suggest the following." He ticked off the points on his fingers as he made them. "Get a new source for your metals. I mean completely new. Get new tools and dies. Hire new technicians.

Fire the present lot. Get a completely different source for your HE, and analyze it microscopically. Remember, it must be kept in a rigidly controlled environment at all times. Finally, involve us each step of the way. If we say something's no good, believe us, if only because we want to see this project completed just as much as you do. Then we can go home and get on with our lives."

Hadid finally asked the one question he'd been dreading. "How far has this set us back, would you estimate, Captain?"

"I really don't know. If we get started immediately, I'd say we could be ready for another test in three, maybe four months. However, that could be an optimistic figure. Like I said, this field demands perfection. There are no shortcuts."

Hadid nodded his reluctant agreement. "Let's call it a day. Thank you, Captain Trader. And my thanks to the rest of you. Praise Allah that today's test was with a dummy package."

"Amen to that!"

Later that night through the prisoners' code Trader and the others learned from Niels Borden that Jallud was expected in camp tomorrow. He also told them that the nuclear device they were being pressed to manufacture was to sit atop an American *Longbow* missile.

Trader was floored by the news. *Holy smokes*, he thought, that madman Jallud's got something really bad in mind. He paced his room while his brain went to work. Who and what were to be the targets? But more importantly, what did Jallud expect to accomplish? He was at a loss for answers, and when he finally went to bed he couldn't sleep. It was a night fraught with demons and images of a man-made nuclear hell. His mind kept telling him that he had to unearth Jallud's secret, then somehow get the word to the outside world and those who could stop the madness before it was too late.

CHAPTER 13

It was the third police car in as many minutes to go whizzing past in the blinding rain.

"That crazy son of a bitch must be doing damn near a hundred," said Specialist Five, Thomas Slattery, U.S. Army, to his companion, Staff Sergeant Gaylord Livingston, U.S. Army, riding shotgun.

"Betcha anything some stupid Kraut's done gone waltzing off the autobahn up ahead," suggested Livingston in a know-it-all voice as he leaned forward for a better look. It was a study in futility. He set off a series of explosions from the wad of bubble gum crammed in his mouth.

"Which means a goddamn delay. *Shit!* I have a date with a big, blond *schatzie,* and I'm supposed to be back in Regensburg by five. Frigging Germans!"

A minute later they rounded a bend only to be confronted by a sea of flashing blue lights.

Slattery began to expertly downshift, using the gears rather than his brakes to reduce the momentum of his tractor-trailer. The last thing he needed — or wanted — was to have his forty-two thousand-pound rig go into an uncontrollable slide on the rain-drenched concrete. By the time he reached the accident scene he was moving at a crawl, the wipers laboring noisily in a vain attempt to hurl water from the windshield. He eased the transmission into neutral and applied the hand brake, but kept the huge diesel motor turning.

Two police officers approached the truck, one on each side. Both carried blue flashing wands, and both made a simultaneous signal for the Americans to roll down their windows.

"Aw, shit, we're going to get soaked!" Those were the last words spoken by Thomas Slattery, and the last heard by Gaylord Livingston. Both were shot simultaneously through their heads and both were dead in the time it took their bodies to slump forward.

Without a word, the officers dragged the bodies from the cab and climbed in. The driver put the rig into the first of its eleven forward gears and started to move the behemoth, wending his way around the assembled cars. Their fellow officers waved them on.

The bodies of the two Americans were dumped into the back of an ambulance already at the scene. The doors were slammed shut, and it, too, sped off into the downpour. Thirty seconds later the cluster of police cars had vanished, along with three American *Longbow* missiles.

*   *   *

Wily von Haart sat in the back of the lead sedan as it raced toward its rendezvous with the U.S. Army truck nine kilometers away. This is just like in the movies, he thought, and we did it all in one take!

The heist had been meticulously planned. Every conceivable contingency had been played out, including one with the possibility of the real police coming upon the scene. He had even scripted a scenario with the Americans having an armed escort, something which had *never* happened. However, the caper had gone off without a hitch; *and in less than two minutes!*

Traffic had been stopped a mile away on both sides of the autobahn so as to prevent anyone from viewing the fake accident scene. But the growing line of motorists noted with satisfaction that the police had everyone moving again within minutes.

And all the while Wily monitored the real police radio frequencies.

His group arrived at the abandoned government agriculture station moments after the American army truck. Wily watched intently as it backed up to a tractor-trailer from Poland, the lettering on its side saying it was a refrigerated unit owned by a Yugoslavian food cooperative.

While two of his men busied themselves removing plastic magnetized police markings from the row of cars now parked shoulder to shoulder, the rest of his group prepared for the unloading the American vehicle and transferring its expensive cargo to the Polish truck.

Wily clambered into the American rig and trained his flashlight on the contents. His heart missed a beat! There were only two missiles and not the three he had been assured would be on board. *Damn!*

The cargo was tethered to mini-trailers. Each missile was still attached to its mobile launch platform, and between the two was what Wily assumed to be some sort of a controller's station, also on its own trailer.

With little fanfare the items were hooked up to an electric forklift and lifted onto the waiting truck. When both missiles and the control apparatus were secured, the men began loading crates of apples and pears floor to ceiling all the way to the rear doors.

Twenty minutes later, and still in the pouring rain, a Yugoslavian truck loaded with fresh fruit set off for the Czech border and the safety of the Eastern Bloc.

The disciplined group of Germans also departed, brazenly leaving behind the American truck and a stolen ambulance with two bodies in the back.

Wily would be proven wrong about one thing. German helicopters did not discover the missing truck for almost five hours, and minutes after that a very angry four-star American general, known as SACEUR, the Supreme Allied Commander Europe, was on the phone to the Pentagon alerting his bosses to the bad news.

SACEUR was asked to retire the following day.

*   *   *

Wily sat next to Jallud in the back of the air-conditioned Mercedes and watched the trailer being lowered from the Monrovia-flagged freighter, *Africa Star*. Minutes earlier he had informed Jallud that only two missiles were being delivered, and was surprised at the seemingly philosophical acceptance of this news by the Arab seated beside him.

"Of course I expect you to reduce the payment by one third because I did not deliver. It's that simple."

Jallud silently followed every move of the stevedores. A tractor unit was backed up to the trailer, and the driver jumped out of the cab. He began coupling air-brake lines and electrical connections for the lights.

Jallud came to a quick decision. Good chance he would

need Wily's services again, so best make him beholden. "No, Wily, you acted in good faith. It's not your fault there weren't three missiles. The money's been fully earned and the balance will be deposited in your account as promised."

"That's extremely generous of you, Herr Jallud. It's always a pleasure doing business with our Libyan friends. I only hope you-know-who takes the loss as graciously." He reached over and shook hands. "I must be getting to the airport. *Auf Wiedersehen!*"

Jallud tailed the missiles to the military airfield south of Benghazi, staying as close as a wary mother hen until everything was loaded onto the C-130. He remained parked next to the runway until the plane was airborne and began its southerly track toward the base in the desert.

It was now time to phone Gaddafi. He gave instructions to his driver then sat back against the comfortable leather cushions and dreamed of the grandeur that was soon to be his.

* * *

What is it about this man that puzzles me? Bakktari wondered. He was sitting at his desk, dressed in operating room scrubs, and studying the black and white photo in the manila folder before him. "John Waltensperger," he whispered, "what secret are you hiding from me? You certainly gave us all quite a little scare this morning." He began to read.

JOHN WALTENSPERGER

Born September 12, 1937. Nothing known about his parents. Graduate of the U.S. Military Academy at West Point, but requested and was granted a naval commission in 1958. Attended flight school. Became a pilot the following summer. Several operational carrier assignments noted. Selected to attend graduate school at MIT. Graduated with a master's in Nuclear??? Physics. Worked at the Naval Weapons Institute for a while, then in the early sixties went back to MIT for a doctorate which was followed by two more years at the Weapons Institute.

Considered to be a 'fast burner' by Navy standards. Promoted to his present rank of commander in early 1971. He had remained current in the F-4B Phantom jet, and had been assigned to the carrier USS Oriskany *on a deployment to join the Seventh Fleet in the South China Sea. Commander Waltensperger was shot down over North Vietnam later that year. A partial clipping from* The Dallas Times *stated that he had been selected for astronaut training by NASA, said training to begin after his Southeast Asia tour was completed. The article concluded with the observation that his wife and children were already living in or near Houston, Texas.*

This guy's not much of a known quantity, Bakktari concluded. He was studying this particular folder simply because of the events of the past few hours.

Waltensperger had been trundled into the clinic in the wee hours of the morning doubled over and writhing in pain. The technician on duty had recorded a temperature of 105 degrees. He also noted that the patient's abdomen was taught and the skin as dry as parchment. Thankfully, Bakktari had been called immediately and had diagnosed acute appendicitis. He in turn called for the chief surgeon to come, stat, and within forty-five minutes the two of them had operated. The appendix had already ruptured, spilling poison into the abdominal cavity. However, both doctors felt confident that the patient would recover completely. To ensure that outcome, he was being flooded intravenously with antibiotics.

A very worried Trader had been given permission to see the patient in the recovery room.

"He should recover fully, Captain Trader. Believe me, Dr. Safarad is a first class surgeon, and we operated in time." Bakktari was confident in his prognosis. We're just puzzled there was no warning. That's rather unusual."

"My thanks for your help, Doctor. I didn't know what was happening. I thought Commander Waltensperger was dying!"

"Well, technically speaking, I guess he was," Bakktari replied. He patted the American's shoulder. "Your friend will be fine. Now you go back to work. You can come and visit tonight. I'll see to it personally."

"Thanks again, Doc, I know the others will be relieved to

hear that John will be okay."

Trader relayed the good news to the others. However, he was worried about the possibility of Waltensperger being disoriented and confused when he woke, which meant he could start mumbling God-knows-what while still in a drug-induced state. He could let it slip that he wasn't a nuclear physicist but rather an astrophysicist, and if someone hearing this realized the significance of what he were saying, then all hell would break loose.

An hour later Jallud paid a visit to the patient, unbeknownst even to Bakktari.

* * *

"Tell me, what am I to expect? Will I see a big explosion?" Jallud directed his questions to Captain Trader, rather than to Hadid who was hovering annoyingly close.

"If we see even a hint of an explosion, it will mean we've failed."

"Explain."

"We're hoping to contain the rather formidable amount of kinetic energy which will be generated within the sphere. We want to make sure all of the explosive force is directed inward even though it will detonate at a speed of nine thousand meters a second. If the shock wave is contained within the sphere, we'll know for sure the housing is structurally sound. Then we can move on to the next stage."

"And you are confident it will be so?" There was a definite edge to Jallud's voice. It was now the middle of December, and as far as he could tell, nothing of substance had been accomplished in nine months. Gaddafi was getting impatient and angrier by the day.

"The Americans have tested and approved the manufacture of our sphere every step of the way, Excellency," Hadid said, hoping to shirk any responsibility in the event of failure.

"Then let us see what we shall see, Captain Trader. Commence."

"Doctor?" Trader deferred the honors to the Arab

scientist.

The countdown sequence started, and the firing order was given. The brightly silvered sphere shook violently in its constraints, but held together.

"*Bravo!*" Hadid yelled out, delighted and relieved that his head would remain affixed.

Jallud ignored him. "So, what does it mean, Captain?"

"It means that you have a sphere capable of housing the implosive power necessary to start a chain reaction. It means you're on your way."

"So, we can have a warhead put together in a matter of days? Weeks?"

Despite himself, Trader had to laugh. "I'm afraid not. When the real Plutonium core is in place, the detonation of the high explosive must be timed so that the shock wave crushes the trigger mechanism inside, causing the material to detonate uniformly. For our initiator, or trigger, we'll be using a highly radioactive isotope of Polonium buried within Beryllium which will absorb the alphas from the Polonium while emitting its own neutrons. These two elements must come together in exactly the right mix in the blink of an eye, because that's what it takes to reach a temperature capable of starting and sustaining a chain reaction. All we proved today is that our sphere will contain the force required to do the job."

Hadid's head bobbed up and down in silent agreement.

Jallud was having none of it. That was not what he wanted to hear. "I haven't a clue what the hell you have just said, and I have no intention of trying to understand the physics. But here is something I do understand. It is now December. I want a test of a real weapon by the end of February."

"What the hell are you saying?" asked a startled Trader. "You can't possibly mean that you want to set off a nuclear explosion just to satisfy your curiosity that the damn thing works!"

"That's exactly what I mean! Otherwise, how will I know for sure that you've done your job? Am I to take you at your word because you're an officer and a gentleman? Don't make me laugh!"

"You honestly think you can set off a nuke right here in the middle of the desert and that no one will notice? Don't make *me* laugh!"

Jallud's jaw twitched violently. His black eyes turned to slits. Hadid instinctively began backing away.

"Don't bait me, Captain Trader. If you are not prepared to test by the deadline I've just given, I do not even want to contemplate the consequences. It is my considered opinion that you are stalling. Keep in mind the penalty for such behavior." He motioned impatiently to his driver. "My suggestion to you and your men is that you all start to work harder." With a disdainful glance toward Hadid, he added, "I suggest you do the same."

Hadid began to bow. No longer able to contain his anger, Jallud lashed out and struck the side of Hadid's lowered head, knocking him to the ground. He stood over the fallen man and yelled in Arabic for a full minute, barely pausing to catch a breath. When he was finished, he kicked Hadid in the head then spat at him. He turned to Trader. "The end of February, Captain. Remember that!"

*   *   *

Darkness found Trader and Sweringen huddled in front of their building a few hours later. The night was bitterly cold. A strong wind blowing from the North was roiling the sand, causing a sea of silica to slash and sting all exposed flesh. They knew they would soon have to retreat back to the safety and warmth of the building.

"How's the project coming along, Tim?"

Sweringen placed his mouth close to Trader's ear. He had to yell to be heard. "I've surprised myself with what I've been able to do, Jim. I've drawn a good picture of the cockpit from memory, and I think I've got it ninety-five percent. I've used that picture to go over my procedures. I'm building a pretty comprehensive Dash-One checklist."

"I knew you could do it. Look, you heard that lunatic this afternoon. Time's running out. We're going to have to get at least one of us out of here, and that plane is going to be our best bet."

"I know. I'm putting in some long hours at night on this thing. Have you had a chance to speak to Niels?"

Trader nodded, head bowed, eyes barely visible slits. "Yeah, and he says that Jallud yelled at Hadid that he just might have to kill one or more of us to make his point. And we both know the son of a bitch is crazy enough to do just that."

"Goddamn it!" Sweringen howled at the night, his words immediately lost to the wind.

"Amen to that. That's why we do have to prepare the men for the worst. I plan to pass on the information to the others later tonight. And I don't mind telling you, I'm really scared for all of us."

CHAPTER 14

Jallud felt the full weight of the pressure being brought to bear by his Supreme Leader. Those days of euphoria had long ago given way to reality, and reality was not a friend he could embrace. Gaddafi was furious upon hearing the latest news from the desert.

"Don't come sniveling to me with tales of what you cannot do," he hissed. "If you're not up to the task then tell me, and I'll replace you with one who is. Either the Americans are fooling you, or they're incapable of achieving what you've promised. If that's the case then I must conclude my investment will have proven to be a poor one."

"They will deliver, Excellency. I, Jallud, guarantee it." Jallud did not care for the turn the conversation had taken, but what could he have done differently? What if he had said nothing of the setbacks only to have that eunuch Hadid go slinking off to Gaddafi behind his back? Or worse yet, that pip-squeak Bakktari!

Jallud was dismissed with a flip of Gaddafi's wrist. He backed away, outwardly calm, inwardly seething.

As he rode through the teeming, noisy, and chaotic streets to his own home, his thoughts harkened back to how the dream had been born. The world had seemed so perfect then.

* * *

WINTER-SPRING, 1970

Colonel Gaddafi had been in power six months in those first heady days of March 1970, when quite by accident Jallud overheard some soldiers reminiscing about the most miserable experiences of their careers. One told of a time several years earlier when he had been posted in the desert as a guard for a geological team. Nothing could be worse than that, he had assured his fellows.

Jallud had invited himself into their conversation. "How right you are, Sergeant. I know, because I, too, was there. In fact, I commanded the unit."

"I remember, Major! Was it not as bad as I have just

described?"

"No, Sergeant, it was worse!"

The small knot of men laughed and slapped at their knees, comrades-in-arms, elite members of an elite fraternity.

Jallud had chatted idly with them for a few more minutes and then departed to take up another of a thousand important missions of state. However, for the rest of the day his mind kept returning to the conversation and the miserable hellhole called Tejerri.

As fate would have it, he was again reminded of Tejerri later that evening during a formal dinner for visiting communist party ministers from Mao Tse-tung's China. The president of the university, seated on his right, was the evening's host. He began telling of a dream one of his professors had espoused, a dream to turn a remote corner of the kingdom into an oasis. And this idyllic creation was to be birthed by nuclear power. Of course, it had been so much rubbish, the wild imaginings of an old, crazy scientist, but for a brief moment in time the doddering fool had held the ear of the king, and that was all that mattered.

"What happened to him?" Jallud wanted to know.

"Killed in a plane crash at the site. A place called Tejerri. About a year ago."

"Could we have built a nuclear reactor? Do we have such a capability?"

"I don't think so," was the honest reply, "but if I remember correctly, he wanted to get the Americans to help him with the project."

Jallud gave an involuntary laugh. "Fat chance of that now!" He waited while his host sipped his Turkish coffee and spooned mounds of flaky baklava into his mouth.

"By the way, who was the head of the physics department at the time?"

"A doctor named Hadid. In fact, he's still there. A good man, Hadid. Trained in Italy. Not brilliant, but a competent theoretician nonetheless."

Jallud had made a note of the name. An idea had been born.

*   *   *

He paid Hadid a visit the following week. The scientist was in awe of his powerful guest. What an honor! To be singled out for consultation by one so high in the new government. Minister Jallud was so cultured, so charming, and so full of knowledge of Italy. Why, he seemed to know all the same haunts that Hadid had frequented as a student. And he even had an Italian wife! This could be a friendship well worth cultivating. Wait until he told his own Farina of this meeting! Farina loved following the doings of the rich and powerful. And Minister Jallud was both!

"So, you're telling me that, yes, we could build a reactor, but it would mean absolutely nothing if we didn't have a source of fuel, namely Uranium 238?" Jallud asked.

"That's correct, Minister. The rest of the technology we could buy on the open market. But, alas, without the Uranium isotope 238, it would all be for nothing."

"This Uranium, is it tightly controlled?"

"Indeed it is. Every single gram is accounted for. However, more than that, some reactors also produce another element even more powerful than the Uranium in their fuel rods. The process, called fission, creates a waste product called Plutonium. These reactors are called breeders, and the Plutonium they create is the stuff of nuclear bombs. Of course, this material is even more closely guarded than the Uranium. It would never be allowed to fall into the wrong hands!"

"So what happens to this Plutonium? For example, there must be reactors in Europe that produce the stuff. Where does it go?"

"It all goes to America for reprocessing. The Americans have total control. Except over the British, who reprocess their own and make nuclear bombs with it."

Jallud was enthralled. "How about the French? Do they willingly turn this Plutonium over to the Americans? Sure doesn't sound like something the French would do, especially since they detonated a small bomb back in Nineteen-sixty."

"They're supposed to, but everyone wonders if maybe

they haven't been diverting a few milligrams here, a few milligrams there, so that over time, *voila,* they will have enough Plutonium to make a weapon a lot more powerful than a Uranium bomb. That's what a lot of scientists suspect, but no one's been able to prove it. Not even the Americans."

"What about the Jews? Do they have a bomb?"

Hadid's eyes darkened. "Nobody knows about the Jews. Rumor has it they acquired a working bomb in nineteen sixty-seven, but, if true, it's the most closely guarded secret on earth."

"Let's suppose for argument's sake they don't yet have a bomb. Would you say they're getting close?"

"If they can get their hands on enough Plutonium, they'll make a bomb. They'll never admit it if they do, even to the Americans. I can tell you with all the confidence in my soul that if they don't already have it, they're working on it day and night. It's the number one priority item in Tel Aviv."

Jallud stood. "Thank you for your time, Doctor, you've been most enlightening." He shook hands, started to leave, stopped, turned, and asked almost casually, "If I got you the Plutonium could you make me a bomb?"

"Yes," Hadid whispered an immediate answer. "Yes, I most assuredly could build you a bomb."

Jallud smiled. "Keep what we've spoken about to yourself. Tell no one, Professor, I'll be in touch. Meanwhile, I want you to dust off the old professor's plans to build a reactor in the desert at Tejerri."

"I shall get started right away, Minister. However, I must warn you. Such an undertaking will be enormously expensive."

"That, my good fellow, will be my worry, not yours. Good-bye, Doctor. You most definitely will be hearing from me."

*   *   *

SUMMER, 1970

Oh, the power of money to loosen tongues, Jallud had reasoned correctly. It turned out the information he had sought was really not such a closely guarded secret after all. It was exactly as Hadid had explained. The spent Uranium turned into a substance called Plutonium from the European reactors was indeed shipped by surface vessels to America, ending up at Oak Ridge, Tennessee, where it was reprocessed. The new Uranium began life all over again as fuel rods, while the Plutonium found a home either in a warhead for an American nuclear bomb carried by B-52s, or perched atop an intercontinental ballistic missile buried in a silo on the American plains.

He had also learned that the spent nuclear material was removed from the European reactors encased in special lead containers, then transported by truck to any of a half-dozen ports where it was placed aboard a ship. And off it went to America. Of course, a very limited number of vessels were contracted for this work, and the companies that owned them were well-compensated even though the atomic material being shuttled between continents was deemed perfectly safe. More often than not, the crews were aware of their special cargo which was packed alongside hundreds of tons of assorted merchandise being traded with the New World. The only concession agreed to by the several governments was that foodstuffs would not be shipped at the same time.

Jallud studied all the ports, and decided to zero in on Marseilles, a busy, rough-and-tumble port city in Southern France, perfect what he had in mind. Close to the North Africa coast, it was but a short sail to the Straits of Gibraltar and from there, out to the open Atlantic.

His informants had told him there would be a shipment of Plutonium leaving Marseilles for the United States on June 30 aboard the French freighter *Galaxie*. The sailing schedules for these special ships were known months in advance by the European Nuclear Regulatory Commission. This was a must, because the agency also had to know when fuel rods were to be downloaded in the various reactors so that it could coordinate the delivery and shipment of the rods. *Galaxie* would be transporting four-hundred-and-two point-two kilograms of Uranium, and twenty-three point-one-five kilograms of Plutonium during this particular sailing. Not an unusual load, Jallud was told.

Jallud's plan had been audacious, but not foolhardy. True,

split-second timing was of the essence, and each member of his away-team had to know what to do and when to do it. And as in all things, practice made perfect.

*   *   *

At a few minutes past twenty hundred hours, Greenwich Mean Time, on June 30 1970, the freighter *Galaxie* was hailed on a discreet frequency from a nearby vessel broadcasting a low-wattage signal. She was well into the open Atlantic and heading west. The sun would be setting shortly, and the red sky foretold of a fine day ahead.

"*Galaxie, Galaxie*, this is *Raven*. Do you copy?"

"*Raven*, this is *Galaxie*. Go ahead."

"My compliments to the master. Please inform him that I need to come aboard. The code word for the day is *Pluto*. I repeat: *Pluto*. I will rendezvous in fifteen minutes. Expect a boarding team of seven. Please tell the captain there is no cause for alarm, but my team needs to inspect the packages. Of course, as per regulation, no further transmissions as of this moment by your vessel to anyone until I release you."

"Understood, *Raven*."

The ship's radio operator knew that *Raven* was the name given to Nuclear Regulator Inspection Teams, and immediately informed the captain. *Galaxie* hove to, and waited for its visitors.

The one hundred foot sea-going launch carrying Jallud and six others dressed in orange colored cotton jumpsuits, white rubber boots, white cotton gloves, respirators, and all lugging Geiger counters and various other instruments, made its way to *Galaxie* and secured lines to the freighter. Jallud cautiously led his team up the metal ladder and onto the main deck. He deferred to the man beside him, Doctor Hadid.

"Captain, we need to inspect the packages," Hadid announced in flawless French to an apprehensive but not yet alarmed master. "A couple of the dock handlers at Marseilles tested positive for radiation after you were loaded this morning. It was an only an infinitesimal jump in the readings, but enough that we were concerned for your safety. I thought it prudent to take a few minutes to make a check. Better safe than sorry, *non?*"

"Yes, of course. Thank you."

Hadid flicked on his instrument, which immediately began to cackle. The captain jumped back.

"Not to worry, *monsieur*. All you are hearing is the presence of normal background radiation. Such is found everywhere on earth. In some places it is more pronounced than others, but it's entirely natural and normal."

Hadid was sweating under his mask. He had to shout to make himself understood. His body was pumping so much adrenaline that it required a conscious effort to keep his voice from rising to an unintelligible squeal. "Let's take a look at the packages, shall we?"

Captain Auguste Boland led Jallud and Hadid to the forward hold. Several members of the crew, driven topside out of curiosity, stood watching the six garbed figures. A few lit up cigarettes. All remained silent.

The nuclear material had been the last cargo hoisted aboard so that it would be the first off in the port city of Charleston, South Carolina. It was firmly secured in a special lead-lined vault built into the hold, where it sat in six lead-lined cylindrical containers, each stenciled with numerous black and orange triangles, the international symbol for radioactivity. Hadid marched confidently ahead of the captain and Jallud, and toggled a switch on his counter. It began to emit the same sound and cadence as it had done on deck. He began moving slowly about the confined space, nodding his head as he went.

"That is background," he called out. "Now I will test for any other source of radiation." He flipped another switch and his machine exploded into a wild cacophony of sound. The needle jumped to the left as if spring-loaded, and pegged itself at the edge of the window. Boland paled. Hadid walked slowly and purposely around the area, as the machine in his hand continued to sound its terrible warning of impending doom.

Walking back to the captain, Hadid turned the device off. "Well, there's a small leak, but nothing serious. Still, we must take care of it."

"But the noise! It sounds like we have a very serious leak.

I would suspect we're awash in radiation!"

Hadid laughed behind his mask, and shook his head vigorously. "No, no, Captain. The instrument is extremely sensitive, that's all. I'm sorry if it alarmed you. You are all perfectly safe. But as I said, we can take care of it in a matter of minutes, and you'll be on your way in no time." He patted the man's shoulder to lend physical support to his words.

"You can do that here? We won't have to return to port?"

"Trust me, Captain, this is nothing serious. However, I would ask that you assemble the crew on deck so that we can test them. Strictly a precautionary measure. It'll only take a moment, then they can return to their tasks."

"How large a ship's company do you have, Captain?" asked Jallud, hoping to put the man at ease with small talk.

"Nineteen, including me."

"That's all it takes to run a ship this size?" Jallud feigned amazement as he looked over the immaculate five hundred-foot vessel.

Boland smiled. "Automation. She almost runs herself." He turned to Hadid, face serious once more. "And if the men test positive, what then?"

"Then we simply wash them with soap and water and test them again. Believe me; we are looking at infinitesimal traces of radioactivity at the worst. There is no cause for alarm."

"Soap and water?"

"That's it."

Boland shook his head in awe as he pulled a CB radio from his pocket and spoke to his first mate. "Henri, all hands to the fantail. I want everyone there in two minutes. No exceptions."

Two minutes later, all nineteen men stood in a tight, straight line, shoulder to shoulder, awaiting inspection.

Instead, they faced mayhem. Four of Jallud's men had furtively removed machine pistols from their bags, and when Jallud had raised his hand above his head, they began firing into the assembled crew. Some broke ranks and tried to run, but were quickly dispatched. They dropped heavily to the metal deck, most dead before they slammed into the steel plates. A few started to scream, but their cries died in their throats.

The carnage continued until Jallud terminated the activity with a wave of his hand. He nodded to one man who set to the task of putting a bullet into the heads of all nineteen figures lying in obscene pools of their own blood and gore. Jallud wanted to make sure there would be no survivors.

The others in his group ran to take up new tasks. One raced to the bow crane and maneuvered its arm over the forward hold, while another began to prepare the containers for hoisting over to the deck of the waiting launch. Two more began dragging the bodies of the crew, like so many sacks of garbage, into the enclosed passageway which led out onto the fantail. They were joined moments later by two more men who had come aboard from the launch for this singular, gristly task.

"You want all the containers, correct, Hadid?"

"Every one of them. We can use the Uranium after we learn to reprocess it."

Twenty minutes later Jallud's mission was complete. His last act was to have the men place dynamite charges in the three holds then open all the seacock valves to allow the ocean to pour into the doomed vessel. The corpses were shuttered fast behind watertight doors, body heaped grotesquely upon body, secure for eternity in their final resting-place.

The launch pulled away rapidly. In the fading light Jallud heard the muffled explosions rip the *Galaxie* apart. He stood in silence and watched through binoculars as the freighter slipped beneath the swells. It had taken him less than half an hour to become the proud possessor of fissionable nuclear material. He was now on his way to a membership in the world's most exclusive club.

Ten days later his precious cargo was safely ensconced in old, abandoned, dry wellbores, deep in the Libyan Desert at a place called Tejerri. Here the canisters would remain entombed while a city sprang up around them—a city which would soon be linked by rail to the rest of the country; a city whose singular runway was again made serviceable, a runway capable of landing huge transports around the clock. Gaddafi gladly committed millions of petrodollars to the project, and by the summer of 1972, the desert at Tejerri was teeming with life.

*   *   *

Galaxie vanished from the face of the earth along with all hands. But in certain circles, and behind some very tightly closed doors, intelligence officers pondered the fate of the ship and its secret cargo. They did not draw comfort from their conclusions. After much analysis it was agreed that the *Mossad,* Israel's intelligence service, had pirated the nuclear cargo, after killing the crew and scuttling the ship. No other nation was up to such a task.

*   *   *

DECEMBER, 1973
(The present)

Jallud smiled at the remembrance of it all.

"Well, you haven't seen anything yet," he crowed in full voice. He was once more in fine spirits as his car crunched its way up his graveled driveway. "And as for you, Captain Trader? Well, I think it's time for another little demonstration. Correction. It's well past time."

He whistled the Colonel Bogie March as he jumped out of the car and bounded up the several steps to his front door.

CHAPTER 15

MARCH, 1974

The pressure on Jallud was now intense. He had become a permanent fixture in the desert, hounding everybody who crossed his path. There was no escaping him. The facility was on a twenty-four hour schedule, and the prisoners were putting in grueling hours. His deadline for a nuclear detonation was fast approaching.

The Americans had finally been told the bomb would contain seven kilograms of Plutonium, and they had calculated that the yield would equal that of the atomic bomb which had been dropped on Hiroshima.

Trader knew there was no way in hell such a blast would go unnoticed.

Early one Sunday, the pilots walked into their conference room to find Jallud and Hadid already there. From the look on Hadid's face it was obvious he'd been on the receiving end of a severe tongue-lashing.

Jallud, red-eyed, unshaven, and wearing the same clothes he had worn for the past three days, glowered at the Americans as they trooped to their places.

Trader took off his radiation badge, and placed it on the table. "Time for new ones, Doctor," he said quietly. He was aware that Plutonium was now being handled in the facility, and the knowledge made him nervous. He suspected that a good number of the technicians did not have a solid understanding of just how deadly the stuff was. Not the fodder of pleasant dreams.

Hadid only nodded.

Jallud walked over to Trader, his face flushed with suppressed anger. "The good doctor here keeps telling me that there is nowhere we can test the fruits of your labor, Captain. He insists there's no way we can set off a bomb to see if it works. He tells me that it is his expert opinion that we must be satisfied that the weapons we create for our protection against the Jews will work. Is it possible that this could also be a reflection of your expert opinion as well?"

Trader could see Jallud was approaching a state of complete meltdown. In nuclear terms, his mass was going critical. "What Doctor Hadid says makes sense," he replied in a quiet voice. "Remember, we're talking about detonating a static device. We're all sure of the physics. We know we have it right, and we're positive it'll work. But that's a lot different from arming a missile and having it detonate as planned."

Jallud wheeled and faced the trembling Hadid. "You told them we would be arming missiles? *You told them that?*"

"Of course he did," replied Trader. "We've been working on the detonation mechanism for weeks now. Do you honestly believe that just because you can set off a nuclear explosion in a tower that the same mechanics would work in either a bomb or a missile? The son of a bitch could end up spewing Plutonium all over the place, poisoning the land for thousands of years. No way, Jose. *There's no frigging way!*"

Jallud dragged a chair to where he was standing, and sat heavily. "You know the type of missiles we have?"

"*Longbows*," said Trader without hesitation. "Intermediate range missiles with a useful radius of about five hundred kilometers. It's field launched, employs a liquid propellant, and contains a somewhat sophisticated mechanical guidance system. A first cousin to the *Pershing* if I remember correctly."

"Do you know how many we have?"

Trader immediately smelled a trap. Hadid had let it slip they had two missiles, but decided not to divulge that information. He shrugged his shoulders. "The doctor never said, but if I was a betting man, I'd assume a half dozen, probably more."

Jallud spoke rapid-fire to Hadid in Arabic, his voice a harsh whisper. He spoke for a solid two minutes. Hadid only nodded.

He wheeled back to Trader. "We *are* going to detonate a bomb, Captain. That you can be sure of. Even if I have to transport it on my back to your Washington, DC, and explode it on the steps of your Capitol, then that's what I'll do. I, Jallud, guarantee it!"

Trader realized this was no idle threat. The man was mad enough to try just that.

Niels Borden grabbed center stage. "What the hell," he began, "why not see if we have a real live bomb on our hands. I say it's put-up or shut-up time. Mr. Jallud here wants a demonstration of good old Yankee know-how. Me too." He paused and looked Jallud in the eye. "We've been here almost a year. Our war's long over. I'm tired, and I want to go home. Mr. Jallud promised us that as soon as we helped him with his project, we could leave. Does that promise still stand, Mr. Jallud?"

"Of course it does, Commander. All I ever wanted was your help to enable my impoverished country to live in peace with her neighbors. We know the Israelis will soon have a bomb. We only want the same protection for ourselves. And of course I want you all to return safely to America and your families, and just as quickly as possible. Sixty days, tops. That would be my guess."

The honeyed words of a disciple of Niccolò Machiavelli's *Prince*, thought Trader.

Eight pair of eyes had shifted to Niels Borden. What had he picked up in the one-sided conversation between Jallud and Hadid only moments before? Trader knew it was obviously something not good. He felt his chest tighten. Niels was putting his commander on alert. He would just have to trust his friend on this. "What do you suggest, Niels?"

"Skipper, Mister Jallud demands a demonstration, so I say Mister Jallud gets a demonstration. All we have to figure out is the when and the where."

"Give me a minute to think about it." Trader closed his eyes and began a seemingly absent tapping of his fingers on the wooden table. Looking at his reposed face, it was impossible to know that his brain was in turmoil. His hands slowly asked the question which was now on each of their minds.

'T-r-o-u-b-l-e?'

He sat far back in his chair, eyes still closed, and remained that way for an eternity. No one spoke. Finally, he pulled himself to an upright position and caught Niels Borden's eye in the process. Niels gave an almost imperceptible nod. *Yes,* the nod said. *Yes, there sure as hell is major trouble afoot!*

Trader spoke. "Okay, Mr. Jallud, let's test. Here's what I'll need. Bring me all your maps and nautical charts. Bring me everything you have showing every continent and every ocean. I'll find you the right spot, and I'll do it in such a way that no one will know who was responsible for the big bang we're sure as hell are going to make."

"Now you're talking, Captain Trader!" Jallud sprang from his chair, face suddenly rejuvenated. "See, that wasn't so hard. We all get what we want, but most importantly, you all get to go home!" His body was still visibly tense. "You shall have every map and chart we've got, and they'll be in your hands within a half-hour. And if you need more, why, all you have to do is ask, and I'll have more flown in."

* * *

"We'll need six to eight hours for setup once we're at the site," Doug Gilchrest was saying, rolling a chewed-up pencil stub in his right hand. "The most important requirement will be the availability of an adequate electrical power source, one which must remain uninterrupted all the way up to the moment of detonation. No electricity, no bang."

"And no prying eyes," added Gerry Glasstner. "We can't have every Tom, Dick, and Harry looking over our shoulders."

"And we've got to transport the package from Point A to Point B without raising any suspicions," Mark FitzGerald chimed in.

"You guys are all for showing me how easy this is going to be, is that it?" Trader smiled as he spoke, even though his tone was serious.

"You know what we mean, boss," Walter Boyd said.

"Of course I do, Walt. And of course all the points you guys have raised are valid. In fact, I've been scribbling them down as fast as you made them. Each must be considered."

Their conference table was laden with several piles of maps, charts, ocean current studies, and even a few computer enhanced photographs of the earth taken by Gemini and Apollo astronauts over the course of several missions.

Trader stretched and pulled at the closest pile. "Gentlemen, let the games begin."

*   *   *

Four hours later they had their answer, and an hour after that were ready to explain it to Jallud.

"This is our recommendation," Trader began, standing by an easel and armed with a wooden pointer whose tip rested on a large Mercator projection map of the area where the South Atlantic and the Indian Ocean become one. The tip of the African continent was visible, displaying a detailed look at the last speck of continuous land, namely the Cape of Good Hope. "We propose setting off the device here, south of the fortieth parallel. You'll want to be well out of the shipping lanes, if for no other reason than to avoid injuring innocents should something go wrong."

"Continue, Captain."

"Our thought is to use a spot somewhat north of the Prince Edward Islands. Our reasoning is that once the explosion takes place, the whole world will know about it within minutes. Washington and London will speculate that maybe a Russian nuclear submarine blew-up, which of course Moscow will deny."

Jallud was radiant. "I love it! Go on, go on, Captain Trader."

"The weather's still pretty good right now in these latitudes, but it's something we can't take for granted. Storms come rolling in off the Antarctic without warning, and when that happens you can easily experience seas running to sixty or eighty feet in a good blow. That's why it's called 'The Roaring Forties.'"

While Trader was talking, Jallud had gotten out of his seat and was now standing directly in front of the map, his face mere inches away from the dot marking the Prince Edward Islands lying just south of the Agulhas Basin. He began to frown.

"I don't see any other island here, Captain Trader. Do you know of another island?"

"No, there's no secret island out there. We have something else in mind." Trader nodded to Niels who took

Trader's place in front of the map.

"What we propose is setting off the device on the deck of a ship," Niels began. "It'll give us the stable platform we require, but more importantly, we'll have a continuous flow of electrical current which we'll need to detonate the bomb. Lastly, we can operate in those waters secure from prying eyes."

"And the world will think this is a Russian sub exploding?"

"Well, that's certainly one scenario that'll be bandied about. Another might be that the South Africans or Indians have set off a nuke. Or the blame could even go to the Israelis. Hell, there'll be as many theories as there are people working on the theories. But you can bet your bottom dollar no one will ever suspect the Libyans."

Jallud beamed with pleasure. "I salute each and every one of you."

"Thank you for your expressions of confidence. May we continue?"

"Please, by all means."

Walter Boyd took over. "We envision using a pretty fair-sized ship because of the need to transport quite a load of equipment for final assembly and detonation. We'll need a crew of ten scientists at the very least, plus, of course, the members of the ship's crew. Remember, all of them must be evacuated at the last minute. This is not a suicide mission."

"So we will need to send two ships into the area?"

"We were thinking of a submarine. In fact, it would be advisable to have the bomb delivered by sub to the South Atlantic. Less chance for an accident, or for discovery, or for a million other things which could cause problems. The sub can stand off several miles at periscope depth then dive deep immediately upon confirmation of the explosion. It would be well below the depth of any serious shock wave, and everyone would be out of harm's way."

"Anything else?"

"Just small details which still need to be worked out. For example, you could maybe use the ship to refuel the submarine on the outward journey, and it could also deliver more fuel to the sub just before it sinks. That way you would only need one hook-up to get you home. Little things like that."

"I see." Jallud stared at Trader for a long minute, then asked, "How many of you will need to go along? You know of course, I don't have a great deal of faith in Doctor Idiot Hadid."

"I haven't thought about that."

"Well think about it, Captain. Pick three men. No more. They will be held responsible for the safety of those left behind. I need not dwell on what I mean. I can tell you one thing right now. You, Captain Trader, will definitely not be a member of the away-team. Oh, and one last thing. How long do you need to put this all together?"

"Four days. You can transport the package and scientists to the port by air. You'll need to alert the submarine, pick out an expendable vessel to be the platform, and arrange for refueling of the sub on its homeward journey. Things like that. Plan on fourteen days travel time each way to and from the site. Everything should be done by the end of the first week in March. You only miss your deadline by a week."

"We'll meet back here in the morning." Jallud stood and stretched, emitting a loud, pleasurable groan. "March starts the holy month of *Ramadan,* the month of prayer and fasting for all true believers. The timing is indeed auspicious."

* * *

Late that night, Niels Borden tapped out a long recital of what he had overheard that afternoon.

"Jallud told Hadid that it was his intention to kill Waltensperger before sundown to show the rest of us that he meant business. His plan was to shoot him right there in the lab. He said that if he ever discovered that Hadid had told us that he had only two missiles and only enough Plutonium left after this test for two weapons, then Hadid would be beheaded. Lastly, he said that when the time comes to dispose of us, he still hasn't made up his mind whether or not to kill Hadid, because he obviously has a big mouth. That's why I forced the issue. Sorry if it was the wrong move, but I thought it our best one, considering the circumstances. I knew I had to buy us all some time."

"You did the right thing," Trader tapped back. Then he tapped for many more minutes. "Tim, we have to get you into that supply plane and out of here within the next couple of weeks. We have enough information to take to the outside world, and stop this maniac. At least we know their arsenal is limited, so we have to find a way to make sure those weapons never work. Because even two nukes the size we're talking about could kill hundreds of thousands of innocent people."

He continued to tap. "The guys on the sub should look for a way to escape, but frankly, I don't expect that to be possible. I absolutely forbid any heroics. No suicides in an attempt to destroy the sub. Let's all get out of this in one piece. Now let's sleep. God Bless America."

Waltensperger trembled as he lay in his bed. "Why was I picked to be shot?" he whispered to himself. "What the hell did I do to piss-off that maniac?"

*   *   *

Tim Sweringen had made good use of the few hours they had had the maps and charts in their possession. While the others had pondered over the how and the where to detonate the bomb, he had pored over every available chart of North Africa. What he discovered left him depressed. He had huddled with Trader, and under the cover of a stream of loud chatter from the others, he had whispered his misgivings.

"Jim, this is literally the worst place on earth to try to get a plane out of. Flying south is out of the question, and so is east towards Egypt. If I stand the slightest chance for success, I'll have to get out of Libyan air space as quickly as possible, and that means going west by northwest into Algeria. But, between here and there are the Ahaqqar Mountains, and some of those peaks are damn near ten thousand feet high! On top of all that, there are no navigation aids in this part of the world, so I'll be flying blind. I'll run out of gas long before I reach civilization. It's like the devil himself hand-picked this spot for that whacko to build his bomb."

Trader listened to his friend, and thought of all the hard work that had gone into this project. Over the months, the group had learned that the supply plane came at least twice a week, always landing before nightfall. It remained overnight, and departed at first light. There was no tower to service the field simply because there was no need. Any plane approaching Tejerri wouldn't see any other traffic within a two hundred-mile radius. They had also discovered there was a lone beacon on the field which was turned on about an hour before any landing, allowing the pilots to home in on its signal. Crude but effective. There were fuel tanks holding twenty thousand gallons next to the strip, the Jet-A kerosene being brought in by rail.

"Tim, if you think we should scratch the idea, then that's okay," Trader whispered back. "Like I said before, I don't want any heroics, and I don't want any suicides. From what you're telling me, suicide is what this mission's shaping up to be."

"Nah, boss, that's just the downside. The upside is that it's theoretically possible, and hey, who knows? If I can make it into Algeria, maybe I'll get lucky and put her down near an army outpost or something. We're running out of time. I want your permission to go."

"Can one man really handle the C-130?"

"I can't lie to you, skipper. Two men would make the chance for success a hell of a lot better. I could fly and give instructions to a second pilot, telling him what to do as far as flap settings, fuel transfers, powering up and acquiring navigation aids, *if* we find any en route. Two guys would better the chances for success by a factor of ten."

"That's what I'm figuring, too. If you go, and that's still a big *if*, then I want Waltensperger to go with. I think Jallud's onto him, and I suspect he knows that John's not a nuclear physicist. I think he figured it out around the time John was getting his appendix out. So, if there's going to be another butt in that plane, I want it to be his. And he's as good a pilot as the rest of us."

"Roger, that, skipper."

"Let me change the subject for a moment. I've decided that Doug Gilchrest, Nick Wolfe, and Gerry Glasstner will go to set off the bomb. Gerry and Jim have first rate minds and Doug has a solid background in electrical engineering, and that expertise will be critical. What are your thoughts?"

"Good choices. But how about Niels? He's pretty damn sharp, too, you know."

"Hell, I know that. He could go and do a bang-up job, no pun intended. I need him here to eavesdrop. So you agree with my choices?"

"Absolutely."

"Then we've got to think about getting you and John out of here while those guys are away. With *Ramadan* just around the corner the timing is perfect. From what Niels tells me, the faithful have to pray and fast every day for the whole month, and folks are only allowed to eat after sundown. A man who has to fast for twelve hours, day after day, soon becomes tired and rundown. That plays into our hands. You should be able to get that bird out of here and into Algerian airspace before anyone could do anything to stop you."

"I'm counting on the crew to fuel the plane immediately after landing," Sweringen said. "I know that's what I'd do in order to get off the deck as soon as possible the next morning. Because if that hog ain't gassed, then, brother, we're shit out of luck!"

Sweringen retired to a corner of the table to study his emergency procedures from memory for another hour, while Trader rejoined the others. He prayed for guidance, just as he did most times he found himself faced with hard choices.

* * *

On March 1, 1973, a high-speed microburst signal was sent from a submarine deep in the South Atlantic. The message made no sense whatsoever to those who intercepted it in the National Security Agency building outside Washington DC, as it downlinked from a spy satellite. *AAAAAAAAAAAAAA.* Fourteen repetitions of the letter A? Who had sent such a message? What could it possibly mean?

In Tripoli, Jallud knew.

AAAAAAAAAAAAAA spelt success! It was confirmation that he had just been admitted into that most exclusive of clubs. And, in all probability, he had beaten the Jews to the punch!

What an honor to be able to deliver such great news to the Supreme Leader on the first day of *Ramadan!* It meant total vindication for all his hard work.

CHAPTER 16

Bakktari relayed the news to the prisoners left behind in the desert. He bumped into the six as they were leaving their building after dinner, going out for a breath of fresh air before retiring for the night. It was the first week in March, and all knew there wouldn't be too many more evenings like this to enjoy before the weather again turned the desert into a furnace.

"Good evening, gentlemen. Our friend Jallud asked me to tell you that the demonstration went off without a hitch. There most assuredly was a nuclear explosion. He's in the capital for the Holy Month, but I'm here to say he's one happy fellow! He sends his congratulations on a job well done."

"And how about you, Doctor? Do you feel like dancing in the streets?" Trader asked.

"Let's walk." Bakktari set the pace, and the Americans fell in around him.

They were filled with mixed emotions. The professional scientist in each was proud that the group had been able to accomplish so much in so little time. Yet each felt the same terrible sense of foreboding.

"No, Captain Trader, I don't feel like dancing in the streets. Truth is, I'm not at all convinced that I can any longer condone what's going on. I did in the beginning, but not now. Of course, if our friend Jallud heard me say this, he would have me shot as a traitor."

"Doctor, this whole adventure can only end badly for all concerned. I don't mean just for the people of your country, but for the entire world. Jallud is quite mad, and we all know that he wants an atomic arsenal not to defend, but to terrorize." Trader spoke in a quiet voice as he walked beside the smaller man in the twilight of the day. "Look around you, Doctor. Go on, take a good look while there's still light. This facility was built for one purpose, and one purpose only. It's a war machine."

"I know that, Captain, and I'm distraught with the knowing I aided that thug."

"Think of the hundreds of millions of dollars that have

been spent funding this lunatic's dream," Trader continued. "Money that could have been so much better used in countless other ways. Ways which could have truly helped your people. Instead, we have this place. It's a tragedy of unspeakable proportions, Doctor."

The fading light betrayed Bakktari's face and the misery he felt. "Everything you say is true, Captain Trader, but what can I do? I'm now as much a prisoner as all of you."

"What does Jallud intend to do with the missiles once we arm them?" Trader asked.

Bakktari shook his head. "I don't know. He once said something about blackmailing the Western Powers, but I am no longer someone he confides in."

Trader decided to go for broke. "Then help us escape. Better yet, come with us. Do the right thing, Doctor. Help us put an end to this madness before it's too late."

Bakktari stopped. "I can never leave, Captain. *Never.* I have a wife and five children in Tripoli, and they are as much hostages as you are. As me. They guarantee my good conduct in Jallud's eyes. You know, it was Colonel Gaddafi who directed me to become a part of this project. He said he needed me to keep an eye on Jallud. Even the Supreme Leader recognizes that the man is certifiable. Nevertheless, Jallud does have his uses, and he certainly gets things done. He'll stop at nothing to achieve whatever it is he sets out to do. He becomes driven."

"You know of course, he plans to kill us as soon as we arm his missiles?"

"I hope not, Captain Trader. Believe me, I pray every day that won't happen."

"You understand he can't let us go. Do you think for one minute that your Colonel Gaddafi could explain to the world how a bunch of American prisoners from Hanoi ended up in his hands? You know, and we know, the U.S. would bomb both Libya and Vietnam back to the Stone Age if such information became known. No, we're dead men walking, Doctor Bakktari. That is unless you help us get out of here while there's still time."

Bakktari broke down completely. Huge sobs wracked his

body. "I can't! He'll kill my family. I don't care about myself, but I cannot face my Maker knowing I was responsible for the deaths of innocents. I'm sorry, but I just can't."

Trader realized that he had pushed the doctor over the edge. He backpedaled, hoping to salvage something from the situation. "Hey, Doc, it's okay. Really. I understand what you're saying. Let me ask you this. Will you try to help us as long as you don't compromise the safety of your family? If nothing else, at least don't be against us."

Bakktari sniffled loudly, then rubbed the back of his hand across his nose. "Fair enough," he replied weakly. "I'm not a strong man like you pilots. I wish I were. And I can tell you another thing. Jallud is insanely jealous of you men. You are all a type of man he knows he'll never be, and it gnaws at his soul. Especially you, Captain Trader."

"Doctor, there's nothing special about us," said Trader. "We're unfortunate souls swept up in this raging torrent of events that's way beyond our control. We're only trying to do the right thing. Heck, we put our pants on one leg at a time, just like you do." As he spoke, Trader punched Bakktari playfully on the shoulder.

Bakktari smiled. "I'm truly sorry for any part I've played in all this. I hope you can somehow find it in your hearts to forgive me."

"Nothing to forgive," Doug Gilchrest said. "We've always looked on you as a stand-up kind of a guy."

"Hear! Hear!"

"Look, a shooting star!" FitzGerald exclaimed as he pointed skyward. Everyone followed the direction of his finger, and there in the night sky, a brilliant star transcribed an arc of fiery beauty, its tail lighting up the firmament.

"Nope, that's a comet," John Waltensperger corrected in a voice filled with wonder. "Just look at that tail, would you. Has to be at least several million miles long!"

The men stood mesmerized and silenced by the heavenly display. Long after the comet had disappeared below the horizon on its voyage through time, all remained mute.

Finally, Bakktari broke the collective reverie. "I must be going. I'll try to help you any way I can. It might not be much, but I'll at least try. That's my promise to you." He waved to the group as he departed for his Jeep.

The Americans stood huddled together and watched the dim red taillight slowly fade from view. Before anyone could comment on the conversation that had just taken place, a single light appeared low in the night sky several miles away. It was a plane.

"Can't ever remember seeing a night landing since our arrival in the dark a lifetime ago," Mark FitzGerald said. "I didn't even realize the field was lighted."

"You're right," Trader replied. "I'd expect to see a ground-glow effect, but everything's black."

"Think it's the C-130?" said Waltensperger.

"Gotta be," Sweringen replied. "Probably a crew that's flown in here dozens of times to be confident enough to try a night landing in the middle of nowhere. Yeah, it's the Hercules all right."

Trader followed the plane's progress all the way to the ground, and it wasn't until the aircraft reversed its four huge turboprop engines that he was able to finally hear the distant roar.

Sweringen glanced instinctively at his left wrist, looking for the watch he hadn't worn in eight years. He cursed under his breath at his forgetfulness. "I guess it to be about six-thirty," he mused aloud. "Give or take a half-hour."

"What you got in mind, Tim?"

"I'm thinking tonight had better be the night, Jim. In view of what Bakktari just told us, and in light of the fact that we all know what Jallud has up his sleeve, I'd say it's time John and I hightailed it to see if we can get help. If we can make it safely into Algeria, we can alert NATO and have a whole damn division of paratroopers here before Jallud even knows we're missing!"

Trader smiled in spite of himself. He had no illusion that any such force would arrive in time to stage an effective rescue. Anybody left behind would probably be taken from the complex and killed. However, he had no intention of giving voice to his thoughts. He squinted into the darkness toward the spot he envisioned the plane to be. Had to be a good two miles away from where they stood. Although there wasn't any evidence of patrols and guards, it stood to reason they did in fact exist. He did some quick calculations, then spoke.

"Let's say it's seven o'clock. Now, give them an hour to off-load whatever it is they're hauling, then another hour to refuel for tomorrow's takeoff. Throw in another two hours after that for everybody to leave the area, it should take us up to eleven o'clock. Let's say you got to the plane about one or two o'clock. If all went smoothly, how long do you think it'd take to go through your checklist, fire her up, and start rolling?"

"Forty minutes," Sweringen said. "Of course, once I begin to crank over the number three, the noise will be enough to wake the dead. Then the whole base will know the plane's getting ready to leave. I'm hoping to get the other three turbines on-line lickety-split, and I want to be rolling while still doing the last of my pre-flight checklist items. I just want that beast in the air as quickly as possible, and pray John and I can clean her up as soon as I have some altitude. My biggest concern is the mountain range directly to the west."

"You could end up killing yourselves," replied Trader, worry creeping into his voice.

"I know, skipper, but we've got to give it a go. This could well be our only chance, and we have to grab the moment. What do you say, boss?"

Trader sighed. "I say do it, Tim. We'll leave a light on in one of the rooms so you can at least use that as a bearing to get out to the runway. I guess you'll need about an hour to reach the bird. My only advice is that you take your time re-familiarizing yourself with the cockpit before turning over the noisemakers. Other than that..."

"Thank, Jim."

"Okay, that's it then," Trader said. "I vote we all try to get some shuteye. I'll wake you guys at midnight."

Trader turned toward the steps followed by the other five. His heart was pounding. *At last we're taking the initiative,* he thought. He prayed he wasn't sending his friends to their deaths.

*   *   *

The parting was both low-key and brief. Handshakes and salutes all round, followed by a momentary group prayer asking for God's deliverance.

"See you in a couple of days," Trader said in a subdued voice. "God bless America, and God bless you both."

"God bless America," they whispered back, and a second later were swallowed into the night. They took a bearing from the light left on in Gerry Glasstner's second story corner room.

"We'll keep the light over our left shoulder," Sweringen said, setting a course towards the runway. It was ink-black on the desert floor, even though the heavens were ablaze with stars. There wasn't a moon, and the going was slow. Twice they had to drop to the ground and lie motionless to avoid being spotted by roving patrols. The guards were in Jeeps, and they made no effort to hide their presence. Their headlights gave the Americans ample warning. Both times they roared past the prostrate forms at about forty miles an hour, the occupants huddled low out of the slipstream, bundled in heavy winter parkas.

They, too, had dressed as warmly as they could, and although the earlier breeze had diminished, it was now bitterly cold. On and on they tramped, conserving energy by keeping conversation to a minimum. A little over an hour later, they stumbled onto the runway.

"*Hot damn!*" Waltensperger whispered in delight, and slapped Sweringen's back. "Now all we gotta do, partner, is follow this yellow brick road to frigging Oz."

"I hear you, loud and clear."

It took another ten minutes to find the plane. It was parked on a huge circular concrete pad, its bulbous nose facing toward the edge of the runway two hundred feet away. They flattened themselves against the ground and remained motionless for several minutes, straining to hear any evidence that there might be guards nearby. Nothing. Not even the sound of animals in the desert.

"Let's go for broke." Sweringen got to his feet and headed

towards the barely visible Hercules, crab-walking in an uncomfortable crouch. He reached the crew door, and holding his breath, jiggled the recessed handle. The locking mechanism disengaged with barely a squeak.

They clambered inside, locking the door behind them. They made their way into the cockpit, breaths short and ragged, their excitement fueled by rivers of adrenaline.

Sweringen lowered himself into the left seat, then turned and grinned at Waltensperger. "Ain't she the prettiest seventy-five thousand pound baby you've ever seen?"

"I'll let you know once she's in the air and shows me her stuff. Until then, I'm from Missouri!"

Sweringen chuckled, then turned serious. "Okay, let's see if there are any flashlights hidden in the storage bins." He began to rummage. "Also, look for charts, John. Doesn't matter what they are. I only want to use them to cover the windows so that we can use the flashlights. That is, if I can ever find the damn things!"

However, it was Waltensperger who found two of them on his side of the cockpit. They spent the next few minutes covering the multiple windows with maps and other papers. Only after both were completely satisfied with their efforts did they click on their lights.

They came face-to-face with the plane's instrument panel, home to a thousand dials and switches. Behind the copilot's seat was another complex station for the engineer whose job it was to monitor the four engines as well as other mechanical and electrical systems. This was definitely a plane made to be flown by a full crew, but both pilots were undaunted by the scene before them.

"Okay, I suggest we use one light at a time," said Sweringen. "If one goes on the fritz, we'll still have a backup. I'd rather not switch on any interior lights, because we'll need all the battery power we've got to turn over the engines."

"Right!" Waltensperger snapped off his flashlight and began an intent study of the panel in the yellow glow from Sweringen's. He had no experience with transports, but nonetheless was able to make immediate sense out of ninety-percent of what he saw.

Sweringen dug into his pocket and extracted the notes he had painstakingly assembled from memory over the past several months; notes he had hidden inside two of the hollow metal legs of his bunk bed.

"Here, hold the light, John, and I'll get started on the checklist. Try to relax. We've got plenty of time, so let's get ourselves real familiar with this baby." He shot a look towards the mechanical clock. "Oh-two-twenty-two hours, local. Three hours or so until first light. Good! We can go slow, and get our procedures down cold. I'm not going to do a walk-around inspection before we're ready. Then we'll remove pins and chocks. Remember that there will some things we won't be doing, like setting our navigation systems, or clearing our flight plan. Okay, let's start our first run-through."

"Fuel-check."

"Check. Full load, thank God!"

"Ramp and door controls, neutral."

"Check."

"Hydraulic panel, set."

"Check."

"Parking brake, set and pressure checked."

On and on they went, working their way down the checklists Sweringen had drafted from memory. Sweringen kept up a running commentary, explaining procedures, pointing out the gauges and switches to his copilot.

Before they knew it, the clock read four forty-five.

Sweringen removed a chart covering the pane of glass directly in front of him and peered into the night. He saw only darkness. "My gut feeling is we can move this bird onto the runway with just our taxi lights and still be pretty safe. I really hate to think that we need to wait for first light if only because we have no idea what time the crew plans on getting out of here."

"I agree. Let's do our exterior preflight now. We need to get this baby rolling. I know I can back you up, Tim."

"Good man! Okay, let's go do our walk-around and prepare to exit this hell-hole."

As Sweringen was about to get out of his seat a beam of

light suddenly cut in front of the windscreen, illuminating the entire cockpit. "Jeeze, it's one of the patrols," he whispered.

Both scrunched low in their seats, listening as the Jeep slowly circled the plane. They heard it make another complete circuit, then it seemed to crawl to a halt somewhere near the tail. They could only speculate that maybe this meant that the crew had arrived for an early departure. If so, the game was up. They heard a sudden burst of laughter followed by a voice bursting into song. The Jeep sped away, the sound of its engine fading fast.

Both exhaled loudly and in unison to cover their fright.

"Let's give it five minutes before going outside," Sweringen suggested.

"Okay by me," Waltensperger whispered back.

They tiptoed from the plane and made their inspection, taking pains not to rush, removing pins, and inspecting flight surfaces as they went. They paid particular attention to the landing gear, and ended by removing the chocks from the wheels. Wordlessly they climbed back into the plane, locked the door, and strapped themselves in. They removed the remaining papers from the windows and jammed the wad into a receptacle on Waltensperger's side of the cockpit.

Sweringen looked across at his friend. "Ready?"

"Ready? Heck, yes, man, I'm ready! Do it!"

This time they called out the checklist for real, methodically powering up the systems in preparation for Sweringen's command to engage the number three self-starting unit.

The moment finally came to turn over the first turbine.

"Clear number three engine."

"Number three clear and turning." Sweringen replied.

The internal power unit labored noisily to provide a positive flow of air through the engine's multistage turbines. The huge jet turbine began to whine, and the four-bladed propeller started to turn, ever so slowly at first, then faster and faster. Sweringen kept his eyes glued to the instruments, watching as the self-sustaining energy began to build rapidly, waiting for a reading that would tell him the engine was capable of operating under its own power. At just the right moment he released the ignition switch, satisfied with the indicated increase in engine exhaust temperature. He advanced the throttle and simultaneously cut the starter switch.

Both men broke out in a sweat despite the cold.

Sweringen turned his attention to the number-four engine and began the ignition countdown procedure again. It wasn't until he was bringing power to the last of the four turboprops— the number one engine—that he noticed lights coming on all over the base. Because of the noise in the cockpit, he did not hear the many sirens around the perimeter wailing the same song of panic.

"Flaps fifty percent, auto pilot off, brakes, checked!" Sweringen yelled reminders to himself. "Look at your hydraulic pressure. Make sure your trim tabs are set. *Go, go, go!*"

The huge plane lurched forward as he brought the throttle quadrant up to a suitable power setting to taxi. Hot diggity-dog! He was actually moving!

A Jeep careened wildly into view on his left side, a soldier standing, grabbing onto the windscreen for balance. The man hurled invectives in their direction at the top of his lungs, but they heard nothing.

The plane bounded forward, Sweringen guiding it toward the runway and freedom. He spun onto the long ribbon of concrete, and headed erratically toward the right shoulder, knowing in an instant that he had over-shot his turn. He pulled back on the throttles, allowing the plane to slow down, thus giving himself the moment he needed to correct his mistake. He found the centerline and held the plane steady, making sure his nose wheel was covering the now-visible painted white ribbon beckoning to be followed to freedom.

Two Jeeps dashed madly in-and-out of his field of vision, each filled with soldiers brandishing weapons, all frantically signally for him to stop.

Sweringen advanced the throttles to full power and the huge plane began to accelerate down the runway, lights now ablaze on the wings and nose wheel, illuminating the track for him to follow. He whooped in delight!

Faster and faster the Hercules went, the Jeeps still keeping pace. Then the soldiers began firing. Shots came whining into the cockpit, but in the commotion of the moment neither man heard them. Then the firing was directed toward the wheels.

Waltensperger called out their speed..."Forty knots...fifty...sixty..."

"Holy shit!" Sweringen yelled in anger and fright as the plane started to veer to his right. My right main gear's been hit, he thought wildly, seeing in his mind's eye the heavy caliber bullets finding their targets beneath the opened wheel doors. Sweringen fought the giant with all his strength to retain directional control. It was not to be. The C-130 screeched in violent protest as it careened off the right side of the runway, colliding violently with a Jeep as it went, turning the vehicle into a fireball before casting it into the night like so much rubbish.

"Hang on, John!" he screamed as he pulled back on the throttles. *"Condition levers, feather! Pull the goddamn fire handles, now,"* he yelled to himself at the top of his lungs. He grabbed the four red fire handle switches on the overhead panel, cutting off all fuel flowing to the turbines. However, in his haste he also yanked the fifth handle, which serviced the gas turbine compressor. *"Get on the brakes,"* he bellowed. The out-of-control plane bounced wildly off the concrete ribbon, trailing a meteor-like shower of sparks and hot metal from the collapsed and shredding main landing gear. The Hercules skidded into the darkened desert at seventy knots. With no hope of regaining control, Sweringen held on for his life.

Suddenly, something long and dark tore through the right windscreen, shattering the double layer of glass and the metal frame. Out of the corner of his eye, Sweringen saw the object slam full force into John Waltensperger, decapitating his friend.

"Johnnnnn!" he screamed.

Then his universe went mercifully black.

*　*　*

Trader stood outside his building and watched as scores of vehicles converged on the distant runway. Sirens continued to wail, and a pall of heavy, black, oily smoke began to rise from the desert floor in the first light of dawn. He knew what it meant.

*   *   *

One hour later Jallud was called in the capital by his chief of security and told that two of the Americans had tried to steal the C-130, but had failed. One pilot was dead; the other only slightly injured. Four soldiers had also died, and the plane had been destroyed.

Jallud was numb with rage. He asked if the runway was serviceable. He was assured that it was.

"Which American was killed?"

"Waltensperger. He burned in the crash."

"And the other? Which one is he?"

"Colonel Sweringen."

"His condition?"

"Banged up. Some minor burns. We got him out before the plane exploded. He'll live."

"He'll wish he hadn't, especially when he finds out what I have in store for him! Keep them all locked up until I get there. Expect me shortly."

The chief of security took that last statement to mean that Jallud would be in the desert some time before nightfall. However, he announced his presence well before then, arriving in a two-seat, French-made *Mirage* fighter three hours later.

Jallud knew what he was going to do, and no one would stop him. The remaining prisoners would come to see death as a welcome friend before he was through with them. Especially that miserable pig Trader.

CHAPTER 17

It was the not knowing what had happened to Sweringen and Waltensperger that tormented the four remaining prisoners every waking moment. Confined to quarters, they had nothing to do but think.

Jallud made his appearance on the third morning.

"It is time for you to go back to work. Hadid's waiting. When the others return from the submarine we will have a meeting."

"What happened to Colonel Sweringen and Commander Waltensperger?" Trader asked.

"Commander Waltensperger is dead, and you killed him. As for the colonel, he's in the infirmary. His doctors assure me he'll live." Jallud's tone was matter-of-fact. He could have been discussing the weather.

"I'd like to see him."

"Captain Trader, you have tested my patience since that first moment I had the misfortune to set eyes on you. I had hoped that with time you would come to display a sense of understanding of what was necessary to ensure your continued well-being. Now, because of your stupidity, one man is dead and another is injured, to say nothing of four dead soldiers from my command. You, Captain Trader, have done enough damage. You will not see Colonel Sweringen until I say you may. Until then, you have work to do. I want the first two missiles operational by the beginning of June. Your bus is waiting. This is the end of our conversation."

They followed a humdrum existence for two weeks, going to the labs every morning; coming home every evening at sundown. No one was allowed outside after dark, and each had to be in his room by nine o'clock.

On March 19, the three Americans returned from their submarine voyage. On the first night back they were brought up to date through the tapping of the prisoners' code.

Dawn found the morale of the seven remaining Americans at its lowest ebb in a year.

* * *

Three days later, on a Sunday morning, Jallud sent the guards to line the prisoners up outside their quarters. A short time later, he pulled up in a Jeep. Seated beside him on the narrow back seat was Tim Sweringen. He was pale, haggard, and had evidently lost weight, but it was the rather sizable bandage on his head that caught the attention of his friends. Trader instinctively sprang forward, but before he could take a third step, he was roughly pushed back by one of the soldiers.

"You men will move only if I give you permission to move, is that clear?" Jallud vaulted over the side of the vehicle, extracted a box from the dust-covered floorboards and placed it on the ground. Crouching low, he methodically unpacked several electronic components, which he attached to a circuit board.

While the Americans stood in silence, a brand-new Mercedes flatbed truck carrying half a dozen heavily armed soldiers pulled into view. The troops disembarked and took up positions around the pilots.

"Colonel Sweringen, get out of the Jeep." Jallud straightened up as he spoke, brushing imaginary dirt from his starched uniform pants. Holding what appeared to be an electronics package of some kind, he took a moment to extend and adjust a telescoping antenna. Satisfied, he turned to Sweringen.

"Colonel Sweringen, it would seem from your recent escapade that you no longer like my company. So I say consider yourself free to leave."

Sweringen stood immobilized, a dazed look blanketing his face.

"Off you go, Colonel," Jallud prompted, not the slightest hint of anger in his voice. "Start walking. You couldn't wait to get out of here a couple of weeks ago so now's your chance to finish what you started."

"Stay where you are, Tim," Trader called out.

Jallud whirled, and in an instant stood nose to nose with Trader. "If you open your mouth one more time, I personally will shoot you. Do you understand me?" He spun and faced Sweringen again. "Colonel, if you don't start walking, I will shoot

Captain Trader where he stands. You have until the count of three."

"Okay, I'm going!" Sweringen winked at Trader, then managed a grin. "Boss, I really was getting tired of this place anyway. Promise not to do anything foolish on my behalf." He paused long enough to hold himself at attention, and saluted the line of officers.

They came to attention and returned the courtesy.

"Hey, Jallud, here's my salute to you!" Sweringen laughed loudly at his tormentor, and raised the middle finger of his right hand. *"Up yours, you certifiable maniac!"*

"Run!" Jallud screamed. He slammed the box he was holding into the chest of the nearest guard, and wrenched the startled man's carbine from his hands. He pointed the weapon toward the ground close to Sweringen's feet, flicked it to full automatic and began firing. The sand flew in geysers, goading Sweringen into action. *"Run, you whoremonger!"* He loosed another burst over Sweringen's head.

Sweringen took off, zigzagging in order to escape the next burst of fire. He stumbled as he went, almost falling, but regained his footing and continued without a backward glance.

Jallud, his composure somewhat recovered, roughly took back possession of the electronic box.

"Pay close attention, gentlemen," he called out. "I think you are all going to be impressed with my little demonstration."

Sweringen was a hundred yards away and running in a straight line.

"Now for the moment of truth." Jallud flipped a switch, causing a small red light to glow on the face of the box. He smiled as his thumb hovered over a solitary, rubber-encased button. Then, with maddening slowness, his thumb came down, sending power flowing through the circuitry.

A hundred and fifty yards away, in the time it took an electronic signal to reach a receiver implanted in Sweringen's body and act on its command, his head blew apart. Skull, brain, hair, face, and bandages all disintegrated into a score of bloody pieces. The force of the blast hurtled the still-running body hard onto the ground. It was a scene out of hell itself.

Jallud placed the palm of his left hand on the tip of the antenna and effortlessly collapsed the thin metal rod. He flipped a switch. The red light faded, then winked out.

"That's another man you've killed, Captain Trader. My guess is you won't be happy until all your friends are dead. But I'm going to make sure that doesn't happen. You see, I'm going to outfit you with the same explosive device in your neck that the late Colonel Sweringen was kind enough to volunteer to test for me. My original plan was to give each of you one. But I think one for you will be enough to keep the others in line."

"You are certifiable," Trader screamed as he sprang forward and smashed Jallud on the jaw with such force that he heard bone crunch as the Arab fell to the ground. Trader was on top of him in a flash, a mass of swinging arms and kicking legs. A soldier jumped forward and hit him squarely on the back of the head with his rifle butt. Trader collapsed, falling hard on top of the unconscious Jallud.

The several guards on the perimeter pointed their guns at the remaining prisoners, daring them to make a move.

"Stand fast! That's an order!" Colonel Boyd yelled for all to hear. He threw up his hands in surrender. "Don't shoot! Hold your goddamn fire!"

The Libyan officer in charge began hollering in a high-pitched voice, trying to draw order from chaos. He ran in circles, pushing and shoving his men, commanding them to secure their weapons. When order was partially restored, he directed two soldiers to place Jallud into the back of the Jeep, and two more to dump Trader onto the flatbed truck. "Go to your house! Stay there! Do it now!" he screamed at the Americans in a falsetto.

"Okay, everyone inside. Goddammit to all to hell!" Boyd led his men away from the carnage; his anger and shock making him shake uncontrollably. "How in the hell did this happen?" he bellowed. Can someone please answer me that?"

No one could.

*   *   *

Trader returned two weeks later. His head had been

shaved, but the stubble of white hair peeking out between the bandages gave testimony to new growth. He also carried a surgical incision at his groin where he'd been told by Jallud a transmitter had been embedded. Thin, twenty-carat gold wires had been threaded up to his neck where a small but powerful charge had been secured. Lastly, a battery pack, similar to one used to power a pacemaker, had been implanted into his upper chest. He'd been told he could be killed anywhere in the Northern Hemisphere with the flick of a button. The transmitter Jallud showed him was programmed to send its signal up to an American satellite, bounce off, and return to earth to ferret him out no matter where he was. Part of Trader's mind told him that Jallud was full of shit, but another more rational part, asked if he really wanted to take the chance? The technology needed for such a task was really quite simple. Trader opted to believe.

Jallud had met with him in the infirmary three days after the operation. Painfully talking through a jaw that had been wired shut, he hissed, "I will be like this for a month, Trader, then, Allah be praised, I shall be better. You, however, will be my prisoner until I grow weary of you. And when that day comes, poof, you shall be gone. Just like that," he added, with a snap of his fingers. "Live with that thought, Captain. You will never know when your last moment on earth will be." He tried to laugh, but the pain in his jaw made him wince. "But before you go to the hell you deserve, you will pay for what you have done to me. I, Jallud, guarantee it!"

*   *   *

"My condition changes nothing," Trader told the group his first night back. "If any of you finds a good opportunity to escape, I am ordering you to seize the moment and go for it. Getting word to the outside world is paramount. That, gentlemen, is not a topic open for discussion. Now, has anyone come up with a plan to make sure the *Longbows* won't fire?"

That was their dilemma. Hadid had passed on to them all the technical literature he could find regarding the *Longbow,* and because they had two actual missiles, the Americans were able to study the item first hand.

Colonel Boyd briefed Trader on what had taken place in his absence.

During the past two weeks, and ever under the watchful eyes of Hadid and his staff, the prisoners had carefully taken apart then pored over the many components of the *Longbows*, testing each with the precision of watchmakers, then reassembling when satisfied. They did this one missile at a time, so that if they made a mistake they would always have one assembled unit to turn to for guidance, and correct any assembly errors.

On Trader's first day back, Walter Boyd asked Hadid: "Doctor, what range do you want to arm the missiles for?"

"Why do you need to know that, Colonel Boyd?"

"Just asking," Boyd replied in an easy manner. "The liquid propellant's kind of volatile. More missiles blow up during the fueling process than at any other stage. You don't want to on-load more of the stuff than you have to. Static electricity is your worst enemy, and in dry air like we have here, well, you can't be too careful."

"I'll keep that in mind."

Later that night Boyd tapped to the others. "I almost blew it today," he confessed. "I really didn't give a shit about the propellant; I was wondering about the guidance system and how it's coupled to the altimeters. I realized that Hadid was zeroing in on me, so that's when I opened my trap. All that talk about fuel volatility was so much smoke-and-mirrors to cover my tracks and get Hadid's mind onto other things." He continued tapping. "I'm convinced our best bet is going to be in altering the preset altitude parameters which will relay the command for detonation sequencing to begin. Which means we need to get to the altimeters. Once we do, we can re-calibrate them so that if the missiles are ever launched, they'll explode at apogee, and not at the settings laid-in for either a ground burst or an airburst. There'll still be an explosion, but it'll take place fifty-plus miles above the earth."

"I was surprised to see that they use mechanical altimeters in the *Longbow*," tapped Mark FitzGerald. "Seems kind of out of date. Electronic altimeters would be better. More reliable."

"Not true," Niels Borden chimed in. "One of the projects I worked on was a study of the effects of electromagnetic pulse. It's called EMP for short. This was back in sixty-seven; two years before I joined you guys in Hanoi, but the all the eggheads were taking it very seriously. In a large-scale nuclear attack, the theory says that the first side to get its missiles off is at a great advantage, because the EMP generated by nukes can screw up electronic signals for days. Rather like what solar flares do. They've actually caused the North American Air Defense Command to get false-positive readings, and more than once we've erroneously concluded that the Russians had fired off a salvo in our direction. Luckily, the computers caught the errors in time. No, the more mechanical components in a missile the better. At least until someone figures out a way to overcome the effects of EMP."

"You could be onto something, Walt," Trader said. "Let's face it. Jallud and Hadid will naturally assume we'll try to sabotage the initiator simply because that's the one area they know jack-shit about. They'll double and triple-check our work on that component every step of the way. But if we can fuzz-up the command program, we'd go a long way to accomplishing what we need."

"There's not an altimeter in the world I can't scramble," Walter Boyd continued. "I can do it in such a way that it could be bench-checked from here until hell freezes over, and the best technicians in the world would insist that it's perfect. Only thing, if it's put in an airplane and you believe what it tells you, your flight will end with you going to meet Jesus."

"Let's call it a night," Trader finally tapped. "We'll sneak a peek at those altimeters tomorrow, and figure out a way for Walt to do his stuff. God Bless America."

                              *   *   *

Gaddafi's rubber-stamp cabinet, The General Peoples Committee, acceded to his every demand. This government was at the center of most of the nefarious schemes dominating the world's political stage. Although the Supreme Leader kept a low profile, he took delight in the havoc he was wreaking.

Gaddafi was on the brink of his greatest triumph. The

world would soon bear witness to his true might and to the glory that rightfully belonged to him as the ruler of the Arab world. One name would be repeated in reverence for all time: *Muammar al-Gaddafi.*

He assembled his cabinet on the second day of June to present his plan for the destruction of Israel and the transfer of power from Washington to Tripoli. After greeting his ministers, he turned the meeting over to Jallud.

"Gentlemen, very soon there will arise a new world order, and the heart will reside here in Libya." Jallud reveled in his position at center stage. His mouth had healed well. Occasionally his jaw would ache, but his doctors had assured him the discomfort he felt would disappear with time.

The assembly murmured among themselves, not knowing what to make of Jallud's opening statement. They looked toward the Leader for a cue on how to react, but Gaddafi sat Sphinx-like.

"My friends, if I could have your attention, I'll explain how what I've just said is a statement firmly rooted in fact, and not one born of idle fantasy. I'm proud to announce on behalf of our Supreme Leader that Libya is a proven nuclear power!"

That statement got every ones attention. Low murmurs quickly intensified into shouts. The cabinet members demanded to know more. Could it be true? Was it even possible?

"Both possible and true," Jallud replied as soon as the room had quieted. "Now, I must insist there be no more interruptions until I am finished. Then you may ask all the questions you wish."

Gaddafi nodded his approval, and the room became still.

"For too long we've been humiliated by the West," Jallud said, warming to his task. "The Americans, along with their European and Jewish puppets, look upon the planet as a bed of oysters, a bed whose resources are to be harvested for their own enjoyment. Moreover, nowhere is that attitude more evident than here in the Middle East. We Arabs have spent the last fifty years a colony of the West in all but name while it plundered our oil and paid us a pittance for our treasure. For this we were expected to be eternally grateful. Well, those days are over. As you know,

OPEC raised the price of oil last year, thanks in large measure to the demands of the Shah of Iran. And what happened? The West capitulated and agreed to the new price. However, their silence was a ruse, meant to throw us off guard. We all know what they're really up to. They're already talking of seizing the oil fields by military means, and, then, under the guise of national security, suck dry our reserves. Their strategy is to pay us only a fraction of its true worth. And when our oil is gone we'll be left without a source of revenue. We'll become beggars on the world's stage."

Heads bobbed in vigorous agreement.

"That will not happen, and we have the means to guarantee it. We now possess a working nuclear arsenal, and we intend to use it if need be, to secure what's rightfully ours. In addition, what's rightfully ours is the gold at the American military installation called Fort Knox, and whatever other bullion is stored in several bank vaults in New York City. That is what we want, and that is what we shall have! Remember, my brothers, we are merely taking back that which is rightfully ours!"

The ministers jumped to their feet, yelling and laughing, clapping and stomping their feet in an unabashed display of ecstasy. Jallud stood back and allowed them to revel to full measure.

"What about the Zionists?" someone called out. "What will we do about them?"

"By the time we are through, America will gladly abandon the Zionists", Jallud yelled back. "Their country will cease to exist and the land will be turned over to our Palestinian brothers."

"And the Russians? What do you think they will do?"

"The Russians will do nothing!" Jallud laughed scornfully. "They have vowed to destroy the West, and this gives them the opportunity to do so without a single Russian soldier having to fire a single Russian gun! Remember, it's the Russians who have the largest supply of gold in the world. Just think of what our action will do to the value of their bullion! The masters of the Kremlin will do nothing to stop us. I, Jallud, guarantee it!"

Gaddafi rose and held his palms aloft for silence. He was

dressed in an army tunic, bereft of insignia save for red tabs on his collar. Drawing himself erect, he slapped his swagger stick once against his leg, then placed the small, ceremonial wooden baton on the table.

"Ambassador Jallud will present our demands to the NATO foreign ministers in Brussels in two days. We have already been assured that he will be granted an audience, even though the secretary-general reminded us that such a request was most unusual. That will be the forum we shall use to let our demands be known. However, Jallud will not inform them that it was Libya that liberated the shipment of nuclear material from a French vessel a couple of years back. They still suspect the Jews, and that error suits our purposes well because we do not want them speculating about just how much Plutonium we have. Jallud will tell them it was Libya that exploded a nuclear device off the southern tip of Africa back in March. Moreover, he will inform them that if our demands are not met, then they can expect nuclear explosions to occur in various countries with monotonous regularity. In addition, they will be told that if they choose to ignore us, then they will do so at their own peril. The Western Powers will quickly be branded as murderers by the rest of the world."

Gaddafi's voice rose in pitch and his eyes shone like black diamonds. "My brothers, our time has come. Israel will cease to exist. Remember, it is only because of the actions of the United States last year that the Arab brotherhood did not destroy the Jews for once and for all. Not this time! When we're finished, the word of Islam will spread to the four corners of the earth, and those infidels who dare defy us will be cut down by Allah's righteous wrath! Allah has chosen Libya as His instrument to spread the truths of the Prophet. The world will listen and obey! Now, join me in a prayer to beseech Allah to guide us well in this most holy of undertakings."

He bowed his head, and the assembled ministers followed suit. They began to pray.

CHAPTER 18

The downpour turned to drizzle as Jallud's Mercedes rolled to a stop under the portico of the building housing the North Atlantic Council in Brussels, Belgium. The fifteen foreign ministers (fourteen members, plus the French minister, whose country had formally withdrawn from NATO in 1967) had just ended the first of their biannual meetings. Throughout the proceedings the participants had expressed their concerns as to the future political well-being of President Nixon. His administration was under siege, wracked by a scandal dubbed *Watergate* which threatened to topple his presidency.

"The ministers are waiting for you, Ambassador. Please follow me." The secretary-general's aide-de-camp set off down the long, carpeted hallway with Jallud on his right. "I trust you had a good flight, sir?" he asked, such requisite small talk coming to him as second nature.

"What? Oh, yes, fine, thank you." Jallud was still gloating over the man's earlier delightful words, informing him that the ministers were waiting. *Won't they be surprised when they hear what I have to say?*

Nevertheless, if they were surprised, they didn't show it. Fifteen ministers and the secretary-general sat mute as the meticulously dressed Arab before them laid out his country's preposterous demands. The more he spoke the less their reaction. Jallud felt a growing sense of unease. Finally, he finished his presentation. "Any questions, gentlemen?"

"Is that the sum of what you have to say, Mr. Ambassador?" the secretary-general wanted to know.

"I hope I've clearly spelled out my government's position. Is there something that needs repeating? Maybe you would like me to repeat myself in French?"

"That won't be necessary. We understand what you have told us, Ambassador. Your command of English is more than passable. Now, would you please wait outside for a few moments? I'll have an aide escort you to a sitting room where I'm sure you will be comfortable. We shall draft a reply for you to take back to your government."

As soon as Jallud was out of earshot, the ministers let loose.

"The man's as mad as a hatter!" exclaimed Sir Robert, the British minister. "He only demands the entire store of gold bullion from Fort Knox! And all that pathetic blathering about scores of nuclear missiles he's ready to unleash. Oh, and lest I forget his last little nugget, we're to abandon the state of Israel and toss out all the Jews, chop-chop! Have you ever heard such bloody rot? What a blasted waste of our time."

"Well, he certainly has nerve," added the Turkish minister, who rose, stretched, and lit a cigarette. "From day one, his government has been a blight on the entire Islamic World. An embarrassment beyond words. I agree with Sir Robert. The man's either a fool or mad. Probably both."

The ministers conferred among themselves in like vein for several minutes. Only the Canadian representative remained withdrawn, spending his time writing on a yellow legal pad. Finally, he cleared his throat, pushed back his chair, and rose.

"Gentlemen, I suggest we give credence to what the Libyan gentleman has just said. I, for one, take the exaction most seriously, no matter how preposterous."

"Jean-Paul, surely you don't..." the Belgium minister said.

"Indulge me for a moment." The Canadian glanced down at his notes. "Let's revisit certain events which occurred over the past few years. Events which when studied separately mean nothing, but if you link them together, then a rather alarming picture unfolds."

"Go on."

"A couple of years ago a sizable shipment of Uranium and Plutonium disappeared on the high seas en route from France to America. At the time we all said, 'Aha! The work of the Mossad.' Couldn't prove it then; can't prove it now."

"Still believe it though," Sir Robert grumbled loudly.

The Canadian continued. "Next, about a year ago if my memory serves me correctly, some *Longbows* were pinched in West Germany. Same result. Disappeared into the blue. Only this time, no one blamed the Mossad. No, we all said, 'definitely the work of urban terrorists. Probably Baader Meinhoff.'"

He now had their undivided attention.

"Then in March of this year there was an atomic explosion off the South African coast. No government took responsibility, but we all speculated at the time that possibly a Russian nuclear submarine had blown its reactor. It was even suggested in some quarters that maybe the Israelis had detonated a device. But we never really knew what to make of it, did we, gentlemen?"

Silence.

"Well, we do now, if that Arab in the other room is to be believed. If one puts all those pieces of the puzzle together, then it seems that mad or not, Monsieur Jallud is telling the truth. Which means we've got big troubles on our hands, gentlemen."

There was no light banter now.

"Supposing Jean-Paul's right?" Secretary of State Henry Kissinger said. "I'm not ready to concede that he is, mind you, but if my Canadian friend has hit the nail on the head and correctly linked these events to the Libyans, then what do we do? There's no way my government is going to roll over and meekly give up the gold in Fort Knox to a ragtag band of brigands. To say nothing of abandoning Israel, our only ally in the region."

"We would certainly hope not, Henry," said the West German representative. "I, for one, reluctantly find myself concurring with Jean-Paul's postulation. Somehow the Libyans have indeed manufactured atomic weapons, and I believe they won't hesitate to use them to further their agenda. If that's the case, we are in grave trouble."

"What was Monsieur Jallud's timeframe for a response?" asked the secretary-general.

"Ten days from today."

"And he did say missiles, correct? Not bombs?"

The nuance between words was everything in the world of diplomacy. Wars had been waged because of a misinterpretation of a single word.

"He said missiles all right, Mr. Secretary," answered Kissinger. "And he suggested they have more than just a couple of missing *Longbows*."

The secretary-general rose and continued in a tone to match his troubled face. "It would appear then that we have ten days to find these missiles and neutralize them. I need not remind any of you that Libya is a rather big country, and we don't even know if the missiles are still there. Quite a tall order, especially in light of the fact we haven't a clue as to where we should start looking, and no earthly idea as to what country, or countries, have been targeted if we don't acquiesce to that man's preposterous demands." He shook his head slowly, almost as though the solution was simply not to be found. "I suggest we call Ambassador Jallud back in here and tell him we shall be in contact with his government shortly."

He turned to Kissinger. "Because of your country's position, Henry, I propose your government become the spokesman for the group. We cannot go spinning off in fifteen different directions. We must talk with one voice. Everybody agree?"

All nodded except the French foreign minister. He took a long minute before he stood and reluctantly gave his formal consent. However, it came with a caveat. "I would ask you, Mr. Kissinger, not to take any unilateral action. Remember that we all have a stake in the outcome. It is not simply an American problem, or even a NATO problem. It's a collective one. And let me finish by observing that we've failed to address a very sticky problem, and that is, do we inform Tel Aviv?"

Kissinger replied immediately. "I recommend we say nothing to the Israelis, at least not just yet. Their agenda is not necessarily ours. They could go off half-cocked and create havoc for the rest of us. However, as to your request that everyone here be kept informed at all times, you have my word on it, Minister. Everyone stays in the loop until this is settled. I suggest we inform all our embassies about this, but at the same time they must be cautioned not to let a word leak to Tel Aviv. Maybe some local contacts can come up with a lead, because let's face it, we need all the help we can get, and we need it fast. One final thought. We cannot have the press getting even the slightest whiff of what's going on. Because if they should become involved, then the panic that will surely follow will turn our hemisphere on its ear! Now, let's get that slimy character back in here."

* * *

"Mr. President, the order of business is to buy time," Kissinger said, seated to Richard Nixon's right. President Nixon had assembled his Crisis Management Team, a group composed of all the members of the cabinet; the directors of the FBI, CIA, and DIA; the Chairman of the Joint Chiefs, and several other department heads. Also included were the party leaders of both the House and the Senate. All were visibly shaken by what they had just been briefed.

Kissinger continued. "First, we must open a dialogue so as to have the Libyans think that we're taking both their demands and their threats seriously. Once we have them talking, we can buy ourselves the time needed to find all of the missiles and destroy them."

"And if we don't succeed, Henry?" Nixon asked. "What if we can't buy time and don't find the missiles? What then?" His mind moved to other thoughts. "Why not turn the tables and slam *them* with a demand?" His fist came down hard on the tabletop. "Like maybe a twenty-four hour deadline for them to hand over all of their missiles? Make them understand that if they don't, we'll blow them into oblivion with some nukes of our own. And at the same time we tell them that we have no intention of handing over even one gram of gold. *That's* the only kind of talk madmen like Mister Gaddafi understand!"

Kissinger remained poker-faced. He had heard similar suggestions from this President at the beginning of other crises. It was a macho thing, nothing more. "Mr. President, I've thought of that, believe me, but we can't allow ourselves to even think in those terms. In all likelihood Gaddafi knows we would never turn over our gold, so he sees that impossible demand as merely an opening gambit. He's nothing more than any common blackmailer who starts out asking for the moon but ends up settling for something far less. And like any other blackmailer, once he gets started there's no stopping him. However, my immediate concern is for the safety of Israel. I think Tel Aviv will be his first target. Maybe his only target. Moreover, I wouldn't put it past him to lob a missile in that direction no matter whatever the outcome with us. That's how much he hates the Jews. So you see, it's imperative we locate those missiles and that we do with all dispatch. And keep in mind, Mr. President, there's no way we can know for sure just how many missiles and bombs he might have. We simply can't afford to think in terms of him having only those two *Longbows* stolen from Germany."

Nixon growled his displeasure. He turned to the Chairman of the Joint Chiefs. "Admiral, could a *Longbow* be launched from Libya and hit Israel?"

"No, sir," came the immediate reply. Not from Libya. However, they could launch from Egypt. As you know, their two governments have become quite cozy in the last few months, even to the point of signing an accord to explore the possibility of merging both countries. So, yes, Gaddafi could have access to the territory necessary to launch and destroy Israel."

"Now isn't that goddamn wonderful!"

The meeting dragged on for two more hours. At its conclusion the group was no further ahead than when it began. Exasperation reigned supreme. The last question was posed by the President to Kissinger. "When do we inform the Russians, Henry?"

"Not yet; but my guess is they already know. They have their sources. No doubt they're taking uncommon delight knowing that we are in one helluva pickle. I'm guessing they will let me know shortly that they would not take kindly to any preemptive strike against their friends in Tripoli. Keep in mind, Mr. President, that the Russians have the world's largest store of gold. So for us to lose ours by turning it over to Libya would cause the dollar to collapse thus making their gold increase a hundred-fold in value overnight! A rather bleak scenario, I'm afraid."

"All right, Henry, enough good news for one day. Let's wrap this up for now, but I want everybody back at seven o'clock sharp in the morning and I want some solid answers on how we're going to resolve this thing before it gets completely out of hand." Nixon turned in his chair and scanned the room. "St. James, are you in here?" he called out.

"I'm here, sir." The man in question was standing next to the door by the east wall.

"Ah, there you are, Andrew! Good. I want you, and you, Henry, to remain." He thanked the others who left the Cabinet Room to do the bidding of the most powerful man on earth.

*   *   *

Andrew St. James crossed the room to the mahogany conference table and took a seat across from the secretary. He waited while Nixon scribbled some notes on a yellow legal pad.

Only a handful of people in or out of government knew how Andrew St. James earned his daily bread. Listed as a GS-16 in the White House directory, he was believed to be but another insignificant cog in that giant machine called the federal bureaucracy. His anonymity was treasured by the president.

St. James worked directly for President Nixon and answered only to him. By training, he was an intelligence agent; a man empowered to make things happen. He was a rarity in Washington. He never flaunted his position and never used it to curry favor. President Nixon trusted and depended on this man.

Almost single-handedly, St. James had broken the formidable impasse that had existed for more than two decades between Washington and Peking. By dint of his tireless work, the President had been able to make his historical trip to China the year before, soon followed by a subsequent journeying to Moscow and a breakthrough meeting with Secretary Brezhnev. All this came to pass because of St. James' handling of a debriefing of the most important KGB intelligence officer ever to defect from the Soviet Union. He was Major General Alexsei Zakharov, the number two in the infamous KGB, and the information Zakharov had brought with him from Moscow had been nothing short of riveting. The absolute shocker had been his claim that he had masterminded the Kennedy assassination, and shortly thereafter had brazenly attempted to blackmail the immediate past-occupant of the White House into doing the Kremlin's bidding. President Lyndon Johnson had refused to be corrupted and chose not to seek re-election rather than to succumb to the threats. St. James went on to prove to Nixon that the former president was a true patriot in every sense of the word, his indisputable proof delivered at a time when others were of a different persuasion. St. James had accomplished all this without a scintilla of public praise. Such was his job, and he would have it no other way. And that was why he held such sway with this President.

"Still getting good information from our Russian guest?" Nixon asked, small talk from a man who loathed small talk.

"I am, Mr. President, and will continue to do so for many years to come. General Zakharov has kept to his side of the bargain."

The President nodded, impatient to move on. "Andrew," he said, shifting gears, "I'm going to have you to leave Zakharov to your staff to handle for a while because I need you involved in this Libyan thing. You have the wherewithal to go places and ferret out information that others can't, and you have my personal *imprimatur* to act on your own volition without reams of red tape to impede you. So, as of this moment, you will be working with the secretary until this problem has been put to rest."

"Yes, sir."

"Is that okay with you, Henry?"

"Of course, Mr. President."

"Good." Nixon scribbled something the legal pad then pointed his fountain pen at Kissinger. "Open the dialogue right away, Henry. Tell the Libyans we'll meet with them any time, any place, blah, blah, blah. You know the drill."

Kissinger nodded.

"Second, I think we need a code name for the operation that we can use when we can communicate with each other and with our allies. I thought about it during the meeting and came up with *Operation Midas touch*. What do you think?"

"*Midas touch*," repeated the secretary. He was keenly aware of this president's love for code names. "I like it." The nation's chief diplomat was being most diplomatic.

"Good, then let everybody know." His eyes shifted to St. James. "What's your gut feeling from what you've heard so far?"

St. James shook his head. My gut tells me this insanity could spin out of control and escalate into World War Three. Colonel Gaddafi is an unstable, uneducated man given to flights of fantasy and suffers from illusions of grandeur. If he has the nuclear arsenal he claims—and I believe he well might—then it's only a matter of time until he uses it. Remember, he has no idea how much gold we have or don't have in our vaults, yet he has to know you would never just hand it over. You could tell him that we have no bullion and haven't had any since you closed the gold window two years ago and decoupled the dollar from the gold supply. I certainly don't recommend that course of action, though," he quickly added. "That would give Gaddafi an opening to go to the press with that news and instantly cause the world's financial markets to fly into a tailspin."

"Damn right it would!"

St. James continued. "And as for his demand for us to abandon Israel, I suspect he feels he's on more solid ground there because Tel Aviv isn't exactly blessed with a whole host of friends. But putting that all of that aside for the moment, there is someone, somewhere, who knows something, Mr. President, and that's the someone I've got to uncover. We have to find out where those missiles are located and what targets have been selected. And I must get an accurate count as to just how many he has in his arsenal."

"Dammit, even Gaddafi must realize that if he sets off a bomb we'll retaliate by annihilating him. It's the most insane threat any leader could make."

"Any *sane* leader," corrected St. James. "This guy's certifiable. I daresay his advisors are either scared to death or as crazy as he is. Either way, we have got to play for time."

"Do you really think he would fire a missile at Israel? Nixon asked. "Remember, there were only two *Longbows* stolen."

"Mr. President, as the secretary stressed earlier, it would be a grave mistake to assume that he only has two missiles. He could have secured others from the Soviets; possibly some from the Chinese, or even a few from the North Koreans. Until we know what he's got, I suggest preparing for a worst-case scenario. That way you won't be caught short."

"Do you think you should go to Europe for the time being? That way you'd be closer to the action if something breaks."

"We still have nine days to go," St. James replied, "and I'm hoping Dr. Kissinger will finagle us an extension. So if it's okay with you, sir, I'd like to stay here in Washington, at least for the next few days. I'll need the time to learn all I can about Gaddafi. I want to talk to some psychiatrists to see if they can come up with a suggestion on how to best negotiate with him. I also want to learn more about that shipment of nuclear material which disappeared a while back. I need to do the math to see just how many bombs it could have been turned into. And, lastly, I want to find out just where in the hell this guy got his expertise all of a sudden to become a nuclear power."

"Good points," said Nixon.

St. James continued. "That last item is probably the most important of all. I'm flabbergasted that the Libyans could have perfected the technology. They had to have had help. But, where could it have possibly come from? I predict the answer will prove to be truly frightening. Because if it's Gaddafi today who overthrows a king, then who will it be tomorrow? How about the Shah of Iran? Imagine him being tossed aside by fundamental Muslim terrorists with nuclear ambitions of their own?"

"Now that's one scary thought to contemplate," said Kissinger, "but of course it could never happen," he added, his voice filled with certitude.

Nixon let out a long sigh. "I have nothing further to ask or add so I'll leave you both a free hand. Let me know the minute you have any important information, no matter if it's three in the morning."

"Yes, Mr. President," both men replied in unison.

*　*　*

At that same moment, deep in the Libyan Desert, Hadid was speaking to Trader. "We leave for Tripoli in the morning, Captain. There will be two planes; one for us, one for the equipment. The missiles left by train last evening. Make sure you take everything you need."

"Will we be coming back, or is our work finished here?"

Unwilling to look Trader in the eye, Hadid, mumbled, "I think you'll be going home." He made a big production of stuffing papers into an old, scuffed leather satchel. "The plan is to be airborne at first light."

*   *   *

The prisoners were pensive as they packed their meager belongings, knowing that the next few hours or days would be telling. They were a pragmatic group so there was no cause for celebration this night.

Finally, Trader saw it his duty to lighten the mood. "My bet is we'll be released within days. Let's face it. Jallud has nothing to gain by killing us. The war's been over for more than a year now, and even the North Vietnamese aren't going to worry if we suddenly surface half a world away. So, lighten up, guys, I really think this is it." He didn't believe a word he said.

"At least we know those missiles won't detonate anywhere near ground level, skipper," Boyd said. "As our buddy Jallud likes to say: I guarantee it!"

"Thank God for that, Walter. We're all proud of you. No matter what happens, we damn well know that innocent people won't be hurt if these idiots should ever decide to pop them off. In many ways I'm glad that maniac picked us for his diabolical scheme. At least we had the expertise to make sure his grand design, whatever it is, will fail. So I suggest that maybe we should believe God placed us here for a reason."

"Amen, Captain. I'm not particularly religious," confessed Nick Wolfe, "but I like that idea. It makes everything somehow all worthwhile."

*   *   *

The American pilots and Libyans scientists left in the second plane. As they boarded their transport, they saw the burned and twisted wreckage of the C-130 Tim Sweringen had tried to fly out.

Bakktari surprised the group by showing up at the last

minute. My master calls," he explained weakly. "And faithful little lap dog that I am, I obey."

Trader could see the doctor was upset. His eyes betrayed him; their message was that events were about to be played out. No matter what he had said to the group the night before to cheer them up, Trader now had no illusions. They could all be dead within a matter of hours.

There were a dozen armed guards on board under the command of the chief of security. Trader noted how the crew had made a very public showing of locking themselves onto the flight deck. They were not about to have the American pilots storm the cockpit in an attempt to takeover of the aircraft.

Both planes arrived at what used to be Wheelus Air Base three hours later. In the breath-robbing heat of the early afternoon, a bus pulled up alongside their plane. The men were hot, tired, and parched. The flight crew had forgotten to pack water on board for the long flight back to civilization. The bus ride lasted five minutes.

"Everybody, off, except Captain Trader. You, Captain, have a meeting to attend. But you'll be coming back later." The army major plunked himself down on the bench beside Trader, and grinned, displaying a mouthful of perfect teeth.

Trader felt the tension rise among his friends. This is not the moment to start anything, he thought, and addressed them in a quiet voice. "No sweat, fellows. Get on out of this heat. I'll be back in a jiff." He smiled broadly to include them all, and gave a casual wave. He was a picture of composure; a man seemingly without a care in the world. "See you guys later. And always remember: God Bless America."

*   *   *

The six pilots got off the bus in front of a Spartan concrete building at a remote corner of the field. Jallud was there to greet them. Standing next to him was a tall, slender man dressed as a nomad. His head was covered and his eyes were hidden behind mirrored aviator sunglasses.

Jallud addressed the group. "Gentlemen, your work is finished here and you will be going home today. That was my promise, and I am a man of my word. I have arranged for a flight to take you to Rome three hours from now. I don't care if you tell the world where you've been for the last eighteen months. It no longer matters. You are free to do and say as you wish." He smiled, and pointed toward the building. "Now, go and clean up. Inside you'll find showers, towels, soap, shaving gear and fresh clothes, everything you will need to make yourselves presentable. You will also find refreshments. I'm sure you are all thirsty after your long flight. Go," he repeated in a pleasant voice while pointing to the entrance. "I'll see you one last time with some final words before you leave."

"What about Captain Trader?" Walter Boyd wanted to know.

"Captain Trader is at the airport infirmary having his electronic tether removed," Jallud replied smoothly. "The doctors assure me it is a simple procedure, and insist the captain will be none the worse for the wear. I suspect there are not too many airline carriers that would care having him as a passenger in his present condition," Jallud laughed aloud at his own humor. "He'll be back in time to join you. Now go."

Walter Boyd led the way into the building, skeptical, but hoping nonetheless that Jallud was telling the truth. There really wasn't a need to detain them any longer, he reasoned, and Jallud obviously felt confident that his newly minted arsenal of *Longbow* missiles would keep the American government at bay. But, he was confident that all hell would break loose in the press when it was learned how the North Vietnamese had sold them to the Libyans. Let's just hope that madman keeps his word, he thought as he entered a well-lit room.

Crowding in behind Boyd, the men spotted the table filled with pitchers of iced tea and three large platters overflowing with sandwiches. Seven tumblers had already been filled in anticipation of the thirsty guests' arrival. Two female cooks smiled bashfully at the group and bowed, while a third was caught by the Americans with an upended, half-finished glass of tea at her lips. She swallowed noisily causing some of the amber fluid to trickle down onto her chin. She quickly drew her glass to her bosom as if trying to hide it. She wiped her mouth with the back of a hand and scurried wordlessly from the room. As she stepped into the sunshine she faced west and raised her glass in what seemed to be a salute. The nomad standing in the searing heat several paces away nodded a silent acknowledgment.

"All right!" exclaimed a happy Mark FitzGerald, swooping up the glass closest to him. "Cheers, everybody. Here's hoping my next drink is a scotch and water on our way to Rome." He tilted his glass and began to drink, moving ice cubes aside with his tongue to better get at it.

Within moments all were chugalugging their tea, eager to replace the fluids lost from sweating on the hot flight across the desert.

The group was keyed with excitement. So Jallud wasn't going to kill them after all, each thought in his own way, telling themselves they would believe it for sure once they were in the air and far out over the Mediterranean Sea.

Niels Borden was the first to notice something wrong. A bemused look crossed his face, and he held his tumbler up close to his eyes as if to inspect it. He opened his mouth to speak but managed only a gurgling sound. He dropped the glass and slowly sank to his knees. He reached out blindly for support, grabbed wildly at a corner of the table causing it to buckle, sending pitchers and sandwiches cascading to the floor. *It can't be! I just saw that Arab woman drinking this very same tea!* It was his last coherent thought.

The others stood mute, staring; their minds tried to make sense with what was happening to Niels, but their brains had already started to short-circuit. They peered at one another with eyes fast losing the ability to focus. Their chests began to constrict in hideous spasms, a sign their autonomic reflexes had lost the ability to heed commands from their brains urging them to breathe. Their nervous systems were for all practical purposes already dead.

They staggered and fell as a group, blessedly unconscious before their minds could really come to an understanding of what was happening. Within two minutes of entering the building, all were dead from the effects of the most deadly nerve agent ever created. Sarin. It had been laced into their tea. But not in the woman's.

*   *   *

"Take the bodies far into the desert and burn them before you bury them," Jallud instructed the lieutenant in charge of the small group of guards as he walked among the corpses five minutes later. "Then you will forget where you've buried them. These men must disappear forever."

The lieutenant nodded and saluted.

Jallud went outside and walked back over to the nomad. The man was like a statue.

"It is finished, Excellency," he reported.

"And the one called Trader?"

Jallud smiled. "I have something special in mind for him. There was no need to prolong the agony of those men," he said, jerking a thumb toward the building. "They were nothings. Now Trader, well, that man's a different story. That particular American will beg and scream for mercy before he dies. I, Jallud, guarantee it!"

"Just make sure he's dead before sundown." Gaddafi glanced one last time at the building, gathered in his flowing robes, and headed for his Mercedes.

Maybe it will be a little later than sundown when you meet your end, Captain James Vincent Trader, but not by much, I promise, Jallud thought as he made his way to his own car, delighting in the anticipation of his final confrontation with the man he had come to hate beyond all reason.

CHAPTER 19

Trader had lost all track of time. He was imprisoned on a ship, and all he could say for sure was that it had set sail from the harbor at Tripoli.

There had been no meeting. He had been blindfolded and manacled, flown in the same C-130 to the seaport city; marched onto this foulest of ships and locked in an interior cabin. When he had demanded to be taken back to Tripoli, his captors had beaten him. Later, when he had threatened to complain to Jallud, the guards had disintegrated into bouts of helpless laughter. They had recovered quickly enough to beat him again, this time with more vigor, and when they tired of their exercise they threw him on his bunk, bleeding, battered, and covered with welts.

The ship had been at sea for several hours, and the steady thump of the engine told him it was probably making ten knots, maybe a little more. He also knew the seas were picking up because the vessel had taken on a distinct roll.

A couple of hours ago he had been fed a meal of soup made from some indescribably foul-smelling fish. Because of his many years of imprisonment, he had forced himself to down the mess, much to the amazement and disgust of his captors. He then passed the empty hours worrying for his friends, praying that they had been freed. As to what lay in store for him, he did not care to contemplate. He only knew it would not be pleasant.

He must have dozed off, because something startled him, causing him to jerk upright on the filthy mattress. There it was again. Someone was having a hard time turning a key. The heavy metal door finally opened, and two men rushed in and grabbed him by each arm. Without a word they manhandled him up two levels and dragged him onto the forward deck.

The night was as miserable as the ship. A heavy downpour stung his face, drenching him within moments. His escorts vanished; leaving him quite alone in a black world, save for one ineffectual spotlight swaying wildly halfway up the mast behind him.

"So, Captain Trader. At last, it's just you and me."

Jallud! He turned toward the voice. Peering through the wind-driven rain he spotted his nemesis, legs apart in an attempt to provide a modicum of balance on the heaving deck. His body was outlined by the feeble light. Like Trader, he was fully exposed to the elements. He stood twenty feet away, and had to shout to make himself heard.

"I have dreamed of this moment for an eternity," Jallud yelled above the din. "I agonized for months over how you should die. Then the answer came to me in a dream. He laughed hideously as he stood in the pouring rain; every few moments transmogrified by the streaks of lightning into some grotesque escapee from the netherworld.

"This is a fishing vessel, Captain Trader," Jallud shouted, waving his arms. "It is used to net anything and everything, because the ones who feast on its catch could care less. You see, Trader, as soon as the fish are caught they're cooked, dried, then ground into meal. Bones, skins, heads, guts. Nothing is wasted. To keep the stench down, the meal is then stored in coolers." He stopped to unleash another round of laughter. "And, Trader, you'll love it when I tell you who gets to dine on this feast from the sea! Go ahead, ask me."

Trader remained silent.

"*Ask me!*" he screamed.

"Okay, I'll humor you, you certifiable lunatic. Who is it, Jallud?" Trader yelled back.

"It's fed to the pigs, of course! Those filthy creatures you heathens devour with such relish. Regretfully, there's still a sizable foreign community in our country—Italians mostly—who eat pork. We refuse to allow our precious grain to be used to fatten pigs, so, this has become the mainstay of their diet. And you, Trader, you are going to die here tonight. And once you're dead I'm going to grind you to pieces along with the catch. Then you'll be fed to the swine of Libya. How absolutely fitting an end, do you not agree?"

Something moved in the shadows behind Jallud. Then moved again. It was a person. He probably had been standing there in the shadows for some time, but only because he had shifted his position at the precise moment the lightning had flashed, had Trader accidentally spotted him. No doubt a guard stationed to protect his master.

"But, Captain, I do so want to make it interesting," Jallud continued. "There is nothing sporting in just pressing a button and blowing you apart. Oh, no! No fun in that at all. So here is what I propose." He fumbled at his waist and extracted a pistol from his belt, then crouched long enough to slide the gun across the wet deck plates. It skidded to a halt midpoint between them. "It's loaded, Captain Trader. You have my word on it as a Sandhurst graduate," he mocked. "All you have to do is grab it, aim, shoot, and kill me! Sounds eminently fair, no? Tell you what. If you kill me, then you can grind up *my* carcass and feed it to the swine!" Jallud laughed as though possessed.

Trader's mind was spinning. Revolted as he was at the thought of what Jallud intended to do with him, his brain kept urging him to think. There's got to be a way out. *Think, man!*

A long, brilliant, ragged streak of lightning turned night into day, fully exposing the two men, and revealing a third still lurking in the shadows behind Jallud. The rain pounded faster.

"All you have to do is beat me to the draw," Jallud yelled. "You go for the gun and I go for my trigger to blow your head off!" Jallud held aloft the electronic box. "Nothing could be fairer than that. Are you ready, Captain Trader?" Obscene peals of laughter fought the howling wind for dominance.

Then Trader spotted movement through the rain. Mesmerized, his eyes followed the figure as it left the shadows and rushed toward an unsuspecting Jallud. The smallish man moved at full speed, and without warning hit Jallud full force from behind, slamming his weight into Jallud's legs. Both crashed violently onto the deck, the impact sending the electronic control panel flying out of Jallud's grasp. It bounced wildly across the deck, seemingly in slow motion to a transfixed Trader, then, with one last erratic bounce, disappeared through a scupper and over the side.

"*Nnnnoooo*, what have you done?" Jallud shrieked at the night.

"Jump, Captain Trader. Jump overboard. The others are all dead. Jump! It's your only chance."

Bakktari!

The man who had been reduced to tears because he saw himself as a coward was saving his life!

Jallud had partially extricated himself from Bakktari's grasp, and the two of them, now consumed with a singular purpose were crawling painfully toward the pistol.

Trader sprang into action. Heeding Bakktari's advice he sprinted unsteadily to the railing, grabbed hold, and heaved himself over the side, striking the water headfirst.

Stay away from the propeller, he warned himself. And keep out of the wake vortex or it'll suck you right in. He swam down and away from the ship, quickly becoming disoriented in the blackness. His lungs agonized for oxygen, but still he kept going. Until he couldn't continue. He had to go up, or die. Up he swam; at last breaking the surface, his mouth already fully opened to fill his lungs with the elixir of life. He threw his head back and lifted his body as high as possible away from the waves and gulped in breath after breath, the rasping, tortured sound barely reaching his ears over the roar of the storm.

He could only just make out the ship vaguely outlined by the lightning flashes two hundred yards to his starboard. It was steaming away from him. He had no idea whether or not Jallud would stop the vessel and lower a boat to search for him, and he realized he had to put as much distance between himself and that maniac as quickly as possible. He struck out in a crawl, his body shaking from shock and the coldness of the water.

On and on he swam, the penetrating chill beginning to take its toll. He kept moving, fully aware of being trapped in a vicious dilemma. To remain motionless would cause him to lose all bodily control to the shivering, but to keep swimming would soon exhaust him.

Suddenly, something bumped him. Something huge. He let loose an involuntary yell of fright and frantically began to distance himself from the unknown. However, it found him, and hit him again, harder this time. He lashed out at the enemy with his left hand.

It was solid. Inanimate. Tentatively, he reached out, felt it, and then began to paw wildly at the object with both hands. A log or a pole of some sort. He now saw it as his savior. He began to swim against the waves in a desperate struggle to stay beside it.

"Oh, sweet Jesus, don't lose it!" he commanded himself aloud. "You've got to get on it. Shag your butt on board because if you lose it, you won't get a second chance." He thrashed and struggled in the inky blackness for five minutes, and found himself at the edge of despair. "God, help me," he pleaded.

With one last mighty heave he dragged his body up and onto the log. Something tore at his belly, and he screamed in pain. A protrusion, possibly a large nail, or even a spike, had ripped open his flesh, and he envisioned a wound going deep into his bowels. Somehow he managed to secure himself, and now lay completely out of the water, spent and clinging to the log.

Sometime before dawn the weather cleared and the seas subsided. There were still sizable swells, but nothing to shake him from his perch. He lay with his head to one side; arms and legs flung wide to encircle the log, fingernails like talons, dug deep into the waterlogged bark. He drifted first into a state of delirium, and then slipped into merciful unconsciousness.

*   *   *

With one wild, lucky kick, Jallud's boot found the side of Bakktari's head, stunning him. Jallud lunged forward, grabbed the gun, turned, and began firing blindly. He emptied six shots into Bakktari, and continued to pull the trigger long after the gun could do any further damage.

"*You miserable traitor!*" he screamed at the corpse.

Four sailors came to his side.

"Are you all right, Excellency?" one yelled down at him. "Are you hurt?"

"I'm fine!" Jallud leaned over and spat at Bakktari's body. "Take him below and grind him up with the fish. Go on! Get him out of my sight. Then tell the captain to make for Tripoli."

Jallud began to pound the deck with both fists in an uncontrollable display of fury, oblivious of the storm raging around him.

The sailors wisely left him where he lay.

CHAPTER 20

Spiro Stephanopoulos almost missed the object as it was carried by the swells from his line of sight, but as he turned to step into the companionway, he saw it again, and gasped. *It was a person!*

"Papa, papa!" He dropped the slop-bucket onto the deck and ran toward the wheelhouse, yelling in his high-pitched, eleven-year-old voice.

Hearing his youngest son's desperate shouts, Constantine stepped out onto the wing and looked down at the boy, steeling himself for some frightful revelation.

"Papa, look, a man!" Spiro shouted, pointing and jumping up and down as if possessed.

Constantine squinted in the direction his child was indicating. Even from his vantage point fifteen feet above the deck he could only see incessant swells to the horizon. He smiled and shook his head. He glanced down fondly at the small, upturned face.

"But he's there, papa, I saw him!" Spiro insisted, tears of frustration welling.

Then Constantine spotted the figure. *God in Heaven, the boy was right!* The figure was astride a barely buoyant log as it descended into a trough and out of view. Without a word he stepped back into the wheelhouse and took the helm from Alexander, his eldest. Throttling back the two huge Detroit diesels, Constantine rapidly spun the wheel.

Alexander stepped out onto the wing, raised his binoculars, and began probing the gray, undulating sea. "I have him, papa. Steady, steady," he cautioned, then shouted down to the deckhand who had just stepped out into the open, driven there by all the commotion. "George, stand by with the life ring. There's a man in the water."

George and Spiro each grabbed rings and stood like statues next to the railing, waiting for the figure to reappear.

When he did, he was only a few yards away. He lay face down and motionless, arms and legs wrapped tightly around an almost totally submerged log.

Constantine threw the diesels into neutral, instinctively allowing the current to work with forward momentum to bring the craft alongside the pathetic figure. The man didn't move.

In a flash, George was over the side and into the sea. Spiro had the presence of mind to fling his ring in after him, and as the line snaked out the boy secured the end to the pitted metal stanchion by his feet. By now Alexander had scurried down to the deck. Standing beside his brother, his eyes darted back and forth between both men riding the swells.

"Thank God it's June and not December," he said to Spiro as George reached the man and began prying him from his perch. He started to slide off the log and sink, but George anticipated the movement. He grabbed the man by his hair and worked the ring over his head and down to beneath his armpits with his free hand.

Two minutes later they had him stretched out on the deck. Alexander looked up to the bridge and gave a thumbs-up. Constantine nodded. The wallowing vessel jumped to life. Alexander and George lifted the still-comatose figure and carried him to shelter.

They eased their burden down the narrow companionway, shuffling along with short, jerky steps. They squeezed into the master's cabin and laid the soaking man on the floor. Still unconscious, he began to shiver violently. Alexander lowered his ear to the man's chest, then nodded to himself.

"He's alive, but barely. Help me strip him, George. We have to get him bundled into blankets. Only the Holy Mother knows how long he's been in the water." He turned from his task long enough to shout down the companionway. "Spiro, bring the ouzo, and hurry!" He helped George finish undressing the man. When he was naked they both stared, mouths agape. Huge, ugly, multicolored marks completely covered the torso. Angry, snake-like welts running from his left breast to a point just below his sternum seemed to possess a life of their own as they writhed in tempo with the shivering body. Lower yet, an ulcerous, foul-looking wound wept from his abdomen, and at the edge of this festering mess, what looked like a recent surgical scar. The entire body surface wore a pronounced blue cast, indicating that the blood supply was now being triaged in a life-and-death struggle to keep the vital organs warm. The unconscious stranger was very, very close to death.

At that moment Spiro and Constantine appeared, crowding the small doorway. The youngster's sudden intake of breath spurred Constantine into action. He took the bottle from his son's hand.

"Go up to the bridge, son. Keep a sharp lookout, but don't touch the autopilot. I'll be up in a minute; now off with you," he commanded with a gentle nudge to the back of Spiro's head.

In two short steps Constantine reached the side of the prone figure, and lifted him to a sitting position. Supporting the back and neck with one strong arm, he placed the bottle of ouzo to the man's cracked, swollen lips.

"You two, continue to dry him off, but be gentle. This one's in very bad shape. Alex, get some gauze pads and Mercurochrome for his wounds. It's not much, but it's all we can do until we reach port."

The three worked swiftly and efficiently, and within minutes had their charge in the master's bunk, bundled in all the boat's heavy, woolen blankets. The ouzo had brought some faint trace of color to his face, but every few seconds or so he would shudder involuntarily. However, the shivering was noticeably waning. Still, the eyes did not open.

"I'll set a course for home at once," Constantine said as he scooped up an armful of soggy clothing. Home was a small fishing port just east of Iraklion, on the island of Crete. He glanced at his watch. "Eight twenty-two. If we push it, we can be back by nine tonight."

"Should we radio ahead?" George asked.

Constantine mulled the suggestion. He studied the comatose figure for a long moment before answering. "No, we say nothing. We'll monitor the radio and listen for any news that might tell us who he could be." He shook his head in a wonderment of all that had happened then headed for the bridge, dumping the sodden clothing into the galley's sink on his way up.

*   *   *

It was twilight when they motored into the harbor along with other fishing boats from the village, some abeam, some in line, all chugging with a single-minded purpose through light swells. Dock crews soon busied themselves on the piers unloading holds of fish, expertly preparing the catch for the morning markets.

Twice during the voyage the man had awakened, and both times Alexander had been able to coax a little warm broth into him. He seemed to alternate between fever and chills. Obviously exhausted by the sheer effort of trying to swallow, he drifted back into a troubled sleep, muttering to himself in English.

At a little past eleven, the dock at last deserted, Constantine directed the two men to carry the stranger to his car which George had retrieved and parked a few paces from the trawler.

"Take him home and tell mother to put him in our bed," he said to Alexander. Speak to no one. As soon as I've secure the mooring lines I'll come with Spiro. The walk will do us good."

"How about calling the Frenchman?" Alexander suggested, a reference to the village's only doctor. An alcoholic of indeterminate age, he had drifted into the tiny settlement over a dozen years earlier and had stayed; a man without a past, a man without a future. He treated those cases he could, and those he couldn't he sent to the hospital in Iraklion on the mainland. And the invariable few who were beyond even God's help, those he prepared for burial in his unofficial capacity as undertaker. The usually suspicious, almost inbred villagers had slowly come to accept the hanger-on as one of their own.

"Maybe in the morning, but not at this late hour. I'm afraid our good doctor is by now beyond helping even himself. Tomorrow will be soon enough."

By morning the man had worsened, and Constantine decided it was time for the doctor to be summoned. Spiro was dispatched, and he returned about forty minutes later with the physician. Upon seeing his patient, the Frenchman became the man he must have once been, for he set to work examining the moaning figure before him with professionalism and concern. He worked rapidly, but without haste, cleaning, cutting, stitching and bandaging, issuing sharp orders for items he needed but not readily within his reach. Finally, his task was finished. Laying aside his stethoscope, he turned to Constantine.

"This man desperately needs a hospital, Constantine," the doctor said. "He's suffering from exposure, possible pneumonia, wounds from a very severe beating, and God knows what else. It's more than I can cope with. He needs X-rays, and quite possibly surgery for internal injuries. He must go to Iraklion. I'll telephone for the ambulance."

At that moment the patient opened his eyes and stared at his benefactors. He coughed once, then began to speak in a barely audible whisper. The physician, recognizing English, bent close to the man's lips and asked him to repeat himself.

"Where am I?"

"Crete. You were saved from the sea by these people yesterday," replied the doctor. "You are a most lucky man."

The stranger seemed to take an eternity to digest this information. He feebly licked his lips, smearing the balm that had been put on the raw skin around his mouth.

"Americans. I must speak to Americans," he gasped.

"All in the best of time," the doctor said. "First, we will take you to a hospital." While he spoke haltingly in English, he patted the man's arm, hoping to relay a message of comfort and security.

The agitated man shook his head. "Tell American officials where I am. Very important. My name is James Vincent Trader." He paused to gain his breath. "I'm a U.S. naval captain," he rasped. "Do you understand?" His eyes were now pleading with the Frenchman.

"Yes, yes, Captain James Vincent Trader, United States Navy. I understand. I shall telephone the mainland with that information. Now you must rest. You are safe, and you will be well soon. No more talk. That is an order."

Trader didn't hear. The effort required to pass along the information had depleted him of his last vestige of strength. He was fast asleep.

*   *   *

Shortly after 1:00 P.M., on June 6, 1974, the telephone operator working the main switchboard at the American embassy in Athens answered a long distance call from a man on Crete. The caller was passed along to a junior staff officer, who scribbled some notes as he strained to understand what the heavily accented voice was trying to say. He thanked the caller, and broke the connection. The underling seemed unsure about what to do with the information, but his bureaucratic mind quickly came up with the correct answer: buck the problem upstairs. Sweeping up his notes, he walked jauntily down the hall and into the assistant military attaché's office. He plopped down opposite an army major.

"Hey, Alan," he began, "has anyone misplaced a U.S. Navy captain lately?"

Alan Stanbaugh squinted at the man opposite. "That supposed to be a serious question, or another of your dipshit riddles, Pete? Because if it is, I'm busy as hell and don't have time for games right now."

"No games. The question is legit." Pete handed over his notes and studied the older man's face as he read the message. The major scrutinized each word, reading the contents at least three times. With a slight shrug of his shoulders, he turned and opened a credenza behind his desk and selected a volume from the uppermost shelf. He began thumbing through the pages. Two minutes passed before he closed the book with a loud thump.

"The guy's not attached to NATO, and he's not with the Sixth Fleet. I haven't received a heads-up on any recent aircraft or ship accidents, and I haven't been given a briefing on any Navy brass traveling through our territory, so my conclusion is that this four-striper must be some old retired fart who fell out of his boat while doing a Captain Ahab routine." Stambaugh smiled at his own wit, but only for an instant. He continued in a more serious vein. "We can't just ignore him though, so I'll wire the Pentagon and have them send his biography back to us. Too bad we didn't have his serial number. That would have saved us a whole bunch of time." Pushing back his chair, he headed for the communications room. "I'll take care of it, Pete."

*   *   *

Major Alan Stambaugh was heading across the expansive embassy lobby when a U.S. Marine private flagged him down.

"Message from the Pentagon, Major," he said, and handed over the signal.

Stambaugh read the telex. He read it again, his eyes reflecting his sense of absolute shock.

James Vincent Trader, Captain, USN, serial number 407986309, shot down over Hanoi, North Vietnam, 1 December, 1970. Not repatriated spring of 1973. Still classified missing in action (MIA.) Photo and fingerprints to follow within the hour. Most urgent confirm identity of individual on Crete. Use ambassador's secure line to secretary of state. Kissinger standing by. End message.

Stambaugh flew up the stairs and into the ambassador's suite on the second floor. Pushing into the spacious waiting room, he began talking to the receptionist even as he made his way to her desk.

"Is the boss in, Sally?"

"He's with Colonel Henderson and Spooky," she said, the latter referring to the CIA senior member.

"Got to interrupt. Priority one."

She picked up the phone, dialed the inner office, relayed the request, and hung up. "Go right in."

The ambassador read the telex, then without a word handed it to Henderson, who in turn passed it down the line to the CIA man.

While Stambaugh was briefing the three men as to what little he knew, there was a sharp knock on the door and the same Marine private stepped into the office and saluted.

"Excuse me, Mr. Ambassador. I have a photograph and a set of prints that just came in over the wire from the Pentagon." He handed the envelope to the ambassador who dismissed the man with a "Thanks, Jimmy," while tearing open the flap. The ambassador studied the picture for a moment then turned the facsimile over to Henderson, the air attaché.

"Ever run across him in the course of your travels, Ed?"

"No, sir, can't say that I have."

The ambassador glanced at his watch. "Okay, here's the plan," he announced, directing his attention to Stambaugh. "Alan, take this photo and the prints. Pick up a fingerprinting kit from the immigration folks downstairs, and hightail it to Crete. I'll call for a chopper. You'll take off from the embassy grounds. Make a positive ID of this Trader fellow, then contact me on the double. I don't care about a secure line or not. If this man isn't the Captain Trader in question, start the conversation with these words: 'Good evening, Mr. Ambassador.' But if he is our man, then say, 'I'm sorry to disturb you, sir.' Then talk for a few seconds about anything at all that comes to mind, but obviously nothing's to be said on an unsecured line about who this officer really is. We'll be ready on this end to relay your confirmation back to Washington."

Turning to Henderson he issued more instructions. "This guy sounds like he's in bad shape whoever he is. Regardless, we'll have Stambaugh bring him back on the chopper. I'll want a C-9 Nightingale on standby to take him to the military hospital at Rhein-Main in Germany. Have the helicopter crew proceed directly to the airport with him." The ambassador turned back to Stambaugh. "I'll clear everything with the Greek government and the local authorities on Crete." He silently read the electrifying telex again, then looked at the men grouped before him.

"How in the hell does a missing prisoner-of-war show up ten thousand miles from Hanoi almost four years after capture?"

No one had an answer.

"Now comes the hard part. The waiting."

The ambassador turned his thoughts to a more serious problem. *Midas touch.* No matter who this man might turn out to be, nothing had changed on that front. *Midas touch* was still the number one priority item to deal with, because the deadline for meeting that impossible Libyan demand was fast running out.

CHAPTER 21

The ambassador shot upright in his chair and grabbed the ringing phone.

"I'm sorry to disturb you, sir," said the small voice from far away.

It was Stambaugh confirming that the man on Crete *was* Captain James Vincent Trader! *My God! How could it be possible?*

Stambaugh continued. "My uncle needs me right away in Germany. He's very sick, and I'm told he has to have an operation first thing in the morning. He's been my favorite uncle from as long as I can remember. Full of fascinating stories. A self-made man. Everybody in the family says he's got the *Midas touch.*"

The ambassador was on his feet at that revelation. "That a fact?"

"No doubt about it, sir. A real Croesus."

"You take all the time you need, Alan. I'll let your wife know where you'll be."

"Thank you, sir. I only wish I had time to talk to his doctors. My uncle will need to have the best surgeons. Guys who are good with small details. He has three tumors; all separate, but somehow interconnected. They're veritable time bombs. Anyway, I appreciate the time off, sir."

"Right. Good luck. We'll all be praying for your uncle." He hung up and had his secretary summon the others.

He led them into the Tank, a soundproof room used to communicate freely, secure from prying electronic ears. Every American embassy has such a room. He spoke rapidly, giving a quick synopsis of what Stambaugh had relayed. Then he sprang into action, a general with last minute orders to his field commanders on the eve of battle. "Henderson, call the Rhein-Main hospital commander and tell him we need his best surgical team standing by. Inform him that as crazy as it sounds, the patient seems to have some sort of explosive devices inside him. That's an educated guess based on what Stambaugh just tried to tell me. Can you guys believe this?"

Colonel Henderson started for his own office, but paused at the door long enough to say, "I have a Navy C-9 en route from Aviano Air Base in Italy to pick up Captain Trader. I've also arranged for a priority fueling, and I personally filed a flight plan so that the crew can turn the aircraft around within thirty minutes."

"Good man."

The ambassador picked up his secure line to Washington, noting it was not quite five o'clock in the morning in the American capital. This information could not wait. In less than three minutes he was talking to Kissinger. When Kissinger hung up, he in turn silently counted to three and dialed a special number in the White House, one that bypassed the switchboard. The President answered on the second ring.

"There's no mistake, Henry? The ambassador did say, *Midas touch?*"

"Yes, Mr. President."

"I'm calling St. James right now. We have to get him to Germany. I'll call you back."

"Pegasus, this is *Top Drawer."*

St. James was instantly awake. Nixon was on the line, and using both their code names.

"You're going to Germany," Nixon said without preamble. "Take Two Six Triple Zero," he said, referring to his personal Boeing VC-135-707 aircraft by its USAF tail number, 26000. To the world the plane was known as Air Force One, a designation used by the flight crew only when actually carrying the President. "It's got the most secure communications set-up in the fleet. I'll brief you in the air as soon as I have more details. But it's definitely *Midas touch."*

*   *   *

Air Force One touched down at Rhein-Main Air Base at nine forty-four local time that night. Only a dribble of information had come across the secure communication link between the plane and the White House, but the little St. James had been told shocked him. A Navy prisoner of war, still listed as missing in action, had been found floating in the Mediterranean far from land by Greek fishermen. Apparently he had been implanted with some sort of explosive device, and to really complicate matters, this Captain Trader somehow had information about *Midas touch*. Such was the stuff of fiction!

A waiting staff car whisked him from the base operations building on the flight line directly to the hospital. The medical group commander, accompanied by a man he hurriedly introduced as the U.S. ambassador to West Germany met St. James at the main entrance.

The ambassador spoke. "President Nixon personally told us that you are to have free rein and that you speak with his authority. We will, of course, cooperate fully," The ambassador found himself in awe of this man whom he'd never even heard of before this afternoon.

"Is security in place?" St. James asked.

"Two MP's outside Captain Trader's door around the clock and another inside his room. Others throughout the hospital corridors," replied the hospital commander, Brigadier General Edwin Pierce.

"How is he, Doctor?"

"In bad shape, Mr. St. James. We operated on him early this morning and removed the most fiendish explosive device imaginable. Apparently implanted by some Libyan madman. The trigger was tied into a detonator, which could be activated by a command bounced off one of our satellites. That's all the patient could tell me. It was a real tense couple of hours in surgery."

St. James nodded as the elevator doors opened on the third floor.

"He's one hell of a warrior, though," continued the doctor, his voice filled with genuine admiration as he led his two-man entourage toward Trader's room. There were several large, no-nonsense looking military policemen stationed in the corridor and two more by the patient's door. The guards had been given orders to shoot to kill if any unauthorized person attempted to get to Trader.

"I have no idea what he's been through," Doctor Pierce said in a low voice as they paused outside the door. "No one has attempted to question him. Those orders came directly from the President. We were told that when you arrived, you'd take over. Let me say that I am aware of *Midas touch,* Mr. St. James, and I know that Captain Trader might be in possession of information vital to the continued well-being of our country. Please remember this; he's about as sick as anyone I've ever cared for, so you must be very patient. He's probably still asleep. If so, my professional opinion is for you to let him rest. He'll come around in his own time. It could be an hour, a day, or even several days. I just don't know. But when he does, don't tire or excite him, because the effort could kill him. If it weren't so God-awful critical, I wouldn't allow anyone other than staff within a hundred feet of this door for at least a week."

"I understand, Doctor. Thanks for your honest appraisal."

Pierce nodded to one of the guards, and the man opened the door. In they trooped, and immediately came face-to-face with a giant. The military policeman recognized Pierce with a nod. Two Air Force nurses hovered on either side of the patient's bed, one a major, the other a lieutenant colonel. Both held top secret clearances. If the patient should inadvertently divulge anything of a classified nature while still in his comatose state, those secrets were safe.

"No change, doctor," the lieutenant colonel whispered. "His vitals are stable. Breathing's still a tad shallow, but nothing to cause alarm. He's remarkable."

St. James looked down on the sleeping figure wired to several monitors with green, luminescent screens. He could have easily been looking at a man in his mid-sixties, St. James thought, filled with a sudden and profound sadness. The face was frightfully gaunt, and the cropped hair the color of fresh snow. Even in a state of unconsciousness, it was evident Trader was deeply troubled. His eyes moved rapidly beneath closed lids and occasionally he moaned. It was a pathetic, bone-chilling sound.

St. James stepped back from the bed and whispered to Pierce. "Could he die, Doctor?"

"He could. It's all in God's hands now. We just have to wait. That's always the hardest part."

The doctor studied this man from Washington. Early forties, athletic, but not musclebound. About six foot, lean, maybe one seventy-five, regular features, good looking, a man used to having to make important decisions and make them on the spot. He carried with him an aura of self-confidence, and he definitely had that quality known as command presence. Now he seemed to have reached a decision of some sort.

"I'm going to have his wife flown over immediately," St. James said. "I'll have her here within twenty-four hours. If there is the slightest chance this man is not going to make it, he sure as hell deserves to die with his wife beside him after whatever it is he's been through. That's the least his country can do for him."

"Excellent idea! Wish I'd thought of it," Doctor Pierce said. "Probably the best medicine in the world."

"Good. I'm going back to the plane to speak to Washington. Mr. Ambassador, I'd like for you to come with me to make the arrangements to locate Mrs. Trader and get her here."

"You don't have to go back to the plane; we have secure lines in the hospital," Pierce said.

St. James smiled. "Thanks, Doctor, but I can talk on a direct link from the plane to the Oval Office. No need for special scramblers because they're already in place." He glanced toward the bed. "As much as I'd like to talk to Captain Trader, and believe me, time is very much of the essence; I can see it'll be a couple of hours at the earliest. I'll be back as soon as I'm finished."

* * *

St. James was napping in an adjoining room when a guard quietly called his name.

"Mr. Saint James. You awake, sir?"

"Yes. What is it?"

"Captain Trader's awake, sir. Doctor Pierce said to call you."

He was up and next door in a flash. A quick glance at his watch told him it was almost dawn. He had slept for four hours.

Dr. Pierce looked spent. Dark circles lined his eyes, but he managed a smile for St. James. "Captain Trader woke about five minutes ago. He's still very tired and somewhat disoriented, but definitely lucid. I suspect he'll fall back to sleep shortly. However, it's a good sign. Anyway, you can have a moment to talk to him. But only a moment."

St. James approached the bed making sure not to touch any of the leads attached to the patient. He pulled up chair and sat close to Trader's right side.

"Captain Trader, can you hear me?"

The eyes opened and focused warily on the stranger. The slightest of nods.

"Jim, my name's Andrew St. James. You're in an American military hospital in Germany, and you're safe. No one can harm you again. Do you understand what I'm saying?"

Another nod, but now the eyes had closed.

St. James leaned closer. "Jim, Patricia's on her way. She'll be with you shortly."

His eyes opened fully.

"Pat will be here before nightfall, I promise. Now, how about you going back to sleep and I'll see you later. Don't worry about a thing. Just sleep, okay?"

Was that a hint of a smile? St. James couldn't be sure.

                              *   *   *

Trader woke at midnight, and the first person he saw was his wife.

The senior nurse on duty motioned to the staff to leave the room.

"Jim, I'm here," Patricia Trader whispered into his ear, tears spilling down her cheeks.

Trader's eyes were riveted on hers.

She held his right hand in her left, brought it lovingly up to her mouth and kissed it as tenderly as if she were cradling a butterfly.

His eyes followed her hand and rested on the void left by the missing finger. Tears welled, then cascaded down his cheeks.

She followed his gaze. *"Oh, my God! You knew!"*

He nodded. Then he lifted his left hand from beneath the blankets, and held out his little finger out for her to see.

"It's my ring!"

They both cried, and she buried her head on the pillow next to his.

Finally, she pulled away, and smiling, looked into his eyes. "I'm okay, Jim, really I am." She sniffled, and leaned over and kissed him on the mouth. "Welcome, home, sailor. It's been one heck of a long cruise!"

He squeezed her hand and tried to talk, but no sound came out.

"*Ssshhh!* Everything's going to be okay. The kids are fine. Your parents are fine. Everybody's fine." She managed a small, joyful laugh through her tears. "Go back to sleep. I'll be here when you wake."

And that's exactly what he did.

They moved another bed into his room and the two of them slept side by side, undisturbed for several hours.

*   *   *

St. James was worried. He'd been in Germany for forty-one hours now, and still hadn't been able to really talk with Trader. The President was understanding, and assured St. James that he had full confidence in his assessment of the situation. Nevertheless, St. James had heard the tension in his voice.

At two o'clock in the morning he was summoned into Trader's room.

Patricia Trader rose and shook his hand. "Thank you for bringing me," she whispered. "I'm told the President got me here at your request." She continued to hold his hand. "Jim and I will be forever grateful for your thoughtfulness." A tear fell to the floor.

"Mrs. Trader, please call me Andrew. I'm honored to meet you both." He looked over and winked at the patient. Trader winked back.

"Mrs. Trader, I need to speak to Jim, but I'd like you to stay. I must caution that whatever you hear, and I stress the point, it can never leave this room and never be repeated."

"My name is Patricia; Pat's even better. I understand. All I ask is that you don't tire him."

"I promise." He turned to Trader. "Hi, Jim, let me introduce myself again. I'm Andrew St. James, and I work for President Nixon. He sent me here because we have a problem, and we think that you might have some answers for us."

Trader nodded, fully alert.

"I'd like to ask you some questions, and all you have to do is nod, or shake your head a little if I'm on the wrong track. Don't get frustrated if I don't ask the right questions, okay? We'll have plenty of time later to go into details. Pat will stay and if she thinks that I'm tiring you, she's already told me that she'll toss me out on my ear. Fair enough?"

Trader smiled weakly, and gave a thumbs-up.

St. James glanced at Pat. She nodded. "Jim, did the North Vietnamese deliberately turn you over to the Libyans?"

A vigorous nod.

"Were there any others?"

Another nod. Yes.

"Did they also have backgrounds in nuclear physics?"

Yes.

"Were there more than a dozen of you?"

No.

"Did they take you to Libya to work on some missiles?"

Yes.

"*Longbow* missiles?"

Yes.

Both men stared at each other.

"Just *Longbows*?"

Yes.

"Jim, do they have more than two missiles?"

No.

"Jim, is it possible they could have other missiles that you aren't aware of?"

Trader shook his head emphatically. *No!*

"Thank God!" St. James looked over at Pat Trader whose face was the color of chalk. "Would you like some water?" he asked in a quiet voice.

She shook her head, eyes never leaving her husband's face.

"No. I'm fine, Mr. St. James. Please continue. I'm sorry."

"Jim, do you know a man named Jallud? We think he's some muckamuck in their government. An ambassador. Maybe higher."

Yes.

"You had dealings with this guy?"

Yes.

"We suspect he might be more than just a little crazy. Is that your assessment?"

Yes.

St. James sat back and rubbed his chin. In some respects this was worse than he had dared imagine. "Jim, are you up to answering a few more questions?"

Yes.

"This Jallud character has threatened to shoot off his missiles unless we agree to hand over to his government all our gold reserves in Fort Knox. In your opinion, would he, and could he, carry out his threat?"

"Yes," Trader actually gasped in a rasping, hoarse whisper.

"Please, Jim. Don't talk. Just nod, okay?"

Trader nodded.

"Now comes the million dollar question. In your professional opinion, will the missiles work? No, scratch that. I mean will the *warheads* work?"

Yes!

"Shit!"

Frustration was now written all over Trader's face. His wife saw the change immediately and held his hand tightly. "Don't get upset, Jim. Try to relax. Let Mr. St. James ask just a couple more questions. He'll get to the right one, I promise."

"At least we now know the worst-case scenario, Captain, and believe me, that's huge," St. James said. "The bugger's only got two missiles and not the whole damn arsenal he claims. That tells me our problem's manageable."

"Won't work!" said Trader in a clear voice.

"Won't work?" St. James repeated in a stunned voice.

A nod. Yes.

"But a second ago you said they *would* work."

Yes.

St. James sat back, utterly confused. "Yes, the missiles will fire. No, they won't fire. I've got to admit, you've handed me a real Chinese puzzle." He smiled kindly.

"Jim, did you somehow manage to sabotage the missiles?" The sudden words from Patricia Trader took St. James by surprise.

Yes! He couldn't stop nodding.

"*You brilliant, wonderful man!*" Pat Trader jumped to her feet and showered her husband's face with kisses.

St. James laughed loudly, his face reflecting a sense of pure relief. "If you weren't so God-awful ugly, I'd kiss you myself! Just a couple more questions, then you have to rest. Do I read you right in saying, yes, the missiles are armed, but that you've somehow managed to screw them up so that they won't detonate?"

Again he could see the frustration painted on Trader's face. Then two words: "Up high!"

"Up high?"

Trader nodded, then slumped back, obviously exhausted.

St. James slapped his knee, the sound carrying like a rifle shot. "You've rigged the *Longbows* to explode at the top of their trajectory! Do I have it right?"

Trader kept nodding like he would never stop.

"You're a bloody genius, Captain Trader. Nothing wrong with your noggin!" St. James stood up. "Please rest. With what you've just told me, we're well on our way to stopping this Jallud guy. One last question, Jim. Are the others dead?"

Large tears fell onto his pillow. He nodded.

"I can't begin to tell you how sorry I am. No words can describe what I know you must feel." St. James reached over and gently squeezed the man's thin shoulder. "I'm going to leave you now. I thank you both. And I thank God I had the sense to ask you to stay, Mrs. Trader. You were brilliant! Now I've got to go tell the President, but I'll be back."

*   *   *

"Andrew, our allies are getting nervous," President Nixon was saying. "They haven't heard from us in a couple of days and the word is out that they think I'm cutting some sort of unilateral deal with the Libyans. They're concerned I'm about to give up a good part of our gold and maybe pay off those pricks to the tune of a billion dollars. They all sound panicky. And there's also some rumblings that the Mossad is onto *Midas touch.*" The President's words carried across the ether from Washington and down to Air Force One sitting on the ground in West Germany. The plane had one huge turbine turning to provide independent electrical power. It was also prepared for a quick departure, should the need arise.

St. James had been talking for almost an hour. Both Nixon and Kissinger were in the Oval Office and both were on the line.

"Andrew, the press is asking what Air Force One's been doing in Germany these past few days. Can you do without it?" Kissinger wanted to know.

"*Absolutely not!* We must have this secure link. I can't stress the importance of that enough."

"No more talk of moving Air Force One, Henry," interrupted the President. "It stays there as long as you need it, Pegasus."

"Thank you, sir."

At that moment one of the Air Force stewards came and handed St. James a note. He read it quickly. "I have to go, Mr. President. Captain Trader's awake again and wants to talk. Says it's urgent. I'll get right back as soon as we finish."

*   *   *

St. James found Trader propped up by a half dozen pillows. Dr. Pierce was in the process of replacing the covers, having just completed an examination of the wounds.

"Looking good, Jim. I couldn't be more pleased. Scout's honor." Pierce grinned at his patient, then addressed St. James. "I can allow you a few minutes. The captain insists he exercise his vocal cords, so I gave him my okay. I'll make sure you're not disturbed."

"Thanks, Doctor. Where's Mrs. Trader?"

"My wife took her to the Base Exchange. She had to pick up some toiletries. Women's things. She should be back in a half hour."

St. James turned to Trader, amazed at how much better he looked and said as much.

Trader was able to talk slowly, his voice just above a whisper. But the words were clear. "Did Jallud give you a deadline, Andrew?" he asked without preamble.

"Ten days. We have a little over four left."

"Did he mention a target?"

"Not yet, but we're sure it's Israel."

Trader shook his head. "I don't think so. Gaddafi won't hit Israel. At least not first. England, maybe; France, maybe; the States, maybe. Now, Jallud sure as hell would hit Israel but he's not in charge."

"Why do you say that?" St. James was intrigued with Trader's line of reasoning.

"Because they will move the missiles by submarine, and Gaddafi won't let himself get trapped in the Mediterranean Sea. He knows we could hunt him down there. Jallud would love to target Israel, but I don't think that's what Gaddafi has in mind. He'd rather hand the country over to the Palestinians than turn it into a wasteland. I think Jallud will be ordered to head out to the open Atlantic. That way Gaddafi will be free to target wherever he wants."

"Jesus! If you're right, then we've got it all wrong."

"Andrew, maybe it's already too late. I hope not. But if I'm right, I also have a plan."

"Fire away, Captain."

"I'm positive he's going to use a submarine. He has an East German crew and they're good. That's how he got us out of North Vietnam. But I can tell you all about that later." Trader paused to sip some water through a straw, barely more than a swallow, but enough to wet his throat. He continued. "Your best bet is to monitor the Straits of Gibraltar. Don't let anything out of the Med without making a positive ID. In fact it would be a good idea to ask our allies not to move any of their submarines until further notice. That way, any sub passing into the Atlantic will be our man. Or maybe a Russian," Trader conceded. "But our boys can make a positive identification in no time, and confirm make and class. We would know in a second if it were a Ruskie. Most of their boats are nukes; this Libyan boat is a diesel."

"I'm with you so far. Go on."

"Have a couple of our hunter-killer submarines lie in wait off the Strait. I'm guessing we still have a substantial naval presence at Rota, on the southern coast of Spain. Get a couple of those boats into the area. You could have them on station within hours. It'll be a piece of cake for them to lock-on to that diesel sub. When they do, that boat sure as hell won't be able to shake them."

"Go on."

"Once they confirm it's the Libyan, they signal it to surface. If it refuses to obey; blow it away. No second chances, Mr. St. James. Waste it! That's the only way you'll be sure those missiles are destroyed."

"Can they be launched from a sub?" St. James asked. I thought *Longbows* were strictly surface-to-surface?"

"They are. However, Jallud will use the sub to transport them to rendezvous with a freighter at sea, then launch the missiles from its deck. He'll have instant long-legs, and at that point, he can roam anywhere he wants. Unfortunately, I was the one who gave him that idea. We exploded a test device using that method back in the spring."

"Off the South African coast?

"Yes."

"Do you think he's already made his move?"

Trader thought about that for a long moment. Finally he sighed, then shrugged his shoulders. "I just don't know. My bet is that he's not one hundred percent sure I'm dead. He has to know there's that outside chance that I'm not. So, because of that, forget the four more days. This guy is insane in every sense of the word and he's liable to strike at any time, with or without Gaddafi's approval."

"I'm moving right now on your recommendation. I'll advise the President."

"Pat says you have Air Force One on the ramp. True?"

"I confess," said St. James, grinning widely.

"I'm impressed, Mr. St. James."

"We flyboys have to stick together."

"You're a pilot?"

"Not anymore, but yes, I flew F-100s a lifetime ago. Had to punch-out over France after a midair collision and screwed up my back. I was permanently grounded, so I left the Air Force and drifted into this line of work."

"I say 'thank God' you did. You strike me a one hell of a troop, Mr. St. James."

St. James laughed. "Well, on that note, I hereby declare this meeting of the mutual admiration society closed." He laughed again. "Really, I've got to get moving. I'll use the hospital as my headquarters until I have Jallud, dead or alive. I promise to keep you informed every step of the way. Get well, okay? Your country needs you."

With a wave he was gone.

CHAPTER 22

Although his heart was pounding, Commander Anthony Graham, USN, skipper of the *USS Snook* said in a matter-of-fact voice, "Give me a fix." This *had* to be it. He had been positioned outside the Straits of Gibraltar for seventeen hours now, monitoring everything moving in either direction. He hovered at a depth of two hundred and fifty feet, compensating for current-induced drift by calling up minimum power from his nuclear reactor. His friend, Derek Heywood, skipper of the *USS Scorpion,* was to his port. Both boats were Skipjack Class SSNs, the most potent, most lethal submarines on earth.

Graham's crew was taking everything in stride. The men had made final preparations to leave their base at Rota, Spain, for a three-month cruise, but orders came at the last minute directly from the Chief of Naval Operations diverting the *Snook* and the *Scorpion* to this new assignment. Both skippers had been told to ready their torpedo tubes for conventional weapons, namely Mark 48s, and to take up a position outside the Straits. Once underway, they had been informed that their assignment was to find, identify, and track a diesel boat operated by the Libyan government. Once positive of the identity, they were to inform the Commander, Submarines, Atlantic (COMSUBALT), and await further orders.

"Bogey, bearing one seven zero degrees, skipper. Range, eighteen thousand. Depth, one five zero feet. Speed, twelve knots. Jeez, he's a noisy bugger! That's our baby all right!"

"Good work, Chief," Graham said to his most experienced sonar operator, then turned to his executive officer, Lt. Commander Forrest Everhardt. "Prepare a message for the boss. When you're ready, we'll slip up to periscope depth and transmit."

"Aye, skipper."

"Now we'll just tag along until further orders. I'm going to take a quick once-around with the Chief of the Boat."

* * *

The Libyans had broken off negotiations earlier in the day.

"Your government is not taking us seriously," the Libyan ambassador admonished Kissinger. "You will soon see that was a mistake." He stormed out of the State Department, rudely brushed aside the protocol officer, jumped into a waiting limousine, and sped off to his embassy.

Kissinger arrived at the Oval Office just as the President was receiving confirmation that the *USS Snook* had made a positive identification of the Libyan sub.

"Some good news at last, Henry," Nixon said, then quickly briefed the secretary.

"About time, Mr. President. The Libyans have cut off all communications, and the Russians are dropping hints to the European press that we're desperately short of gold. What's next?"

"The team is meeting in the Situation Room in ten minutes. If I give the order to go for the kill, I don't want any Monday morning quarterbacks weighing in tomorrow. I spoke with St. James fifteen minutes ago and he's comfortable with what we have. Good man, that."

"Yes he is, Mr. President."

* * *

"When do we next hear from the *Sword of Allah?*" Gaddafi had assembled his Revolutionary Council in anticipation of the great event which was unfolding according to plan.

"Not for another hour, Excellency," an army officer replied. "It is scheduled to surface briefly with its position report and to confirm that all's well."

Gaddafi took a red pencil over to the large map of the world spread out on a table and drew a red line from Tripoli across to the Straits of Gibraltar, then a couple of inches beyond. He would lengthen it once the submarine reported its latest position. He looked up at his ministers and grinned. "It looks like Jallud has made it into the Atlantic with no one the wiser."

"Allah be praised, but, remember, Excellency, no one is looking for our submarine!"

"When does Minister Jallud expect to rendezvous with the ship to transfer the missiles?"

"About this time tomorrow," replied the chief of staff. "Then it's just a matter of you selecting of the first target should the Americans fail to come to terms. You've put the fear of the Almighty into their souls, Excellency! Terminating the negotiations was a brilliant move. The infidels will come begging to resume the talks within a matter of hours. They will bend, then break, just as you prophesied."

Gaddafi rose, momentarily fussing with his clothes. "I'll select the initial target tomorrow, but first I must pray. Should anything untoward arise, call me at once."

Everybody nodded. None wanted to be the bearer of bad tidings. It never paid to be the messenger. But in this case, what could possibly go wrong?

                              *   *   *

"The *Snook* will confront the Libyans, and if they don't surrender and surface to be boarded, then it's to be destroyed. Is that correct, Admiral?"

"Yes, Mr. President. And the *Scorpion* will standby in case its presence is required. Both skippers are solid men," replied the Chief of Naval Operations.

"Then these are my orders. Contact both subs and inform them of the rules of engagement. They will have total freedom to act as their judgment dictates given the tactical situation as it exists at any given moment. The skippers don't have to call back to me for further endorsement. They're empowered to shoot to kill if the situation warrants." His eyes darted around the table, in search of a sign of dissent. "Everyone agrees?"

Multiple heads nodded.

"I can't hear you, gentlemen. Does everyone agree?"

"Yes, Mr. President," all parroted in unison.

"How about you, Andrew?" the President asked into the speakerphone.

"I say, yes, Mr. President," St. James replied from Germany.

"Good! Now we wait." The President rose. "I'll be in the Oval Office if you need me, Henry."

                              *   *   *

Ping!

"What in the name of all that is holy was that?" Jallud asked, standing shoulder to shoulder with Captain Dieter Weir in the cramped control room of the *Sword of Allah*. He had been in rare form these past few days. Trader was now a distant memory, a nuisance, a fly which had been disposed of with a flick of his wrist. So, too, the rest of the Americans. Only thoughts of Bakktari would bring his blood to an instant boil. However, that particular traitor had been dispatched of in a most fitting manner.

Now, he, Jallud, stood on the verge of greatness. His name would be whispered with reverence for a thousand years. Lately, he'd been fighting forces inside his head; forces which spoke most clearly telling him that it was he, not Gaddafi, who was the Great One. He had tried to resist those sirens but they gave him no peace. So he started to make plans.

Ping!

There it was again! The noise reverberated throughout the boat's hull. He looked to Dieter Weir for an answer.

Weir reached above his head and hit the klaxon, bringing the boat to general quarters. "Mr. Jallud, that sound means that the Americans have found us."

"*Impossible!* No one knows where we are. Not even the Supreme Leader will know until we surface to give our next position report."

Ping! Ping! Ping!

"Then I suggest you tell that to the Americans, because they most definitely have found us. That is their active sonar you hear. They will make hard contact with us momentarily."

The pinging became more rapid.

"All quiet," Weir ordered, and every man on board stopped what he was doing. Everybody listened to the message coming across the deep in Morse code, sounding off their hull. Heinrich Webber, the communications officer began writing rapidly on a pad.

He tore off the page and handed it to Weir.

To commander Libyan submarine from commander USS Snook. Surface immediately.

Prepare to surrender your boat to a boarding party. This warning will not be repeated. End message.

"Well, that's it then," said Weir. "Mr. Grundhauser, prepare to surface the boat."

"*Stop!* You'll do no such thing! I'm in command here." Jallud was not about to see his dream end with a whimper and not a nuclear bang. "You will outrun the American, Captain Weir. You will lose him. That's an order." His face twisted with rage. He looked wildly about the small control room, his mind racing. There was no way he was going to allow this boat to surrender. "Prepare your torpedoes. We'll blow them out of the water. *Attack!*" he screamed, spittle flying.

Weir answered Jallud as though he were a child. "No, Mr. Jallud, I will not attack. I will not sacrifice these men. What you are suggesting is suicide. That boat out there is a Skipjack Class attack submarine. I recognize its name, and it has no equal. She is the cat and this boat is the cornered mouse. The *Snook* can destroy us at will. It is over."

"*You have torpedoes! Fire them before she fires at us! Do it now!*" Jallud screamed.

Weir shook his head. "I am not prepared to die for a lost cause. And neither is any member of this crew. Unless we take immediate steps to surface the boat, the American captain will kill us. The next sound he wants to hear is us blowing our ballast. That will tell him we intend to comply. And I assure you, Mr. Jallud, I will obey." He turned from Jallud as if he were now nothing more than an irritant. "Stand by to surface!" he called out for all to hear.

Weir had his back turned when Jallud whipped out his pistol, and shot him once, shattering his spinal cord.

"You miserable coward! You don't deserve to command. Grundhauser, take over."

Dieter Weir crashed to the deck, moaning in mortal agony.

"Put that gun away, you bloody fool! Goddamn it, you'll kill us all!" Grundhauser hollered at the top of his lungs.

Pandemonium reigned. Men clawed at each other as they

raced out of the control room and away from the madman in their midst.

At that moment, the *Sword of Allah* no longer had a human hand guiding it. The submarine tilted forward and began descending at a rapid rate.

"Get back here, all of you," Jallud screamed. "Get back here," he repeated. "It will not end this way, I, Jallud, guarantee it!"

Many crewmembers stumbled and fell as they lost their footing, but all knew they were now in a desperate battle to save their very lives.

"Everybody back to his station," Grundhauser yelled as he staggered forward and grabbed the helm. "We're losing the boat! Get on those dive planes!" He pulled back on the yoke, struggling with all his might to bring the *Sword of Allah* back onto an even keel.

"Put that gun away, you bloody moron before you kill us all!"

Jallud was beyond reason. "Are the torpedoes ready to fire?"

"Yes, Excellency," stammered a terrified Libyan sailor from his battle station.

Jallud lurched forward the few paces necessary to do what he knew he must. His fingers found the firing button for the first loaded tube. He slammed his fist with all the force he could muster onto the red handle. The boat lurched slightly aft and sideways from the sudden release of thousands of pounds of compressed air from the torpedo tube.

"*Noooooooo!*" Grundhauser wailed, going into shock. "You've just killed us all!"

In a blinding flash of insight Jallud realized the German was right. Grundhauser's face became Trader's, and he knew in that instant the significance of what he was seeing. It meant the American had won, and in winning had dashed his dream of eternal greatness.

And the atheist Grundhauser began to pray aloud to a Creator he had been taught from infancy was but a figment in the imaginations of fools.

*   *   *

"Holy shit, skipper," said the stunned sonar operator on the *Snook*, "someone just fired a gun over there!"

"It's got to be something else," Graham replied. "No one would do that on a sub."

"Definitely a gunshot, Captain," the rating insisted. "No doubt in my mind. There's all sorts of shit going on. People yelling and screaming their heads off. Sounds like a goddamn mutiny, *SIR!*"

"I hear you, Dixon, and, yeah, I believe you. It's just so stupid. Good work."

"Captain, they've just fired a torpedo. It's off and running but heading away from us. It's like they just blew one out with no target in mind or anything. Next one might have our name on it though, skipper."

Graham made a decision. "Standby tubes one and three. Do you have the plot, Number One?"

"Ready on your command, skipper. Short range attack mode," Eberhardt answered.

"Fire one!"

The boat rocked as the torpedo raced out of its tube, rapidly unfurling a thin, snaking, guidance wire in its wake.

"One away, sir!"

"Fire two!"

It was a repeat performance.

"Both torpedoes running true, Captain."

"Roger, I copy, Number One."

Because of the distance, he didn't have long to wait. The sonar operators wisely turned down volume control knobs and removed their headsets in anticipation of what was to come.

Everyone heard the two explosions, yet none aboard the *Snook* took the slightest pleasure in what they had just done. True, that boat was the enemy, but it was brother submariners who had just lost their lives. The men on the *Snook* stared at one another. Silence reigned supreme.

Graham broke the spell. "Secure from general quarters.

For what it's worth, good job, everybody." He addressed his executive officer. "You have the conn, Mr. Everhardt. Standby to surface and get ready to transmit a message to Washington. I'm going to my cabin to draft it."

"Aye, skipper, I have the conn."

*   *   *

President Nixon showed no emotion upon hearing the news. He was in the Situation Room, and the Chief of Naval Operations had just informed the group of the signal from *Snook.*

"Now we can move onto more pressing matters." Nixon looked at the secretary of state. "Henry, inform our allies it's over."

"Yes, Mr. President."

He turned to his secretary of the treasury. "George, the Russians aren't going to be happy that they've again backed a loser. They'll really run with that rumor now, telling everyone we have no gold, so let's put them in a box. Arrange for a guided tour of Fort Knox for the press corps. I want them to get inside the vaults and see for themselves that we still have our gold reserves. No touchy-feely stuff, mind you, and no souvenirs, but they're to be allowed to take all the pictures they want."

The secretary wore an unhappy look. "You know this has never been done before, Mr. President. In fact, the only time a civilian has been inside the vault was when President Roosevelt paid a clandestine visit in April, 1943."

"I'm aware of all that, George," replied the President, a hint of exasperation creeping into his voice, "but there's a first time for everything. I need this to prevent a panic in the world's monetary markets. And, George, I want it done deal before the week is out. Understood?"

"Yes, Mr. President."

"Anything else, gentlemen?"

All shook their heads.

"Meeting adjourned. I know you have work to do."

*   *   *

"How about both of you flying back to Washington with me on Air Force One?"

"Are you serious?" Pat Trader found herself instantly transformed into an awe-struck kid.

"Absolutely. The plane has to go back and we have tons of room. You, Jim, have a bed waiting at Bethesda Naval Hospital. I've already cleared it with the President and he insists you use his on-board suite."

"Oh, my, what do you say, Jim?" Pat asked.

Trader smiled at his wife. "Jim says thanks. I'd love to go home on Air Force One."

"Okay, we'll be leaving in about an hour. Dr. Pierce is sending a flight surgeon and two nurses along, so he's in essence saying you're fit to travel. He'll be dropping in to say his good-byes shortly."

"Thank you, Andrew, for everything." Pat reached up and kissed him on the cheek. "Will we see you again after we get back to Washington?"

"I hope so. In fact, you should count on it."

"That'll be great. I second what Pat said. Thank you for everything."

St. James turned serious. "There are a couple of things I need to go over," he said in a suddenly subdued voice. He walked over to the window and stared out at the sprawling hospital grounds while collecting his thoughts. Then he turned to Trader. "Jim, we can't tell the press what really happened to you. At least not yet, and possibly never. We cannot talk of your being sold to Libya, to say nothing of your friends who made the ultimate sacrifice. Quite frankly, the President doesn't know how he's going to handle that. However, we do plan to destroy that facility in the desert. It'll be reduced to rubble before the week is over. So, in some small measure their sacrifice will not have been in vain."

St. James turned and stared out the window once more, but continued talking. "President Nixon has clamped an *Ultra Top Secret* classification on the circumstances surrounding your sudden appearance. The Pentagon will release a statement this week to the effect that you had escaped from North Vietnam just before the peace treaty was signed. The story line will be that you had an accident which caused amnesia. You have worked as a deckhand for the last few years, traveling all over the world, unaware of who you were, or where you were from. A few days ago you were swept overboard during a storm in the Med, and when you came to, you'd regained your memory. I know it's weak, but we think it'll wash. At least we hope so." He turned to them both and correctly read the concern in their faces. "I'm not thrilled with it either, but I'm afraid this is something bigger than the three of us."

"It stinks, Mr. St. James," Pat Trader said in a voice filled with bitterness and bile. "The North Vietnamese and the Libyans should be held accountable for murder!" She was close to tears. "How many other American prisoners have been sold by North Vietnam to how many other countries? How many other Jim Traders are out there, slaves in every sense of the word? Men who gave their all for America, only now to be abandoned and discarded in their hour of greatest need? Who is looking out for them, Mr. St. James? Can you answer me that?" She was now crying. "I repeat. It stinks!"

St. James shook his head miserably. "I don't have an answer, Pat. The President put out the word, and he was most emphatic. He's the Commander-in-Chief, and as such he has that right. Look, because of what's happened to Jim, we know with certainty now that we will never believe the Vietnamese when they tell us they have made a full accounting of all our prisoners. But I also know this President, and I'm here to tell you this; as long as he's in the Oval Office he won't rest until he has the answers. This chapter is far from closed. Mr. Nixon just needs time, so please trust him on this. Both of you. The tragedy of Vietnam will not end until we have a full accounting of our missing and our dead. You must believe that. We all must."

"Promise me we won't let the world forget, Andrew," Pat whispered through hot tears. "Don't allow those lives to have been given in vain. Please, please, find a way to get the truth out. We're counting on you. Just find a way."

St. James nodded. "I promise, Pat." He then smiled at them both. "Now, how about going home? It's past time, wouldn't you agree?"

THE END

Author's Note

The Twilight of the Day is a work of fiction. The author did draw on certain truths to give the story an enhanced sense of reality while other facts have been tweaked to embellish the narrative. The aircraft carrier *USS Ranger* was indeed conducting air operations against North Vietnam in November 1970 when Captain Trader was shot down. However, in 1974 the holy month of Ramadan started on September 17th and not on the first day of March as written. Historical characters are presented as themselves; all others are the creation of the author.

* * *

A shipment of Plutonium did disappear on the high seas during the timeframe covered in this story. The culprits were never found. Because of the sensitive nature of the ship's cargo, it was decided at the highest levels of government to concoct the story that the ship was lost with all hands during a storm.

* * *

Tactical missiles capable of carrying nuclear warheads were stolen from a West German depot; their theft attributed to urban terrorists. The missiles were never recovered.

* * *

A mysterious nuclear explosion did take place deep in the South Atlantic, but later than written. Speculation at the time of the incident as to whom or what was responsible was just as described by the author.

* * *

President Nixon ordered the depository at Fort Knox be opened to the press corps in 1974 to squelch rumors that the gold reserves of the United States had been severely depleted. Such an action had never before been taken; nor has it since been repeated.

* * *

The Twilight of the Day

To our brothers left in Limbo
Whose tormented souls we pray,
Have found a peace so well deserved
At the twilight of the day.
Abandoned, then discarded,
So much chaff upon the wind,
For Duty, Honor, Country,
Was the crime of which they'd sinned.
Thus through days of endless terror,
Amidst nights fraught full of fears,
It was their faith in God and country
That sustained them through those years.
While their tortured cries of anguish
Fell on cruel, unheeding ears.
*   *   *
Seasons turned, their numbers waned,
All hope grew dim in hearts remained
In dungeons hidden from the light
Of all but God's omniscient sight.
There would be no accounting,
No one cared to know their plight.
They simply were expendable
To jackals guised as men,
Abandoned and forgotten
To a cause all claimed no ken.
Each had learned too late in horror
There'd be no respite from his fears,
While their tortured cries of anguish
Fell on cruel, unheeding ears.
*   *   *
And from the splendor of their temples
All that while a world away,
Self-serving kings and emperors
On mock-bended knees did say;
Let's put this time behind us,

We must close this chapter now,
Those self-anointed monarchs prayed
With heads too proud to bow.
They beat their breasts in false lament
And shed reptilian tears,
From behind the ramparts of their castles
Amidst approval from their peers.
While those tortured cries of anguish
Fell on cruel, unheeding ears.

*   *   *

But in a Pantheon of Heroes
Men with names not to be found,
Lie now with Hector and Achilles
Free from pain on hallowed ground.
Those long-abandoned warriors
At last unfettered, freed to stand,
Now heed the call from Gabriel
To grasp God's guiding hand.
They have finally found their solace,
They have earned their Promised Land.
Here given nurture by the Savior
Who dried their eyes of untold tears,
For those tortured cries of anguish
At last fell on God's all-heeding ears.

*   *   *

Ian A. O'Connor

Author's Biography

Ian A. O'Connor is a retired USAF colonel who has held several senior leadership positions in the field of national security management. His expertise in countering nuclear, biological, and chemical warfare threats from those who wish us harm helps convey that special sense of reality and urgency in his soon-to-be released page-turning, international thriller, *The Barbarossa Covenant.* Ian is the author of *The Twilight of the Day,* and *The Seventh Seal,* and is the co-author of *SCRAPPY: A Memoir of a U.S. Fighter Pilot in Korea and Vietnam.* He is a member of Mystery Writers of America and lives in Palm Beach Gardens, Florida, with his wife, Candice, where he is working on his latest Justin Scott thriller, *The Masada Option.*

Visit Ian at: www.ianaoconnor.com
Contact Ian at: ianaoconnor@ianaoconnor.com

Made in the USA
Monee, IL
23 July 2023

39767420R00127